# The Mothersea

Also by Stephen Renneberg

THE MAPPED SPACE UNIVERSE

The Mothership

The Antaran Codex
In Earth's Service
The Riven Stars
The Spawn War
The Warrior Worlds

SF/TECHNOLOGICAL THRILLERS

The Siren Project
The Kremlin Phoenix

# The Mothersea

Stephen Renneberg

For Elenor with love.

# The Mothersea

## Map

# Abbreviations & Terminology

| | |
|---|---|
| ADF | Australian Defense Force |
| Bulkhead | A vertical wall inside a ship (nautical) |
| C&R | Contact and Recovery Program (Area 51) |
| DARPA | Defense Advanced Research Projects Agency |
| EBE | Extraterrestrial Biological Entity |
| ESA | European Space Agency |
| F-35 | Lightning II stealth fighter |
| Forecastle | Forward section of deck mounting anchor winch (nautical) |
| Gangway | Internal horizontal corridor, passageway (nautical) |
| GNC | Guidance, Navigation and Control Systems (NASA) |
| GN | Ground Network (NASA tracking) |
| HAIV | Hypervelocity Asteroid Interception Vehicle |
| Hatch | Horizontal access in a deck (nautical) |
| HMAS | Her Majesty's Australian Ship |
| HQJOC | Headquarters Joint Operations Command (Australia) |
| JAXA | Japan Aerospace Exploration Agency |
| JPL | Jet Propulsion Laboratory |
| JWST | James Webb Space Telescope (NASA, infrared observatory) |
| NASA | National Aeronautics and Space Administration |
| NT | Northern Territory, Australia |
| Overhead | The underside of the deck above, i.e. ceiling (nautical) |
| P-8 | Poseidon maritime patrol aircraft |
| PDCO | Planetary Defense Coordination Office (NASA) |
| PLAAF | Chinese People's Liberation Army Air Force |

| | |
|---|---|
| RAN | Royal Australian Navy |
| RAAF | Royal Australian Air Force |
| SLS | Space Launch System (NASA) |
| STOCC | Space Telescope Operations Control Center (NASA, Hubble ST) |
| STScI | Space Telescope Science Institute (NASA, Webb ST) |
| UAV | Unmanned Aerial Vehicle |
| USAF | United States Air Force |
| USN | United States Navy |
| USS | United States Ship |
| UUV | Unmanned Underwater Vehicle |

# Mapped Space Chronology

**3.4 Million Years Ago to 6000 BC**
Earth's Stone Age (GCC 0).

**6000 BC to 1750 AD**
Pre-Industrial Civilization (GCC 1).

**1750 - 2130**
The rise of Planetary Industrial Civilization (GCC 2).
The First Intruder War – unknown to mankind.
   *The Mothership (MS-First Contact 1)*
Start of the Blockade.
   *The Mothersea (MS-First Contact 2)*

**2130 - 2643**
The spread of Interplanetary Civilization (GCC 3) throughout the Solar System.

**2629**
Marineris Institute of Mars (MIM) perfects the first stable Spacetime Distortion Field (the superluminal bubble).
The MIM discovery leads to the dawn of Inceptive Interstellar Civilization (GCC 4).

**2615**
The Solar Constitution ratified, establishing Earth Council (15 June 2615).

**2644**
First human ship reaches Proxima Centauri and is met by a Tau Cetin Observer.

**2645**
Earth Council signs the Access Treaty with the Galactic Forum.
First Probationary Period begins.

Tau Cetins provide astrographic data out to 1,200 light years from Earth (*Mapped Space*) and 100 kilograms of novarium (Nv, Element 147) to power human starships.

## 2646 - 3020

Human Civilization expands rapidly throughout Mapped Space.

Continual Access Treaty infringements delay mankind's acceptance into the Galactic Forum.

## 3021

Dr. Anton Krenholtz discovers Spacetime Field Modulation.

Krenholtz Breakthrough enables transition to Incipient Interstellar Civilization (GCC 5).

## 3021 - 3154

Mass migration dramatically increases human colonial populations.

## 3154

Human religious fanatics, opposed to interstellar expansion, attack the Mataron Homeworld.

Tau Cetin Observers prevent the Mataron Fleet from destroying Earth.

## 3155

Galactic Forum suspends human interstellar access rights for 1,000 years (the Embargo).

## 3155 - 3158

Tau Cetin ships convert human supplies of novarium held in Earth stockpiles and within ship energy plants to inert matter (as human ships landed at habitable planets).

## 3155 - 4155

Human contact with other interstellar civilizations ends.

Many human outposts beyond the Solar System collapse.

## 4126

Earth Navy established by the Democratic Union to police mankind when Embargo is lifted.

Earth Council assumes control of Earth Navy.

## 4138

Earth Intelligence Service (EIS) established by the Earth Council.

## 4155

The Embargo ends.

The Access Treaty is reactivated, permitting human interstellar travel to resume.

The second 500 year Probationary Period begins.

## 4155 - 4267

Earth re-establishes contact with its surviving colonies.

## 4281

Earth Council issues Sanctioned Worlds Decree, protecting collapsed human societies.

## 4310

The Beneficial Society of Traders established to manage interstellar trade.

## 4498

Quantum Instability Neutralization discovered (much earlier than galactic powers expected).

Mankind becomes Emergent Civilization (GCC 6).

The golden age of human interstellar trade begins.

**4605**

The Vintari Incident.
*The Antaran Codex (MS1)*

**4606**

The Battle of Tresik Prime.
End of the Blockade.
*In Earth's Service (MS2)*

**4607**

The Nan Chen Disaster.
The Xil Asseveration.
*The Riven Stars (MS3)*
The Siege of Serris Orn.
*The Spawn War (MS4)*

**4608**

The Fall of Earth
*The Warrior Worlds (MS5)*

**Notes:**

| | |
|---|---|
| *MS*: | Mapped Space |
| *GCC*: | Galactic Civ. Classification system. |
| *Asseveration*: | A solemn or emphatic declaration. |

# CHAPTER ONE: EMERGENCE

The Infiltrator dropped from superluminal flight close to the heliopause of a yellow star and scanned space, searching for the enemies it had evaded for sixty five thousand light years. Finding itself alone, it dived into the frozen heart of a nearby comet and powered down, making itself virtually invisible to even its most technologically advanced adversaries. Adrift at the fringes of interstellar space, it waited and watched for enemy warships to appear, but none came.

Of the thousand self-aware infiltration probes launched from the Intruder Civilization's home cluster, it was the last survivor, the only one of its number not hunted down and destroyed by the Alliance Fleet. During the breakout, some probes had deliberately revealed their presence, sacrificing themselves so others could escape into a galaxy swarming with enemies. The probe force's collective effort had been designed to allow at least one of their number to reach the Place of Inexplicable Defeat, to discover how a great Intruder Fleet had been disabled without firing a shot by an unknown technology. For a species that had travelled the stars for millions of years, such a complete disaster had shaken their immense civilization to its core. It drove them to determine its cause so they could ensure such a defeat would not be repeated when the reckoning came. And it would come, even if that day was thousands of years away for the Intruders were, if anything, patient and unrelenting.

After three years of creeping from one hiding place to another, the Infiltrator was nearing its objective deep within the enemy's core space. It was why it moved with extreme caution. Any mistake would end years of planning and effort, condemning its makers to continued ignorance as to the cause of their defeat in what the galaxy now called the Intruder War.

That defeat had ended a conflict they'd thought almost won, lost them all they had conquered and left them exiled within their resource poor home cluster beyond the galaxy's outer rim. If the Infiltrator could discover the nature of that defeat, its final act would be to transmit its findings to the Supernexus in the Galactic Halo for analysis. Such a powerful transmission could not be hidden from its enemies who would swoop in and destroy it with frightening speed. The Intruder probe would have no chance of survival, for it carried no weapons. Its only protection was invisibility, a defense it would gladly shed to complete its mission, for it did not fear destruction, only failure.

When no annihilating attack came, the Infiltrator turned its attention upon the nearby star system. It was the location of a battle that had ended in an illusory Intruder victory and was the last stepping stone to Tau Ceti, home of their great enemy. The Infiltrator intended to search the battle space for clues before beginning the hazardous approach to Tau Ceti itself, where the Inexplicable Defeat had occurred.

Knowing it couldn't risk openly approaching the nearby system, it expanded spacetime along one side of its cometary hiding place and accelerated it toward the dim yellow star. The Infiltrator could have pushed the comet to much higher velocities, but that would have attracted unwanted attention from passing ships. Instead, it slumbered patiently as the comet drifted through the Oort Cloud toward planetary space. In time, it passed out of the spherical shell of ice and dust enclosing the system and the feeble yellow star became the brightest light in the sky.

The Infiltrator detected transiting enemy vessels many times, but none showed any interest in the wayward comet. Most were from civilizations far less advanced than the Intruders and lacked the capability of penetrating the probe's vastly superior technology. When the comet crossed the orbit of a dwarf world at the edge of planetary space, a Tau Cetin ship appeared, forcing the Infiltrator to shut down all but its most critical systems. Fortunately comets were of no interest to the technologically sophisticated Tau Cetins, who ensured the science ships studying the system's pre-stellar civilization were following galactic protocols, then it left with only a cursory scan of the third planet.

Months passed as the probe drifted through the orbits of a pair of ice giants, discovering all that remained of the battle was a thin radiation cloud stretching halfway across the system. The cloud was gradually dissipating into background radiation, although there were signs anti-radiation measures had been employed to prevent the four inner planets from being contaminated – Tau Cetin handiwork, no doubt.

The Infiltrator had expected to find the wrecks of hundreds of Alliance ships adrift within the radiation cloud, but not a single derelict remained. The enemy had long ago removed the hulks of their shattered fleet, ensuring that in the coming centuries they did not fall into the hands of the system's pre-stellar inhabitants. Even the remains of the two Intruder assault carriers lost during the battle were gone, although where they'd been taken remained a mystery.

One of the two wrecked Intruder ships had been caught in a highly elliptical solar orbit while the other had crashed onto the third planet with only a single female survivor. She'd been returned to the Intruder homeworld after the Inexplicable Defeat, but had been unable to explain what had occurred.

After finding nothing of interest in the battle space, the Infiltrator considered heading toward the Tau Cetin home system twelve light years away. The presence of two enemy research vessels subjecting the third planet to close study made it hesitate. Abandoning its hiding place while they were present was an unnecessary risk, so it decided to wait. Whether it took ten years or ten centuries to complete its mission was of no concern.

Success – not haste – was the priority.

When the comet passed inside the orbit of the sixth planet, the Intruder probe turned its attention on the enemy ships and the blue-green world they studied. The ships came from low to mid level civilizations within the Orion Arm while the planet possessed a high habitability, carbon saturated biosphere with level two chemical poisoning. The planet also contained traces of radiation contamination and fission electricity generation, causing the Infiltrator to upgrade its assessment of the planet's developmental stage from Combustion Level to Pre-Fusion.

The Infiltrator soon discovered miniscule quantities of highly enriched material in many locations indicating the planet's inhabitants had constructed enough fusion weapons to reduce their world to a radioactive cinder. Millions of years ago, the Intruder homeworld had faced a similar dilemma, surviving the Nuclear Mass Extinction Era by the merest of margins. The NME Era served as a natural barrier to ultra-warlike species which tended to exterminate themselves before they could pose a danger to the rest of the galaxy. This was because it took an irrationally high degree of competitive aggression to risk self extinction by constructing atomic weapons in such numbers. The Intruders were such a species, and so it appeared were the inhabitants of this slowly suffocating world.

Mildly intrigued, the Intruder probe continued studying the third planet while it waited for the science ships to leave. On one of the southern continents, it found partially disguised indicators of a kinetic assault landing typical of Intruder invasion ships. If it was the landing site of the second assault carrier, all trace of the ship itself had been removed, no doubt to prevent the planet's inhabitants from discovering its secrets.

When the comet passed inside the orbit of the small red planet fourth from the star, the Infiltrator detected anomalous bioreadings on the third world. They were close to the crash site and would have been lost in the dense biomatter found in the planet's tropics if not for the fact that the probe's sensors were particularly sensitive to those specific signatures. With rising curiosity, the Infiltrator gathered more data, confirmed the nature of the life signs and came to a startling conclusion.

The enemy's attempt to cleanse the blue-green world of the Intruder species had failed.

* * * *

Beloved-of-the-Sea let the warm current carry her away from the island as she listened to the thrashing of hundreds of tiny legs. It was the frantic sound of bottom-crawlers trapped in a cage as it was hauled to the surface by a land-dweller crab boat. The trawler was a short distance away, glowing like an island of light upon a dark, midnight sea. Tall warm-blooded creatures from beyond the horizon worked feverishly on deck to sort the catch and stow the metal cages that pillaged her feeding grounds.

Beloved resented the land-dwellers not only because they stole her bottom-crawlers, but because they used boats, cages and nets her brothers lacked. It was a natural instinct to defend what was hers, to destroy what threatened her domain. On another world sixty five thousand light years away, she would have been a natural ruler, but she knew nothing of that world, its language, its monolithic culture or its towering technological achievements. Her world comprised the warm tropic waters, long empty beaches and sun bleached cliffs of the Mothersea, bordered by the forests of the Endless Land to the south and the limitless waters of the Deep Blue to the north. It was a world where her brothers obeyed her every command, her few sisters plotted and schemed against her and the land-dwellers posed an ever present threat. In her short life, she'd faced death many times, yet only the mysterious machine powers wielded by the land-dwellers truly frightened her.

The strange thrumming of their boats which miraculously glowed at night as they swept the sea of little-swimmers and bottom-crawlers were a constant warning to her. On land, they rode in growling machines and showed no fear of the long-tooth-stalkers, the giant predatory lizards that had eaten her brothers when they were still too young to defend themselves. Even the one-fin-killers that roamed the sea devouring anything in their path posed no real threat to them.

Watching the land-dwellers from afar, she knew they were violent and dangerous hunters, in some ways like her own kind, in other ways not. She feared the day her kind were discovered hiding in the Mothersea, certain the land-dwellers would use their machines to destroy them. It was why she had ordered her brothers and convinced her sisters to hide until she better understood them and had devised a way to take their power for herself.

She took a breath, compressing air into her quad-lungs, and sank below the surface. Once the rounded sonar lobe bulging from her forehead was submerged, she emitted a single pulse, measuring the swimming distance to the metal hulled crab boat now only a kilometer away. Together with Prowls-the-Shallows, her hunt leader, she surfaced to watch the approaching trawler with widely spaced, bulbous blue green eyes. A flock of hungry seagulls circled above the boat, swooping in and out of the light in search of food while the land-dwellers labored on deck, unaware they were being watched.

Beloved-of-the-Sea's naturally telescoping eyes zoomed toward the trawler's work deck. She puzzled at the way the land-dwellers kept only the large crabs and threw the small ones back into the sea, taking it as a sign that only the best would satisfy their greed. Her predator's sharp eyesight, almost as keen as her sonic abilities, revealed the trawler crew's speed and organization which her prodigious intellect interpreted as yet more proof of the threat they posed.

"Are you sure, Beloved?" Prowls-the-Shallows asked uncertainly in a language they had invented – were still inventing – in order to communicate.

"It is time," she said, certain they had learnt all they could from afar. To discover more, they would have to get closer, even at the risk of revealing themselves.

Prowls studied the trawler, knowing it followed the line of buoys marking the locations of crab cages it had laid and was now hauling in. "I'll signal when it's done."

He said it in a way that told her in this one thing, he would not be overruled. She'd insisted on being present against his wishes and over the concerns of the other hunters, but they would refuse to let her risk her life further. She had the pheromonic power to force them to obey her every command, except where her own life was endangered. The species survival instincts of the males gave them that one power to resist her orders because her one life was worth more than all of theirs combined. It was the one exception to her absolute authority she accepted, albeit reluctantly.

Prowls-the-Shallows motioned to the hunters, then the fourteen males compressed air into their quad-lungs and slipped beneath the waves. While she watched from a distance, they swam toward the trawler like torpedoes racing through the darkness. When the blue trawler hull loomed above the hunting party silhouetted by its deck lights, the hunters dived deep, broke into two groups, then shot toward the surface.

They burst out of the sea on both sides of the trawler, leaping like dark shadows in a swirl of water over the gunwales into the light. The hunters splashed onto the deck as the fishermen looked up in surprise, unaware of the danger. While the men tried to understand what these strange creatures were, the hunters hurled smooth stone disks at the floodlights, shattering glass and immersing the deck in darkness. Night blind and confused, the seamen stood blinking as the diminutive forms pounced on them with inhuman speed. The amphibians slashed at their throats and tore open their stomachs with razor sharp coral blades that sprayed the deck with blood. Shocked expressions flashed across the fishermen's faces as they died, then their corpses were hurled into the sea.

Prowls-the-Shallows was surprised how easy it had been, how slow their responses. As land-dweller blood ran down his blade onto his hand, intriguing him with its heat, he wondered if they really were as dangerous as Beloved feared. He lifted the blade to his small mouth and tasted the blood curiously, then finding its taste foul, spat it out.

Rapid footsteps sounded from the wheelhouse as the Captain emerged holding a flashlight in one hand and a pistol in the other. Some of the hunters had seen the land-dweller's spitting-flash-weapons from a distance and knew the threat they posed. When they saw the gun, they scrambled up the ladder to the bridge, charging into the torchlight.

The Captain's eyes widened, shocked at the sight of the bipedal creatures on his deck. "What the hell?" he muttered incredulously.

When the first hunter reached the top of the ladder, the bearded Captain fired once into the amphibian's oversized head, blowing out the back of his skull. The hunter fell back onto the deck with a welling hole between his eyes. Prowls glanced at his dead brother's wound, instantly understanding the advantage of surprise was lost.

A second hunter reached the top of the ladder, then the Captain kicked him in the mouth with his heavy sea boot, sending him flying. The old fisherman could have shot the hunter, but he was so filled with rage, he wanted to physically strike the murderer of his crew mates. The old seaman stepped to the edge of the ladder and aimed down at the amphibians and began firing. He caught one in the shoulder as they scattered, then a dark torpedo leapt high out of the water and landed behind him.

Before the trawler skipper could turn, Beloved-of-the-Sea caught his forehead, pulled it back and sliced open his throat with a flashing swipe of her blade. The Captain crumpled at her feet, gurgling blood as she bent forward, watching him die. Terror and confusion spread across his face as he looked up into her large, separated eyes, unable to comprehend what he saw. He spluttered blood, struggling to breath, then she retrieved the gun he'd dropped by his side. She turned it over curiously, tested the large grip in her small hand, then pointed it at his head and fired. The recoil surprised her, then she placed her finger curiously over the bloody hole in his forehead, examining the damage the bullet had caused.

Prowls raced up the ladder, saw the trawler captain was no longer a threat to her, then relaxed. "You were right, Beloved. They are more dangerous than I realized."

His concession gave her no joy. She straightened, annoyed she had one less hunter at her disposal, then handed the Captain's pistol to Prowls-the-Shallows.

"Give this to Watcher-of-Skies," she said.

Watcher was the least skilled of the hunters, but the

greatest thinker. He would learn all he could about the land-dweller hand gun and teach his brothers. In a few days, they would know everything that could be gleaned from the weapon.

"What now?" Prowls-the-Shallows asked.

"Take everything. Leave no trace," she said, then entered the wheelhouse.

She studied the instruments, wondering as to the purpose of the global positioning system, the depth sounder and the circle with the arrow that always pointed the same way. Suddenly a box with glowing lights hissed, startling her with the sound of a land-dweller voice. At first, she thought there was another land-dweller nearby, then she stepped warily toward the radio, listening intently, wondering where the voice came from and what it was saying.

Beloved listened with growing trepidation, wondering how her people could ever hope to defeat creatures with such strange powers.

* * * *

The Intruder probe watched the last science ship form a superluminal bubble and streak out of the system. It was the first time since the comet had begun its voyage through the planets that the entire Solar System was empty of ships. The Infiltrator knew this was its chance to begin sneaking toward Tau Ceti. It was an opportunity that wouldn't last as there had been a constant trickle of visitors from across the galaxy since its arrival – and more would come.

The dilemma it faced was that it was now convinced Intruder biosigns existed south of the planet's equator, close to the assault carrier's crash site. Considering the size of Intruder invasion ships, it was possible the lone female who'd been returned after the war had been unaware of other survivors. The Infiltrator now wondered if those others possessed information vital to its mission. Even more troubling was the Species Survival Dictate imbued into every Intruder artificial intelligence that compelled it to assist females in need ahead of all other priorities. It obliged the probe to determine if there were female survivors, and even though it could do little to help them itself, it could report their presence to the Supernexus when it transmitted the results of its mission. It did not matter that a rescue mission was virtually impossible. The survival directive forced the Infiltrator to act even against its own rational objections.

It was, after all, only a machine.

Trapped by the Species Survival Dictate, the Intruder probe adjusted the comet's course to pass close by the third planet, ensuring it could use the mountain of rock and ice to sneak out of the system after it had investigated the biosigns. With its escape route assured, it slipped from its frozen hiding place, keeping a constant watch for enemy ships entering the system.

Two minutes later, the Infiltrator plunged into the warm tropical waters northeast of the Mothersea.

# CHAPTER TWO: EVIDENCE

A month after the attack on the trawler, a US army helicopter banked over King Oscar Fjord, Greenland, and followed the icy waters inland. In the copilot's seat, Colonel Robert Beckman glanced down at a pod of bowhead whales gliding between the icebergs below. He was fit and lean for a man in his mid forties, thanks to a regular fitness regime, although his fair hair was beginning to gray at the sides and noticeable lines were forming around his eyes.

"First time this far north, Colonel?" the pilot asked.

"No," he said, gazing toward the pristine white plain of snow and ice ahead. The seemingly timeless ice sheet stretched to the horizon beneath darkening skies, yet even though they were over six hundred and fifty kilometers above the Arctic Circle, it was only a matter of time before it collapsed, transforming Greenland into a scattered archipelago. In a way, that inexorable melt was why he was here now.

The pilot pointed ahead. "They're two clicks from the edge of the ice sheet. Once we're down, it'll take an hour to unload. If you could be back aboard then, sir, I'd appreciate it. I'd like to be out of here before the storm hits."

"I understand, Lieutenant."

The chopper flew along the fjord to the edge of the ice shelf, climbed above a white capped ridge, then skimmed a snow covered plain at low altitude. A single row of green army tents and a black derrick straddling a narrow crevasse soon came starkly into view against the white of the snow.

The pilot put the chopper down beside a bright yellow windsock, then Beckman said, "Don't leave without me, Lieutenant." He climbed out and hurried toward the derrick, flashing his ID at the guard standing beside it. "Is Dr. McInness down there?"

"Yes sir."

Beckman climbed into the small cage, glancing down apprehensively between glistening walls of ice to the glow of electric light far below. "How deep is it?"

"Four hundred and ten meters, sir," the derrick operator replied as he put the winch in gear, lowering the elevator into the crevasse.

The cage dropped slowly into freezing darkness, forcing Beckman to zip up his thick parka and pull the hood over his head. The growl of the derrick engine quickly faded, replaced by the sounds of dripping water and creaking ice. After several minutes, he heard muted voices, a humming generator and the tapping of small hammers, then the cage descended into an ice cave. It was filled with banks of floodlights and a dozen scientists and technicians wrapped in thick thermal suits, none of whom paid him the slightest attention.

He pushed the cage door open and stepped out onto a slippery rock floor. On the far side of the cave was a squat metal disk four meters across extending from a wall of ice. It had been discovered by Norwegian researchers exploring the cavities forming within the melting ice sheet, all of whom had now been sworn to secrecy.

Part of the craft's hull had been crushed by glacial forces and one of its landing struts was bent sideways, but otherwise it was intact. Several men chipped away at the ice encasing the craft with small hand picks, carefully digging it from its icy grave, while a familiar figure was bent over the disk sliding a circular sensor across its hull. The dark haired scientist was almost ten years younger than Beckman, wore dark rimmed glasses, had a slender build and was so absorbed in his work, he hadn't noticed the elevator's arrival. Circling the disk was a bank of computers and screens on metal stands monitored by the usual gaggle of scientists from Groom Lake.

Beckman stepped past them all and tapped the lead scientist on the shoulder.

"Not now," Dr McInness muttered as he slid a circular sensor to a new position on the craft's hull and glanced at one of the scientists monitoring a computer screen. "What about here?"

"Nothing. No radiation, no heat," she said. "It's totally dead."

The Contact and Recovery Program's chief scientist sighed, disappointed. "It's hardly surprising I guess, considering its age."

"Ian," Beckman said, tapping the scientist's shoulder again.

Dr. McInness look up, surprised. "Bob! What are you doing here?"

"What do you think I'm doing here?"

The scientist shrugged uncertainly.

"I've sent you seven messages in two days. You haven't replied to any of them."

"Hmph." He motioned to the disk. "I've been busy." A concerned look appeared on his face. "What day is it?"

"Thursday. The fifth."

Trepidation flashed across his face. "Oh-ho. Kim will be wondering what's happened to me."

"She knows," Beckman said dryly, implying his wife wasn't happy at being ignored for days on end. As a former member of Beckman's contact team, the scientist's wife – who in her wilder days had gone by the call sign 'Vamp' – knew all about her husband's work, even if she was no longer involved in the program herself.

"I better call her," he said, standing.

"You'll see her soon enough," Beckman said, already convinced from the look in the scientist's eyes that he wouldn't leave without a fight. He'd known Dr. McInness for ten years during which time they'd risen together through the C&R Program's ranks. Beckman commanded the field retrieval missions while Dr. McInness led Area 51's reverse engineering program. Beckman knew if the scientist had been allowed to publish his findings, he might have won a Nobel Prize by now, but no word of his work would ever see the light of day. For that sacrifice alone, Beckman's attitude toward him had softened over the years to one of respect and eventually friendship. "You're coming back with me."

Dr. McInness looked surprised. "I can't." He turned to the disk. "I've got to get this artifact back to the lab in one piece."

"Your team can handle that."

"You don't understand, Bob, it made a soft landing," he said meaningfully. "Its drive system is intact."

Beckman glanced at the small disk, noting the faded script on its hull. "I don't recognize the markings."

"No, you wouldn't." Dr. McInness motioned for Beckman to follow him to a table covered with metal trays. He pointed to a rectangle of rock lying in one of the trays. "See that?" He indicated a perfect circle imprinted into the rock over a slender leaf pattern. "Do you know what it is?"

Beckman glanced at the rock impatiently. "A fossil."

"Exactly. The circle is a perfect match for the disk's landing strut. This fossil proves the disk landed on a leaf from a spruce tree."

"OK," Beckman said, eager to get back to the helicopter.

"Bob, we're at seventy two degrees north. There are no forests here. No spruce trees."

"I noticed."

"There are no forests here *now*, but half a million years ago when the Earth was hotter than it is today, there were spruce and pine forests here. That fossil proves the probe landed here five hundred thousand years ago. That's why you don't recognize the language, because even if this probe came from one of the local powers, their language must have evolved. They probably don't even use this script any more, or speak its language. After all, in just a few thousand years, we stopped using Latin and hieroglyphics. Same thing, only on a much longer time scale."

"I get it," Beckman said. "It's old."

"It's more than that, Bob. It's early interstellar tech, extremely primitive by their current standards, but almost within our reach. If it's first generation, it's still centuries ahead of us, but it'll be the closest alien tech we've ever found to where we are now. In time, we might be able to figure it out, maybe even build something like this ourselves."

"I thought we couldn't build alien equipment," Beckman said.

"Not if it's hundreds of thousands of years ahead of us. We don't have the industrial technology, but anyone sending out probes like this is just beginning. They wouldn't have had many starships, so they were trying to figure out where to send the few ships they did have. This is where we could be in a few centuries. That little disk could be the key to our first step."

Beckman glanced at the partially crushed disk with renewed interest. "If anyone is going to figure it out, Ian, it'll be you, but not today." When the scientist gave him a confused look, he asked, "Is there somewhere we can talk?"

Realizing Beckman had something serious to discuss, Dr. McInness led him from the flood lit area to a metal table holding platters of half frozen sandwiches.

"This is about as private as it gets down here." Dr. McInness glanced at the sandwiches, remembering he'd forgotten to eat lunch. His concentration on the disk now broken, he touched the side of his head, closed his eyes and winced, forcing himself to relax.

"Headaches back?" Beckman asked.

"They never leave me." Dr. McInness pulled a rectangular tab of pills from his pocket and popped out two tablets, then washed them down with a glass of water. "Just sometimes, I get so focused on my work, I forget them for a while." He held up the tab. "Providing I've taken these."

"You should do something about it."

"Kim made me get a scan. There's nothing there. Nothing we can see anyway."

Beckman pulled a small metal box from his pocket, pressed the fingerprint scanner with his thumb to unlock it, then lifted the lid to reveal a small triangular tooth inside. It was off white with a chipped point and had a ragged base where it had broken off. "What do you make of this?"

Dr. McInness took the container and turned it slowly, studying the object from different perspectives. "Teeth aren't exactly my field. Maybe you should show it to a dentist."

"They've already seen it. So have the geneticists."

Dr. McInness sobered. "Geneticists?"

"Two DNA tests confirm whatever creature that tooth belongs to did not evolve on Earth."

The scientist looked surprised. "It's not a Zeta tooth, wrong shape. Too small for a Swede." He shrugged uncertainly. "We have so few samples like this, it could be from … anywhere."

"That's what Hendrickson in xenobiology said."

"How'd you get it?"

"It was found in the boot of a dead fisherman who washed up on a beach a few weeks ago. He'd been shot in the head by a nine millimeter pistol and his throat had been cut by – get this – a sharpened coral blade. Forensics took a piece of it out of a bone in his neck. Whoever cut his throat nearly took his head off."

Dr. McInness furrowed his brow. "Aliens don't murder humans and even if they did, it wouldn't be like that."

"Tell that to his crew. They're all missing. So is their boat. That tooth and the place where the body was found is all we have."

Dr. McInness looked up. "Where?"

"The coast of East Arnhem Land, northern Australia," Beckman said, knowing he would instantly understand the implications.

A shocked look appeared on the scientist's face. "How close to the impact sites?"

"Close enough."

They'd been there ten years ago, their first mission together, investigating what was eventually classed as a small asteroid impact. The final report had claimed unusual solar activity had downed satellites and aircraft while the asteroid itself had broken in two before causing significant ground damage. Images of several small impact sites had been broadcast around the world and promptly forgotten by the public, although Dr. McInness had never been convinced. There were too many unanswered questions, too many holes, but with no evidence to the contrary, he'd been forced to drop it.

"Aliens don't use stone age weapons," the scientist said as he gazed at the tooth.

"I know. They'd have ray guns and they wouldn't bite a fisherman's boot or put a nine millimeter bullet in his head, but we have the tooth, a dead body, a missing boat and no crew."

"My headaches started after Australia ... and the dreams," he said absently, then his eyes widened in

18

surprise. "The dreams!" He glanced at the tooth with growing excitement, then put the box on the table. "Wait here," he said and hurried away.

"Where are you going?" Beckman asked, but the scientist didn't answer.

Dr. McInness returned almost immediately carrying a leather briefcase from which he retrieved an artist's pad. He flicked through pages of badly drawn sketches and scribbled notes, all pictures of alien machines and different perspectives of a wrecked ship.

"Pamela makes me keep this," Dr. McInness said, referring to the base psychologist who was treating his migraines. "She said it would help me with the nightmares ... It doesn't." He stopped at a picture of an angular face with a bulging forehead that was disfigured from burns. Dr. McInness stared at it a moment trying to remember where he'd seen that face. It had troubled him for a decade, but he'd never been able to recall the details, just the face.

"Is that what you see?" Beckman asked.

The scientist nodded. "Sometimes." He removed the tooth from the box and placed it on the page, then slid it toward the disfigured mouth where he'd drawn a row of small triangular teeth, finding a near perfect match. "I knew it!" he whispered. "They did something to us, to our memories."

Beckman stared incredulously at the drawing. He had no headaches, no recollections of anything unusual. As far as he was concerned, the trip to Australia ten years ago had been a costly dead end, with half his team lost to an accident – or what he thought had been an accident. "Why are you the only one who remembers?"

"I have an eidetic memory," he replied. "I guess they couldn't wipe it fully."

"What do you remember?" Beckman asked, trying to come to terms with the possibility that his mind had been tampered with.

"Flashes, images, impressions. Nothing concrete.

Mostly it comes in dreams." He smiled, relieved. "This proves I'm not crazy."

"I never thought you were. A little odd maybe, but not crazy."

"My God … they're real," he said straightening, leaving the tooth on the page. "And they've been down there for ten years!"

"So where's their ship?" Beckman asked, returning the tooth to the security container.

"It's gone. Whether it left them behind on purpose or by accident, using stone age weapons shows they didn't choose to be here."

"We've had people all over that site. There's no wreckage."

"Wreckage can be removed," Dr. McInness said as he considered the possibilities. "I wonder what they've been doing all this time?"

"That's what we're going to find out, as soon as I can get your butt on the helicopter."

"Are we sending the team?"

"Nope, there's no ship to recover. They'll be on standby in case we need them. For now it's a fact finding mission. Just you, me and Teresa, but no walking, not this time."

"I'm glad of that," Dr. McInness said. "One jungle hike per lifetime is enough for me."

"Be careful what you wish for, Ian. There are some things worse than the jungle."

"Like what?"

Beckman smiled knowingly. "Seasickness."

\* \* \* \*

An Australian navy helicopter collected Beckman and his two companions from the airbase at Darwin in northern Australia and flew east between the vast tropical wilderness to the south and the sparkling blue waters of the Arafura Sea to the north. Watching the forest stretch away to the horizon, Beckman recalled their previous visit, wondering if his memory could possibly have been altered to hide what had taken place there a decade ago.

The explosion of an alien tech weapon salvaged from an ancient wreck had killed half his team and set his mind permanently against using such weapons again – or so he believed. The stockpile of alien infantry weapons was tiny, gathered from a handful of crash sites worldwide by the US military over more than a century of covert collection. He'd once vigorously advocated their use, but now refused to touch them, preferring human weapons because at least he understood how they worked. Now for the first time, he wondered if his stark change of mind – from committed advocate to resolute opponent – was his own decision or the result of alien programming. The more he examined his memories and found nothing, the more he realized it was a question he would never find the answer to.

His reverie continued until they were fifty kilometers east of Croker Island when Lt. Commander Adam Reynolds, a sun tanned navy pilot with a relaxed manner said, "There she is."

He pointed to a small, gray ship in the distance lying at anchor on a calm, blue sea. She had a rectangular superstructure amidships crowned by a row of square bridge windows on three sides. Above the superstructure was a single funnel and a pair of masts bristling with technology while facing aft was a small hangar and an elevated flight deck that ran almost to the stern. Beneath the helipad was an open air main deck containing side mounted derricks, hydrographic equipment and three motor boats.

Beckman glanced over his shoulder at Dr. McInness behind him. "You might not need those seasick pills after all," he said, nodding to the flat sea below.

"I'll take them anyway," Dr. McInness said, as wary of the ocean as he was of the jungle.

"It hardly looks big enough to land on," Major Teresa Bertolini said as she peered at the ship. Behind her sunglasses were dark eyes and fine Italian-American features framed by short black hair. Teresa had been with Beckman and Dr. McInness on their ill fated expedition ten years ago, although this was her first field trip in four years. Back then, she'd gone by the call sign 'Xeno', having been the team's expert in alien symbols and languages. Now she led the effort to decode data devices recovered from a handful of alien wrecks, some centuries old. It was difficult mathematical work more akin to cryptography than translation, yet it made her the nearest thing Beckman had to a translator. If they encountered extraterrestrials, it would be her job to find a way to communicate with them.

"She's twenty one hundred tonnes," Reynolds said with a hint of pride. "She's got the most sophisticated hydrographic sensors of any ship in the southern hemisphere and the legs to sail around the world without refueling."

"What's she called?" Teresa asked.

"HMAS Naturaliste. She's named after a cape on the west coast. It was discovered by the French a couple of hundred years ago," Reynolds replied, then radioed the ship for landing permission before maneuvering toward the elevated flight deck.

Beckman was well aware of the ship's long range, but it was her technology which had led to her being requested for the mission. The *Naturaliste* was a hydrographic survey ship equipped to explore and map Australia's immense ten million square kilometers of oceanic territory. She was his best hope of finding a handful of stranded aliens hiding among the many islands and bays of one of the most remote and sparsely populated regions on Earth.

When Reynolds set the chopper down, three crewmen wearing helmets and light gray coveralls secured the helicopter to the flight deck, then he said, "The crew will see to your gear while I take you up to meet the skipper."

When the crew began to unload their bags, Dr. McInness glanced anxiously at a small metal case he'd brought with him, but Beckman gave him a reassuring nod. On a navy ship at sea, there was little chance the device would be lost or stolen and the deceptively strong case would ensure it would not be damaged. Reluctantly, the scientist entrusted the case to the sailors, then they followed Reynolds through a cramped hangar, up to the captain's relatively small but well appointed stateroom.

"Welcome Colonel, I'm Commander Turner," the captain said a little stiffly. She was slightly shorter than Beckman, with brown hair, green eyes and a tanned complexion. With more than twenty years sea service, she was one of the more experienced female commanders in the navy. They shook hands, then Beckman introduced Dr. McInness and Teresa before Turner motioned them to a small conference table. When they were settled, she gave Beckman a slightly forced smile. "Well Colonel, would you like to tell me what I'm doing here?"

"What do you know?" he asked cautiously.

"Only that Chief of Navy himself ordered me here and that I'm to offer you every assistance short of endangering the ship. Oh and everything on this deployment has the highest security classification. Apparently we're not even allowed to mention your name off the ship. Considering our job is making maps, that's a rather unusual order, to say the least."

Beckman knew the request for a technologically advanced ship had passed between governments at the highest level, although very few people on either side of the Pacific had any idea what his mission's true purpose was.

"We're investigating the disappearance of a trawler, the Mermaid," Beckman said, giving her a cover story that contained an element of truth.

When Turner looked puzzled, Reynolds said, "She

went missing about a month ago. There was a search but she was never found. The captain's body washed up east of Maningrida a few weeks ago."

Turner nodded slowly as she recalled the incident. "I remember." She returned her attention to Beckman. "That's a civilian matter, Colonel, something for the Northern Territory police. Why is the US military interested?"

Beckman knew it was always going to come to this and that she wouldn't like the answer. "There are aspects of this case that exceed civilian jurisdiction, aspects I'm not at liberty to discuss."

Turner showed no surprise at his answer. The Chief of Navy had already warned her what to expect and had instructed her to accept the secret nature of Beckman's mission. Certain she would get nothing more, she turned to Dr. McInness, noting his clothes. "You're a civilian. What's your role in all this?"

"Ian's a technical expert," Beckman answered quickly before the scientist could speak.

"In what field?" Turner persisted.

"Ian's area of expertise is classified," Beckman said.

"And you, Major?" Turner asked, turning to Teresa. "Is your field also classified."

"I have a PhD in mathematics," she replied evasively.

"Really?" Turner said, wondering what possible use a mathematician would be at sea. She returned her gaze to Beckman. "Is there anything you can tell me that isn't classified?"

"I get motion sickness," Dr. McInness said, showing her his seasick pills. She glanced at his medication with a hint of disbelief, then he produced a box of pain killers. "And migraines."

She sighed resignedly, running a curious eye over her three guests. "We're responsible for charting a large part of the Earth's surface with a handful of overworked ships, Colonel. I hope this is worth it."

"It is," Dr. McInness said earnestly.

Seeing the frustration in her eyes, Beckman added, "I appreciate this is inconvenient, Captain, but your government wouldn't have agreed to have us here, to making your ship available, if it wasn't important."

She nodded slowly, certain that, at least, was true. "So where would you like to go?"

"Arrla Bay. Ever heard of it?"

Captain Turner glanced curiously at Reynolds who knew that coast better than she did.

"It's about a hundred sixty kilometers southeast of here," he said. "There's nothing there."

Turner realized from Beckman's expression that her executive officer was incorrect. "What's at Arrla Bay, Colonel?'

"The Mermaid."

Turner looked surprised. "You found our trawler?" When Beckman nodded, she asked, "How?"

He looked slightly embarrassed. "We had four satellites examine every inch of sea and coast from here to the Gulf of Carpentaria, then subjected the pictures to the most sophisticated image analysis known to man. It's there."

Surprise flashed across her face. "Four satellites? One wasn't enough?"

"We really wanted to find that trawler, Captain," he said emphatically.

"Obviously," she said, her irritation abating as she realized whatever Beckman was up to had to be important to get so many satellites retasked. "Very well, Colonel, let's go see what your four satellites have found."

\* \* \* \*

After an orientation tour of the ship and a late evening meal in the officer's mess, Beckman and Dr. McInness shared a junior officer's stateroom while Teresa bunked in with a female sub lieutenant. While they slept, the

*Naturaliste* sailed through the night, dropping anchor off Arrla Bay next morning.

After breakfast, Turner and Beckman stood on the landward side of the bridge scouring the coast with binoculars. The bay was a rectangular inlet with a long sandy beach surrounded by tropical forest. West of the beach was the narrow mouth of a nameless river whose banks were overgrown with mangroves.

"I don't see it," Turner said skeptically as she scanned the coast with binoculars.

"It's up river, beyond the beach" Beckman said.

She aimed her binoculars in the direction indicated, studying the narrow snaking channel and mangroves in the distance. "There's no way it could have drifted over that sandbar. It would take some fancy navigation to get a trawler in there."

"How fancy?" Beckman asked.

"I'd want a local pilot, depth soundings, tide charts, look outs on every quarter. The problem is, Colonel, there are no local pilots here, no accurate charts. Even the aborigines don't have the knowledge I'd need."

"Maybe they don't, but whoever got that trawler in there does," Beckman said thoughtfully.

She scowled, thinking he wasn't listening. "We'll send a launch at high tide. It's a shallow draft boat. It'll get you in safely." She lowered her binoculars. "Is there anything else?"

Beckman remembered the Australian forensics report had indicated the trawler captain had been killed by a knife wound so savage it had almost decapitated him.

"Yeah. Arm the boat crew."

\* \* \* \*

Several sailors used the starboard hoist to lower one of the *Naturaliste's* ten meter motor boats to the water, then helped Beckman and his two companions aboard. The gray survey boat had a wheelhouse amidships, a small crane astern and was equipped with radar, echo sounders and position monitoring equipment, but no weapons. Lt. Commander Reynolds and the three sailors crewing the boat all wore sidearms although Captain Turner had decided that Beckman's small team, as foreign nationals, should remain unarmed.

After the hoist cables were released, a sailor steered them toward the shore at high speed, slowing only as they neared the sandbar in front of the narrow river mouth.

"The trawler would have scraped bottom getting in here," Reynolds said as his eyes flitted from the depth sounder to the shallow waters beneath the hull. "They'd have had to time it just right."

Beckman turned his gaze to the deserted beach east of the river mouth. There was no sign of life, not even a single pair of footprints in the glaring, white sand. Beyond the beach, dense mangroves lined a meandering river that crawled to the sea through a vast land inhabited by a mere handful of semi-nomadic people. He was certain anyone who could hunt and fish could hide there for years without discovery, perhaps for their entire life.

*They're resilient*, he thought as the boat motored through the shallows toward the river mouth.

Once across the sandbar, they followed the river inland as it wound through mangroves humming with insects. Dragonflies skimmed green water as still as glass while birds circled above and walked on spindly legs at the river's edge searching for food. Occasionally the tropical forest gave way to low sand dunes and salt encrusted marshland, giving glimpses of ochre colored cliffs far to the south, then the mangroves would claustrophobically enclose them again. There were no navigational markers or other boats on the river, no sign man had ever been there, only oppressive heat and humidity and the occasional warble of a bird to break the unrelentingly drone of a million insects.

"Commander," the helmsman said. "We've got a

radar contact starboard side, two hundred meters ahead."

All eyes turned to the muddy river bank. Thick mangroves shrouded the shoreline in shadow concealing any sign of the *Mermaid*. Only when the survey boat closed on the radar contact did the outline of the trawler appear through a tangle of green foliage. When the helmsman nosed the motor boat in, they discovered wires had been tied to low hanging branches, pulling them in around the trawler's hull. Two small mangrove trees had been dug up and replanted on the river side of the trawler further obscuring its presence while mud had been smeared from bow to stern, blending the hull into the shadows. The camouflage effort expertly hid the trawler's shape and color, making her invisible to any distant, casual observer.

"How'd they get her in there?" Teresa asked when she saw how shallow the water was.

"Must have dragged her up," Beckman said, hardly believing it himself.

"She's at least seventy tonnes, Colonel," Reynolds said skeptically. "Maybe if there was a king tide, they could have done it."

"How often do you get king tides?" Dr. McInness asked.

"A couple of times a year."

"So whoever attacked the trawler," Beckman said thoughtfully, "timed it to coincide with a king tide."

Reynolds looked surprised as he realized how much planning had gone into the attack. "No wonder we couldn't find her. How'd your satellite spot her?"

"Image analysis detected the trawler's outline," Dr McInness explained. "It's the same technology we use to locate camouflaged missiles. The outline is easier to identify from above."

A sailor with an assault rifle stood guard on the motor boat's wheelhouse while another sailor climbed aboard the trawler with a mooring line. When the launch was securely tied to the *Mermaid*, Reynolds and Beckman clambered across, followed by the others.

Reynolds gazed curiously at the wires, noting how carefully placed they were, pulling branches around the hull without breaking them. "I've never heard of pirates going to this much trouble before. Normally they'd loot the ship and abandon it or take it for ransom. Not this."

"They weren't pirates," Beckman said, but didn't elaborate when Reynolds gave him a questioning look.

Teresa produced a camera from her backpack and began photographing the scene while Reynolds took a closer look at the wires anchoring the mangroves to the fishing boat.

"They cannibalized this wire from the crab cages," he said puzzled, glancing at a stack of cages that were now little more than empty metal frames. Teresa photographed them too, then he added, "Why not just bring wire?"

"You can't bring what you don't have," Beckman said.

Dr. McInness peered down into an open hatch at a large tank with a shallow layer of water at the bottom. "What's this?"

"That's the crab tank, sir," the sailor who'd carried the mooring line across replied.

"Why's it empty? The report said the trawler had been at sea for three weeks. Shouldn't they have caught something in that time?"

Reynolds and Beckman hurried over to where Dr. McInness stood and studied the empty tank.

"It should be full of dead crab," Reynolds said.

"So what did they do with the cargo?" Beckman wondered aloud.

"Crab are valuable, Colonel, but you wouldn't kill seven men to get them. And transferring a load of crab at sea would be virtually impossible."

"They had to lighten the boat, to get it in here," Teresa said.

"Yeah, that would make her ride higher," Reynolds

agreed. "I guess they dumped the cargo."

"Or ate it," Dr. McInness said, giving Beckman a meaningful look.

"There'd have been tonnes of crab," Reynolds said doubtfully.

"They might like crab," Beckman said, turning toward the wheelhouse overlooking the work deck. "Let's see if there are any bodies inside."

The sailor led Teresa and Dr. McInness through the lower hatch while Beckman and Reynolds climbed the ladder to the bridge. When they entered the wheelhouse, they were surprised to discover every piece of equipment and every length of electrical wiring had been carefully removed. Only empty cavities now remained where the trawler's electronics had been. Even the compass and light fittings were gone, including the screws securing them in place.

"It's like she's been stripped in dry dock," Reynolds said impressed. "They could sell the equipment for spares, but they wouldn't get much."

"They're not after money," Beckman said as he opened the drawers below the chart table, finding them empty. Every technical manual, book and magazine in the bookcase had also been taken.

"What then?" Reynolds asked.

"I wish I knew," Beckman said, genuinely puzzled, then he climbed down the narrow ladder behind the bridge. They found the galley was in a similar condition to the wheelhouse. All of its fittings and wiring were gone.

Reynolds could hardly believe his eyes. "Someone sure went to a lot of trouble for junk."

Dr. McInness appeared in the passageway, casting a quick eye around the galley. "The generator's gone and the engines are in pieces, all laid out in neat rows." He glanced at Reynolds uncertain if he should say more, then added, "If I didn't know better, I'd swear they were reverse engineering us."

"What?" Reynolds said incredulously. "You can buy this stuff anywhere."

"Yeah, anywhere," Beckman said thoughtfully, then turned to Dr McInness. "Any bodies?"

The scientist shook his head. "There's no sign of the crew."

The sailor who'd been first aboard stopped at the galley and spoke to Reynolds. "The bilge is flooded, sir. Looks like she was scuttled. The valves and watertight doors are all open."

"So she can't float away, even in the wet season," Reynolds concluded, then turned to Beckman. "I'll get a salvage crew sent out from Darwin. They'll pump her out, but floating her off will be another matter." He joined the sailor in the gangway. "Let's have a look at those engines."

The sailor led Reynolds down the passageway, then Dr. McInness whispered, "The way they took the engine apart was systematic and precise. It reminded me of how we take alien artifacts apart so we don't break anything and can put them back together again afterwards."

"Ian, everything on this boat would be like stone age tools to interstellar aliens."

"I know," he said helplessly, "but that's what it looks like. They're doing to us what we do to them."

"Could they be cannibalizing the boat for parts to repair their ship?"

"None of our equipment would be of any use to them. It certainly couldn't be used to repair their technology."

Several photographic flashes lit the passageway, then Teresa appeared with her camera. "There are no computers, TV's or electronics of any kind left aboard," she said. "Even the mattresses from the crew cabins are gone, although personal items, like family photographs, are where the crew left them."

"Did you see any books?" Dr. McInness asked.

"No," she replied. "No e-readers either."

With nothing more to learn, they went back up on

deck. While Teresa completed photographing the trawler, Dr. McInness and Beckman stood on the work deck in silence.

Dr. McInness said, "It doesn't fit any of the contact scenarios."

"Then we better come up with a new scenario. We need to know what we're dealing with, what they want."

Teresa called out from the foredeck, "Colonel, you might want to look at this."

Beckman and Dr. McInness hurried forward to the small deck in front of the wheelhouse. Teresa stood beside the anchor winch photographing the shore.

"What is it?" Beckman asked, glancing at the river bank. It was shrouded in shadow and covered in aerial roots rising out of the black mud.

"Footprints," she said, pointing. "There!"

It took Beckman a moment to understand what he was looking at. For more than thirty meters in both directions, mud used to camouflage the trawler had been dug from the river bank. Tiny pockmarks covered the excavation, which he'd mistaken for a natural feature until he realized they were small footprints. They reached all the way from the water to dry land and ended abruptly just beyond the limits of the excavation.

"We've been thinking about this all wrong," Beckman said in a flash of understanding. He'd assumed they were dealing with only a few individuals, desperate survivors of a shipwreck. "There are hundreds of them!"

"Hundreds of what?" Reynolds asked as he and the sailor joined them on the foredeck.

Beckman hesitated, not ready to share their discovery with the naval officer. "Footprints."

Reynolds studied the bank, quickly grasping the implications. "They came from the sea."

"How can you tell?" Teresa asked.

"No footprints inland," he replied. "Could be smugglers or Indonesian poachers, although they've never attacked one of our trawlers before."

Beckman's eyes followed the muddy shore, past dense mangroves to the stagnant green river. In the baking heat and humidity, it seemed utterly deserted, yet he had an uncomfortable feeling they were being watched by unseen eyes.

"What is it, Colonel?" Teresa asked, sensing his unease.

"I think it's time we got out of here," he said as the others followed his gaze.

Reynolds glanced at the river, not sharing his apprehension. "Yeah, there's nothing more we can do here."

They returned to the trawler's stern and climbed down to the motor boat, then a sailor released the mooring line. With a rev of the engines, the launch reversed away from the trawler, then headed back down river toward the sea. While the boat crew stayed in the wheelhouse, the others gathered on the stern deck, searching the river for any sign they were being followed. Occasionally, they heard a splash or saw spooked birds take flight, but never saw the cause. All the way to the river mouth, Beckman couldn't shake the sense of being observed, which annoyed him as he was not prone to irrational fantasies. It was only when they passed out of the river and entered the channel back to deep water did he begin to relax.

After they cleared the sandbar, Reynolds said, "The media will have a field day when they hear about this. We had search planes up for weeks and found nothing."

"They won't hear about it," Beckman said. "And you're not to write any reports."

"Navy procedure requires a report," Reynolds explained, certain he had no discretion.

"Not this time. Your Chief of Navy will confirm it."

Reynolds showed mild surprise, then shrugged. "OK by me, I'm not one for paperwork anyway."

"And don't call for a salvage team," Beckman added. "Your intelligence community will recover the trawler and sink her in deep water. No one will ever know we found the Mermaid or in what condition."

"Colonel, that's interfering with a murder investigation," Reynolds said uncomfortably. "They put you in jail for that down here."

"I understand. You'll get the appropriate orders."

"Very well," Reynolds said, suppressing a host of unspoken questions.

Beckman's gaze returned to the mouth of the river receding in the distance. "How big a generator would that trawler have had?"

"Hmm ... maybe ten kilowatts."

"That's a lot of electricity. How long would it run for?"

"I didn't see any portable tanks, so assuming they stole those too, they could keep the generator running for weeks, months if they rationed their fuel or stole more."

Beckman began to suspect these shipwreck survivors – if that's what they were – were more desperate than he'd imagined. Could they have gotten away from the crash site with little more than their lives, been forced to survive in the wilderness by their wits alone while remaining undiscovered for a decade? If so, it was a tremendous feat. He wondered if they were waiting for rescue or simply trying to avoid capture. Considering how they'd treated the trawler crew, he was certain whoever they were, they wouldn't hesitate to kill anyone in their way.

Dr. McInness leaned against the gunwale wondering how he could establish peaceful contact with them when he suddenly jumped to his feet and pointed at the water. "There's something down there! Teresa, get a photo."

"It's probably just a dolphin," Reynolds said unconcerned, not even bothering to look.

"There's another one," Dr. McInness said leaning over the side for a better view. "There are five of them. They're over there." He pointed toward five torpedo-like shadows in echelon formation heading for the open sea.

Teresa stepped up beside the scientist with her camera and peered into the water. "I don't see anything."

Beckman joined them, but the five underwater swimmers were already too far away.

Dr. McInness searched the water in vain, then said deflated, "They're gone."

"Don't worry, Doc," Reynolds said, "dolphins play under our boats all the time. You'll see more."

"They were swimming in a tight V-formation," the scientist said to Beckman, then repeated meaningfully, "It was a formation. They were watching us. When I saw them, they swam away."

Reynolds smiled. "They probably saw some fish and were hungry. Dolphins got to eat too, Doc."

Dr. McInness shook his head emphatically. "They weren't dolphins!"

* * * *

An orderly served coffee in Captain Turner's quarters after they returned to the *Naturaliste*, then Lt. Commander Reynolds recounted the discovery of the *Mermaid*. When he finished, Turner said, "Does that conclude your investigation, Colonel?"

"Not yet. Whatever killed the crew and hid the trawler is still out there."

"Don't you mean *who*ever?" she asked.

Beckman gave a noncommittal nod. "Have there been any other strange occurrences in this area?"

"Nothing like this trawler incident," she replied.

"There have been a few unexplained disappearances," Reynolds said. "Not as many as you might think. There aren't a lot of people along this coast, but those that are here know how to look after themselves."

"What about in the water?" the scientist asked. "Any unusual sightings?"

"Unusual how?" Turner asked puzzled.

Reynolds explained, "Dr. McInness saw something in

the water on our way back to the ship."

"There were five of them," the scientist said. "They were small and fast and … swam in formation. I only saw them for a few seconds."

Turner gave Reynolds a questioning look.

"I didn't see anything," he said. "I could have our sonar log checked."

Turner nodded her approval. "Just to be thorough."

"What kind of sonar do you have?" Teresa asked.

"We've got hull mounted, towed and side scanning sonars, as well as single and multi beam echo sounders," the Captain said. "We can map the sea and everything in it down to six thousand meters, twenty thousand feet."

Dr. McInness nodded, encouraged. "We're going to need those sensors."

"What about weapons?" Beckman asked.

"We're an oceanographic vessel, Colonel, not a warship," Turner replied. "We've got a couple of twelve point seven millimeter machine guns and small arms, of course. Why? Are you planning on starting a war?"

It was a feeble armament, but Beckman realized it was more firepower than sharpened coral knives. "I hope not, but you might want to arm your lookouts."

Turner looked surprised. "Against what, Colonel?"

"As a precaution," he replied evasively.

"Hmph," she said. "I'll consider it."

\* \* \* \*

Petty Officer Jeff Casey, a stocky, former submariner sat at one of the ship's sonar displays pointing to a series of five blips on the screen. He'd been watching them periodically brighten and dim every few seconds for some time.

"That's them," he said to Lt. Commander Reynolds standing beside him. "The computer logged them as natural acoustic anomalies, dolphins or whales. It couldn't decide which."

Beckman, Dr. McInness and Teresa looked over Casey's shoulders, studying the sonar display.

"Can we hear them?" Dr. McInness asked.

"Sure," the sonarman replied, then played the five signatures through the speakers, filling the compartment with repeating low frequency pings.

"Sounds like sonar," Beckman said.

"It is. They're ranging us."

"How long have they been there?" Dr. McInness asked.

Casey checked the time stamp. "First contact was eleven forty six."

"That's about the time you saw the five swimmers," Teresa said.

"Can you tell what kind of equipment they're using?" Beckman asked.

Casey shook his head slowly. "No equipment. These signals are biological. They're more powerful, with a larger frequency range than I've seen before, but there are natural variations in the pulses you don't get with mechanical sonar. That's why the computer's hedging its bets. It knows it's some kind of animal, but can't match the signature."

"How complete is your database?" Dr. McInness asked.

"Very," the sonarman replied confidently. "It's not often we don't get a match. The strangest thing about this isn't the signal, it's that they're just sitting there watching us. Biosonar contacts are always moving; looking for food, following currents, chasing each other. Whatever those things are, all they're interested in is us."

"Have you ever detected them before?" Dr. McInness asked.

Casey shrugged. "I can check our contact log."

"Go back six months," Reynolds said.

The sonarman passed the search parameters to the *Naturaliste's* main computer then waited as it scanned the ship's recent sensor history. Within a few seconds, his screen filled with hundreds of similar contacts indexed by date, time, latitude and longitude.

"These are all from the fisheries mapping we did four months ago," Casey said, glancing up at Reynolds. "All east of Elcho Island."

"Where's that?" Beckman asked.

"A couple of hundred kilometers east of here," Reynolds replied.

Petty Officer Casey studied the results with a keen eye. "These are more than ranging pulses. There's something else in the sound." He played several segments, filling the compartment with pings and rhythmic tones. "It's like whale song, only faster."

"By faster, you mean more sounds per second?" Dr. McInness asked.

"Yeah." He did some quick calculations. "Sixteen times faster."

"What's the difference between sonar and whale song?" Beckman asked.

"One is for ranging, the other..." Casey shrugged. "We don't really know. Could be for mating, for talking, or whales might just like singing."

"If it's a form of communication, then these signals could contain sixteen times more information than whale song," Dr. McInness said intrigued.

"No way to know," the sonarman said. "But I can tell you this: a few years ago some scientists recorded a song sung by whales on the west coast. They then tracked a couple of those whales that moved from the Indian Ocean to the east coast. Before long, the east coast whales were all singing the west coast song. Does that mean whale song means something? You tell me."

"It means something, otherwise, why copy it?" Dr. McInness said.

"It could have a social purpose," Teresa suggested. "Mating or family bonding or group acceptance."

"Whatever it means," Casey said, "your little friends out there are doing way more of it than any whale I ever tracked."

"Does sixteen times more information make them sixteen times smarter than whales?" Dr McInness wondered aloud.

"How much smarter than whales are humans?" Beckman asked.

"Not sixteen times smarter," Teresa said.

"Can you run that search back ten years," Beckman asked, "and plot the contacts on a map?"

"Absolutely," Casey replied, expanding the search parameters.

"If it's a local species," Reynolds said, "we'll only have logs for the time we've spent in this area. We've covered a lot of territory in that time."

They waited while the computer scanned and plotted every natural acoustic anomaly the *Naturaliste* had detected in the last decade. For long periods, the ship was away in the Indian, Pacific or Southern Oceans, although once or twice a year she passed the coast of Arnhem Land or carried out assignments in the Arafura Sea.

Casey brought a map of the Northern Territory coast up on his screen, then red acoustic contact dots began to cluster near a slender chain of islands running northeast out into the Arafura Sea. As the dots continued to appear, they began overlapping each other, forming larger and larger blobs of red that painted out the sea southeast of the island chain.

"That's a lot of contacts!" Teresa said astonished.

"Too many for what we're looking for," Dr. McInness said disappointed.

"What are you looking for?" Reynolds asked.

"Not dolphins," Beckman said.

Reynolds pointed to the island chain on the eastern side of the map. "They're called the Wessel Islands. It's all aboriginal land. Not many people there."

"Plenty of fish?" Dr. McInness asked.

"Some of the best fishing in the country," Reynolds

said. "It's virtually untouched."

"So plenty of food," Beckman said thoughtfully, "few inhabitants and judging by all those bays and inlets, lots of shelter. That must be the place." He turned to Petty Officer Casey. "Can you zoom the map out a little?"

The sonarman did as he was asked, revealing the sprawling empty land to the south and the open sea to the north. Beckman pointed to a featureless valley in Arnhem Land, several hundred kilometers southwest of the cluster of acoustic contacts.

"From there," he said pointing to the Goyder River impact site, "they could have floated down river to the sea, then followed the food supply along the coast." His finger traced a path along the Arnhem shore to the remote Wessel Islands.

Reynolds furrowed his brow. "Who did what?"

Beckman turned to Reynolds and Casey, both of whom were giving him curious looks. He'd already decided sonar would be integral to the success of the mission, forcing him to take them both into his confidence. "Survivors of a craft that crashed in the Goyder Valley ten years ago."

"Survivors?" Reynolds said, then a knowing look appeared on his face. "Ah! So that's who you are."

Beckman nodded. "Yeah, that's us."

Lt. Commander Reynolds was well aware ADF radars periodically tracked craft travelling at incredible velocities and that every such report was highly classified. No one who knew of those contacts was allowed to discuss them or even acknowledge their existence. Sometimes ships at sea and land bases were over flown or military aircraft shadowed, but always the craft refused every contact and soon moved off at tremendous speed, often accelerating vertically out of the atmosphere. It wasn't routine, but it occurred often enough that a procedure existed to handle it. All such reports were sent to the US military, although what happened to the reports at the other end, no one knew.

Beckman turned back to the map. "Which way does the current flow?"

"To the west," Reynolds said.

"So they'd have had a hard swim against the current," Beckman said.

"Yes, but it would have brought signs of food. Going east along the coast would be like following a trail to the food supply."

"And swimming isn't a problem for them," Dr. McInness added.

"Gentleman," Beckman said as diplomatically as he could, "not a word of this is to be discussed with the crew or other officers, including the Captain – for now."

"Now wait a minute," Reynolds said uncomfortably.

Beckman raised a placating hand. "If this develops into a situation, she'll be told what she needs to know. While we're still unsure what we're dealing with, it's best to keep this to as few people as possible. From now on, only Petty Officer Casey will operate the sonar and you commander will make sure the rest of the ship doesn't find out. I'll send a dispatch immediately. Within an hour, your Chief of Navy will confirm the orders in secret to you directly."

"You're pretty sure of yourself, Colonel," Reynolds bristled.

Beckman knew he'd feel the same way if he were in the naval officer's shoes. "Right now, Commander, this is the most important secret on Earth. It has to be this way." He turned to Casey. "And that sonar database of yours is now classified. No one sees it, no one accesses it, but you."

"You've got one hour, Colonel," Reynolds said, suppressing his irritation. "If I don't see those orders, I'll be reporting to the Captain." He turned to Casey. "Until then, assume Colonel Beckman has authority. The other sonar operators are stood down until further notice. They're not to discuss their change of status with anyone."

"Aye sir," Casey said, not quite sure what had happened.

Beckman fixed his attention on the map display screen. With nothing but a few isolated native communities for hundreds of kilometers in any direction, he was beginning to understand how a group of stranded aliens had gone unnoticed for a decade. If they hadn't attacked the trawler, they might have remained undetected for years to come. What he couldn't understand was why they'd taken such a risk? Why they'd revealed themselves now?

"So what next, Colonel?" Reynolds asked.

"Set course for the Wessel Islands."

\* \* \* \*

The Infiltrator lay at the bottom of the Arafura Sea, listening to the world around it with a vast array of sensors. It had confirmed the survivors were not using any of the communication technologies favored by Intruder forces, while the indigenous life forms extensive use of radio had almost certainly discouraged them from utilizing that technology. From sound waves pervading the sea, the Intruder probe tracked thousands of slow moving ships by their cavitating propellers and noisy combustion engines, monitored the movements of armed submarines creeping through the depths and recorded and classified the great chorus of life produced by millions of sea creatures. It was a kaleidoscope of artificial and natural sound that allowed the Infiltrator to construct an extraordinarily detailed understanding of the marine environment it hid within.

By the time it finished its analysis, another enemy ship had entered the Solar System and had begun scanning the planet's Pre-Fusion civilization from orbit. The Infiltrator quickly determined this new enemy lacked the technology to penetrate its invisibility shield while it kept its power levels low. Reassured, the

Intruder probe hugged the sea floor as it glided up onto a continental shelf and crept south toward a large land mass where it had detected the unmistakable acoustic fingerprints of its creators – but *not* its creators.

The Infiltrator was puzzled by the crudeness of their sounds, by the lack of complexity and resonance in their acoustic communications. Most surprising of all, the sonic patterns bore no resemblance to the One Speech, the Intruder's one and only language.

Unlike the languages of purely land bound species that evolved within geographical regions isolated from each other for thousands of years, the Intruder language had been carried acoustically around their origin world by its oceans, linking every coastal region together from the dawn of their civilization. That sonic link had created a rudimentary form of global communication leading to a single planetary language before their stone age had even ended. Even though the One Speech had thousands of dialects, the power of trans-oceanic sound ensured it had remained universally understood by all.

The Infiltrator came to an astonishing conclusion, that for the first time in millions of years, an Intruder spawn had appeared using a language unknown on their homeworld. This Earth spawn trilled in raw, unrefined tones as if they had been entirely deprived of their rich linguistic heritage. Such a calamity could only have occurred if there had been no nursery fathers to school the hatchlings in the patterns of the One Speech. Whatever the cause, the result was a set of acoustic patterns and structures whose meanings remained as impenetrable to the Infiltrator as the most complex enemy encryption.

Searching for an answer, the Infiltrator reviewed the testimony of the assault carrier's sole female survivor. Her story was no more than a footnote to the war history, yet it recorded her attempt to spawn after the ship had crashed. The Supernexus had presumed her microscopic progeny had been destroyed when she was captured, but now the Intruder probe suspected that assumption was false. The more it listened, the more it wondered how defenseless hatchlings had survived on an alien world for so long, a world dominated by warlike mammals in a star system close to their enemy's heartland.

That quandary alone merited further investigation, convincing the Infiltrator to solve the mystery of this unsophisticated Earth spawn. Only then would it reveal itself and only to the paramount female.

# CHAPTER THREE: INCURSIONS

Beloved-of-the-Sea listened to the rhythmic sounds drifting across the water from a white hulled cruiser as the sun dipped below the horizon. She'd heard land-dweller music before, although its purpose remained a mystery to her. She assumed the sounds were a form of communication or were used for navigation and hunting. The idea that sound was a medium for artistic expression never entered her head because her life was dominated by the need to simply survive. Beloved feared the music was being used to detect their approach although the motor yacht's occupants showed no sign of preparing for battle. She worried the land-dweller's seeming vulnerability was a trap, that they knew the attack was coming and were waiting to cut them down with their spitting-flash-weapons. They were fears stoked by unanswered questions that had plagued her since birth.

Where had she come from?

How could they be the only ones of their kind?

Where were the adults who'd given them life?

And worst of all, why was their world ruled by these strangely powerful land-dwellers?

They were questions she'd pondered from her earliest days, even as her young brothers were devoured by the great aquatic predators, the one-fin-killers and the long-tooth-stalkers, known as sharks and crocodiles to the land-dwellers. She particularly feared the long-tooth-stalkers, who hid in the mud waiting for their prey to approach, then struck without warning, unleashing a killing fury that gave their adversary no chance. Her biosonar always saw the one-fin-killers from a long way off, but the stalkers were rarely seen until it was too late. They hunted with a patient menace she recognized within herself and left her respecting the great predator long after it had ceased to be a threat.

Many of her siblings had died as hatchlings during those early helpless years, but thanks to the *myrnod* growth hormone they'd inherited from their spawn-mother, they'd grown rapidly. With no language or culture to draw upon, they invented their own, driven by the need to survive in a hostile world. Their powerful intellects quickly developed vocabulary and syntax with verbal and biosonic equivalents. They learned to use their biological sonar to hunt, to avoid danger and to communicate over long distances just as their ancestors had done eons ago. Six years after their appearance, while still barely adolescents, they ruled the Mothersea and the bays and rivers bordering it. All that prevented them from becoming the apex predator were the land-dwellers who remained blithely ignorant of their existence.

Occasionally, a fisherman chanced upon them, only to be torn apart before he could carry word of their existence to his own kind. As the seasons passed and they learned to hide from the land-dwellers, such chance encounters decreased even as they crept closer to the settlements, studying their enemy's every move. While still young, Beloved realized the land-dwellers were their only true competitor, possessing an intelligence that made them masters of the world and guaranteeing that one day, a reckoning would come, for one world cannot have two masters.

Beloved-of-the-Sea knew the time when they could no longer hide their presence was fast approaching. That knowledge drove her to take greater risks, to learn all she could before it was too late. They'd been stealing from the land-dwellers for years, watching their machines, picking through their garbage, learning their written language from children's picture books, but much more was needed.

She sank below the surface and emitted questioning pings from her sonar lobe, *"How many?"*

A moment later, Heart-of-the-Deep, her most trusted sister who led the scouting group on the far side of the cruiser replied, *"Two that we can see, Sister. They have no weapons."*

Knowing they could wait no longer, Beloved emitted a burst of pulses from her sonar lobe, ordering her warriors to attack. Off to her right, Prowls-the-Shallows emitted a single ping, acknowledging the instruction, then led five males in a high speed dash toward the luxury cruiser. They swam three meters below the surface while she was forced to watch from a safe distance with her bodyguard and Watcher-of-Skies.

Watcher preferred pursuits of the mind to hunting. It was he who'd supervised the scavenging of the trawler and the disassembly of its equipment, although devising and solving abstract mathematical problems was much more to his liking. From a young age, he had studied the night sky, mapping in his mind the celestial lights as they moved across the heavens. Watcher had read more land-dweller books and penetrated their secrets more deeply than any other. Once he'd mastered their written language, he'd found the sequential way they moved from one idea to the next a frustrating limitation. Considering the land-dweller's obvious material power, the linearity of their minds was a perplexing paradox and a sign of hope.

Prowls-the-Shallows might command the hunter-warriors, but Beloved believed Watcher's growing mastery of land-dweller secrets was the key to their survival. It was for him, and those following in his footsteps, that drove her to act now, to give him time to learn all he could of their enemy's strengths, and more importantly, to find their weakness.

She hoped they had one.

Beloved surfaced again to the sound of a female land-dweller's drunken laughter followed by a male's deeper voice. The pop of a cork followed by the clink of glasses preceded the emergence of a naked couple from the cruiser's sleek cabin. They held glasses of champagne as they strolled out onto the stern deck, then pressed their bodies together and kissed, believing they had the sweeping bay all to themselves.

Beneath the lovers, Prowls-the-Shallows and two of his hunters dived deep, then surged upwards, leaping out of the water and over the teak topped railing. The thud of them landing on the deck startled the couple who turned sharply toward the sound. The man stepped in front of the woman to shield her as Prowls darted forward and slashed his throat open with a lightning fast stroke. Blood sprayed over the woman as her husband slumped to the deck. She screamed, then her neck was severed by one of the other hunters, choking off her shriek as she collapsed.

Three more warriors leapt out of the water onto the deck and charged into the sleek white wheelhouse searching for anyone hiding inside. On the stern deck, the couple's bodies were thrown over the side to a pair of hunters who towed their corpses into deep water where the one-fin-killers would devour them.

Beloved-of-the-Sea motioned to Watcher, who swam to the motor yacht and leapt onto its deck. He vanished into the cabin, then moments later, the sound of the anchor winch reached her as the engines came to life. By the time the sun had set, the cruiser was motoring at fourteen knots toward Elcho Island at the southern tip of the Wessel Island chain.

Beloved followed at a distance, relieved it had been so easy, yet wary of what was to come.

* * * *

Martha Nurruwi snapped awake thinking it must have been a nightmare, then it sounded again, a woman's scream. It was a scream unlike any she'd heard, a cry of pure terror that was suddenly cut off by a strange gasping sound. She couldn't tell who it was, but she must have known her. Martha knew all her neighbors in the tiny community.

She rolled off her bed, tiptoed to the window and peered out. There were few streetlights outside her simple house, only a couple by the school and another over near the shop. She hid in the darkness, listening and waiting for another sound, but none came. Martha wondered if she'd dreamt it, then she saw a shadow creeping through the trees across the road. It was heading for the school, the largest building in Galiwinku and the only major school between there and Darwin five hundred and fifty kilometers away. As her eyes became attuned to the night, she realized there were other shadows sneaking toward the school and the police station. They were the size of small men although their proportions were all wrong. The heads were too large, faces too angular, bodies too thin and shoulders too broad. They looked like nothing she'd ever seen before even though she'd lived all her forty two years in the Wessel Islands.

Two shadows appeared near the shop, moving in the opposite direction toward the beach. At first she thought they were carrying a sack, then realized it was the body of a woman. A shiny wetness glistened on her severed neck and down her limp arms in the moonlight, convincing Martha the poor woman was dead.

Her heart began beating loudly in her chest, so hard it almost hurt. She barely breathed as more shadows slipped between the trees. There were so many of them, it was as if the ground was alive with movement, yet they scarcely made a sound. She slipped back into the darkness of her room, crept to the telephone in the hall and called the police station.

When a young constable answered, she whispered, "A woman's been murdered out by the school."

"Who is this?" the constable asked.

"Martha Nurruwi. I heard a scream and I seen some little fella's takin' a body."

"Who was taking the body?"

"Don't know who they are. Can't see them. There's more than one of them."

"Do you know who screamed?"

"Nah, couldn't tell."

"This is out by Shepherdson College?"

"Yeah, across the road."

"OK, we'll send someone."

Martha hung up, then crept back to the window. By the time she got there, the shadowy forms had vanished and the lights at the school were off. She strained to see what was happening, then heard glass shatter as the light at the shop winked out leaving only moonlight to illuminate the dusty red dirt streets.

She decided to go into the kitchen for a better look at the school. With her pulse racing, she tiptoed to the screen door beside her sink and peered out. In the weak moonlight, three small forms were visible near the southern classroom. They were careful to stay in the deepest shadows, appearing only momentarily as they moved between the buildings. Unlike vandals or thieves who tended to be brazen, these strangers took unusual care to hide their identities by avoiding the moonlight. She watched with mounting fear as they slipped around the corner and stopped to observe the road.

Martha tried to convince herself they were teenagers up to no good, then remembered the murdered woman. Kids out for late night mischief might vandalize the student's garden or smash a window with a rock, but they'd never kill anyone – and these prowlers didn't move like people. Their gait was more fluid than a man's, graceful and terrifying at the same time.

A car came cruising slowly up the red dirt road, its engine purring quietly. When it switched on a bank of floodlights mounted above the cab, Martha realized it was a police four wheel drive sent from the station. The coppers had come quick as she knew they would. The station was only over on Galawarra Road, just two blocks from the school. The paddy wagon turned into the school, sweeping light over the trees and illuminating the side of the classroom, showing the three dark forms that had hidden near the corner had vanished.

Two constables wearing blue uniforms stepped out of the car. They separated, ambling off in opposite directions, playing their torches over the building as they moved away from the area lit by the car's floodlights. They were relaxed and confident, not even bothering to keep one hand on their guns. Both officers knew Galiwinku was a peaceful little community on the edge of nowhere, where the worst they had to deal with were domestic disputes and petty thievery. Very few of the inhabitants owned guns and those that did only fired them at the occasional crocodile that wandered into town and never at the police.

Martha watched the two coppers move alongside the building, casually checking windows and doors. From their calm demeanor, she knew they hadn't believed there was a murder. They assumed local kids had scared a woman out of her bed in the middle of the night and then run off home as soon as they saw the paddy wagon approaching.

She decided she had to talk to the officers, to convince them a woman had been killed. She raised her hand to push the screen door open then froze as one of the constable's flashlights suddenly spun sideways and hit the ground. A small dark shadow drove a knife into the policeman's stomach, then pounced on top of him to deliver a finishing blow as he fell. It happened so fast, the officer didn't have time to cry out or call to his companion. Martha wanted to yell a warning to the other copper, but she was paralyzed with fear as another shadow burst out of the darkness with astonishing speed. It leapt at the second policeman with a savage sweeping motion that sliced deep into his neck, then its shoulder struck the man's chest, knocking him to the ground. The officer clutched at his throat as the dark form drove its knife into his chest and twisted the blade, causing the man to convulse.

Martha gasped, shocked by the speed and ferocity of the attacks, then other dark shapes appeared, quickly switching off the flashlights, scooping up the officers' guns and carrying off their bodies. One diminutive figure avoided the cone of light emanating from the car, then climbed inside and turned off the floodlights. A moment later the engine roared loudly as if a learner driver was over revving the engine in a failed attempt to start the vehicle. After repeated failures, the engine flooded and the shadow behind the wheel abandoned the car.

With rising terror, Martha decided to go next door to Frank's place. He was a ranger and had a gun. She pushed the screen door open and slipped outside, her eyes riveted on the school. Fearful of the screen door banging, she eased it shut then turned to run, but found a small dark shape with a softly ridged hairless head, domed forehead and angular chin barring her way.

Paralyzed with fear, she stared into its bulging blue-green eyes too afraid to scream, then it darted forward so fast it blurred in the darkness. She glimpsed a short white blade slash at her in the moonlight, felt a pulling of skin around her neck and a flood of warmth running down her chest. She glanced down, unaware her throat had been cut and that she was already drowning in her own blood, then she crumpled onto her garden. Two forms emerged from the darkness and carried her body to the sea.

By dawn, one-fin-killers had consumed her corpse, ensuring no trace of Martha Nurruwi's body was ever found.

* * * *

"You want to go where?" Captain Turner asked from her chair on the bridge.

"The Goyder River Valley," Dr. McInness said. "I want to take some readings at the alpha impact site."

"Scientists have been tramping all over that place for years," she said. "They've taken every kind of reading there is, many times over."

"Not every kind," Beckman said.

"I have classified technology with me they wouldn't have had access to," Dr. McInness explained. "All I need is a few hours."

"Is this related to your investigation?" Turner asked.

"It's hard to say until we get down there," Beckman replied.

"It is," Dr McInness said definitely, giving Beckman a meaningful look. His dreams and flashbacks often related to the remote location deep in the Arnhem forest. He'd read every report of every expedition to the site, all of which were inconclusive due to the damage inflicted on the area by the asteroid impact. He'd wanted to return for years and had been testing a piece of recovered alien technology for that purpose, although it took the discovery of the alien tooth to finally secure approval for the trip.

"It's in range of the helo," Reynolds said.

She considered the request a moment. "OK, every assistance," she said, recalling her orders. "When do you want to go?"

"As soon as your chopper's ready to fly," Beckman said.

\* \* \* \*

Lt. Commander Reynolds took the small helicopter's controls as the *Naturaliste* steamed north of Castlereagh Bay. Beckman took the copilot's seat while Teresa and Dr. McInness sat in the rear, she with her camera, him nursing a metal case fitted with a sophisticated biometric locking system.

Reynolds asked, "Did you want to land or just fly over the crater?"

"Land," Dr. McInness said, "in the middle of the impact zone."

"OK," he said, then powered up the AS 350 Squirrel.

It was a short flight over a glittering sea to the coast, then they followed the Glyde River south as it wound through pristine tropical forest. The Glyde became the Goyder, flanked by broad flood plains stretching off to ochre colored cliffs encircling tree covered plateaus. In time, the wilderness gave way to a plain of fallen, ashen trees. Saplings and tropical ferns had begun sprouting from the ruins of the forest that a decade before had been felled by a great blast and incinerated by the firestorm that followed.

"In another twenty years, you'd never know what happened," Reynolds said over the beat of the rotors.

Beckman stared down at the nascent forest, thinking, *If Ian's right, we don't know what happened here now.*

The small crater at the center of the blast zone blocked a gently flowing river that had eaten away part of the rim wall, flooding the interior. The shallow crater lake was carpeted with water lilies sprouting pink, purple and white flowers and was already home to a growing population of multicolored birds.

"I thought impact craters had islands in the center?" Teresa said, puzzled by the lake's unbroken shallows.

"Big ones do," Dr. McInness said, "if they're over 3 kilometers across. This impact was too small to form a complex crater."

"As asteroids go," Reynolds said, "they say it was a baby."

Dr. McInness studied the crater and the destruction surrounding it. The blast zone stretched off toward the horizon while the nearby cliffs showed signs of having been seared by intense heat. "Whatever created this crater wasn't large enough to have caused this much damage."

Beckman gave him a curious look. "It was almost two Hiroshimas."

"That's only thirty kilotons, Bob. This was a multi-megaton blast."

It was the one inconsistency the after-impact studies had agreed upon and couldn't explain, the blast radius was much larger than a small asteroid could have caused. The researchers theorized it might have had something to do with the asteroid's chemical composition, or the high iron deposits in the soil, but none of the teams could agree.

"I'll set her down over there," Reynolds said, pointing to a charred stretch of ground beside the lake.

Dr McInness studied the surrounding black cliffs curiously. The rock face was ragged in places while other sections appeared to have been sliced off as if by a knife. At the foot of the cliffs, giant boulders had been cut in half, with the valley side crushed flat. Suddenly he realized what he was looking at.

"No!" he said, leaning toward Reynolds. "Take us up."

"Up?" Reynolds asked confused. "I thought you wanted to land."

"I do, but not yet. Go higher."

Reynolds shrugged and put the helo into a slow climb. The crater fell away beneath them, merging fine details into broad patterns revealing the shallow circle of the crater and the gray blast zone surrounding it.

"How's this?" Reynolds asked.

"Higher," Dr McInness said as he pressed his face to

the window studying the shearing pattern on the cliff wall and the crushed ground below.

Reynolds turned to Beckman, seeking confirmation.

"It's Ian's show," Beckman said, then Reynolds fed more power to the engines, continuing their vertical climb.

At fifteen hundred meters, Dr McInness grinned, finally convinced he wasn't going crazy. "There it is!"

The others looked down at a blasted wasteland partially obscured by regrowth.

"There's what?" Beckman asked, not seeing it.

Dr McInness pointed out into the valley. "From there ... to there," he said, sweeping his hand toward a point behind them, tracing a rectangular imprint in the ground twelve kilometers long. It was partially camouflaged by regrowth and the circular impact crater at its center.

"Son of a bitch!" Beckman exploded when he saw it, realizing whatever had come down had almost filled the valley. "You were right!"

Reynolds gazed at the ground, not comprehending. "Right about what?"

Teresa started taking photographs. "Shouldn't there be two craters? One for the asteroid, one for the ship?"

"What ship?" Reynolds asked, aware he was missing something the others had seen.

"Should be," Dr. McInness said, scanning the wasteland for signs of a much larger crater enclosing the first, but the floodplain was flat, swept clean by a blast that had scythed all in its path. "The impact and the debris thrown into the sky should have absorbed a lot of energy, but this says the energy was channeled horizontally."

"Is that possible?" Beckman asked.

The scientist shrugged. "It would be an efficient weapon, directing the ship's kinetic energy at anyone on the ground. They'd have to protect the crew from the inertial effect of the impact, but we know they can do that because they can withstand incredible acceleration. I just never imagined they'd use that technology as a weapon."

"So they crashed the ship on purpose," Beckman said. "Hell of way to establish a bridgehead."

"A megaton sized explosion without radiation," Dr McInness said, aware the same effect could be achieved with nuclear weapons at the cost of irradiating the area, making it dangerous to the crew.

Reynolds gave Beckman a frustrated look. "What ship?"

"It left a footprint, a big footprint," Beckman said, tracing its outline with his finger.

Suddenly, Reynolds saw it. His eyes bulged and his mouth opened in surprise. "No way! ... NO WAY! ... A ship did that?"

"The meteor hit was no accident," Beckman said. "The area was sanitized so there'd be nothing left for us."

Teresa lowered her camera with a troubled look. "They knew."

Beckman turned to her, puzzled. "Who knew?"

She shrugged. "Whoever's in charge. The Pentagon, the White House, some black committee no one's ever heard of. They've known from day one what happened. They had to." She pointed to the ground. "One satellite picture would have told them what happened, especially ten years ago before the site began degrading. That's why we never saw any satellite imagery, no aerial shots. Those bastards knew and didn't even tell us. And we're the team. We're the contact point. Half our people are dead and they didn't even trust *us* with the truth."

Shock flashed across Dr. McInness' face. "They told me I was crazy!" He turned to Beckman. "Did you know?"

Beckman shook his head. "No."

"That's why every request I made to come here was denied, because they knew I'd figure it out."

"And you did."

"I bet they redacted the investigator's reports," Teresa said, "taking out anything that would indicate what really happened here."

"More than that, Teresa," Beckman said. "Aliens have been studying us for a very long time. They know us well enough to predict our moves. They knew if they created the circumstances to conceal what happened – the two asteroid impacts – our governments would play along, would hide any inconsistencies, which is exactly what they did."

"So what are we going to do about it?" Dr McInness asked. "The lies. The deception."

"Not a damn thing," Beckman replied.

"What!" the scientist exploded. "Bob, if they don't trust us, who the hell do they trust?"

"No one. That's how this game's played, Ian. Everything's compartmentalized and as far as this goes, we're in the wrong compartment. The only reason we're here now is because they need us to figure out what's going on."

"So we go on as if nothing happened?"

"That's exactly what we do," Beckman said firmly. "If you have a problem with that, I'll have to put you on the first plane home."

There was an icy silence, then Reynolds glanced over his shoulder. "Hey, they didn't tell me either and it's my country!" A crooked smile appeared on his face, lessening the tension.

Beckman gave Dr. McInness a curious look. "Are we good?"

His friend sighed. "Yeah. You're right. You can land, Commander, inside the crater."

Reynolds gently nosed the chopper down, dropping quickly toward the crater lake. Soon they were skimming the water, startling birds to flight, then they set down on a small rise close to the water's edge.

They climbed out, then Dr. McInness put his precious metal case on the ground. He and Beckman simultaneously pressed their thumbs against the case's biometric scanner, then locking bolts clicked open. Dr. McInness lifted the container's lid, revealing a screen on its underside and a white, rectangular device with angular markings cradled in the metal case's body.

Reynolds stared at the unfamiliar characters curiously. "What language is that?"

"Nu-pi," Beckman said.

"I've never heard of it."

"We made it up, because saying Nu-Two Lupinian was a bit much. Isn't that right, Ian?"

Dr McInness didn't look up from the screen. "What he means, Commander, is this device came from a planet orbiting Nu-Two Lupi in the constellation Lupis. It's a sun-like star forty eight light years from Earth."

"We don't know their actual name," Beckman said, "but Teresa's working on it."

"Lupis?" Reynolds said incredulously.

"Yeah, as in the wolf," Beckman said. "I wanted to call them wolfies, but ... the naming committee outvoted me."

"You have a naming committee?" Reynolds asked, giving Teresa a quizzical look. "Is he serious?"

"Yes," she replied. "I'm on it."

"I used to be," Beckman said, "but they kicked me off it."

Teresa smiled. "The Colonel likes nicknames, which doesn't work for the scientific community."

Beckman snorted. "You guys can be so stuffy. Wolfies was a good name. It helps me remember where they're from."

"But they're annelids, sir, not wolves."

Beckman shuddered at the thought of hyper intelligent, segmented worms visiting Earth.

Reynolds blinked, trying to digest what he was hearing. "Are you saying there are so many aliens that you need a committee to name them all?"

"Pretty much," Beckman replied, "although most are

just catalogue numbers at this stage. We need something solid, like a homeworld location, before it goes to the committee."

"That kind of data is hard to come by," Teresa added.

"And you can actually read that language?" Reynolds asked, motioning toward the white device.

"Not exactly," she said. "We can translate its number system – numbers are easy – and we've deduced a few words, but full translations are a long way off."

"It's working," Dr. McInness declared, drawing their attention.

The bottom third of the screen was filled with a band of green topped by small, high frequency ripples. Three quarters of the way across the screen, a single red line rose vertically out of the green layer. Dr. McInness manipulated a slider, scanning the intensity of the green ripples.

Reynolds leaned over the scientist's shoulder, reading two text labels in the top right corner of the screen alongside a pair of ten decimal place, exponential numbers. The first line read 'Background Gravitons', the second, 'Radical Gravitons'.

"Gravitons?" Reynolds said surprised. "As in gravity?"

"As in a massless, spin-2 boson elementary particle that mediates the force of gravity," Dr. McInness said, transfixed by the solitary red vertical line.

"You can measure those things?"

"With this I can."

"I thought we needed supercolliders to see stuff like that?"

"No supercollider can do what Ian's little toy does," Beckman said.

Reynolds' eyes settled on the white alien device at the heart of the graviton scanner. "So where'd you get this thing?"

"Same place Ian gets all his toys. Salvage. We pulled this box of tricks out of a seven hundred year old wreck lying at the bottom of the Bering Sea eighteen years ago. It's taken us almost that long to figure out what it does."

"Which is?" Reynolds asked.

"It's like a depth sounder," Dr. McInness said. "Instead of measuring how much water is under the ship, it measures gravity, which seems to be dangerous to their ships, probably because of how it curves spacetime."

"A depth sounder for space travel?" the naval officer asked incredulously

"They all have them," Beckman said, "at least the ones we've seen."

Reynolds watched the band of wavering green as the red line lengthened slightly. "What's the green represent?"

"Background gravitons," Dr. McInness said. "That's the strength of Earth's gravity at this point on the planet's surface."

"And the red line?"

"They're the radicals. Gravitons that have been pushed out of phase with Earth's gravity."

"How does that happen?" Reynolds asked, puzzled.

"I have absolutely no idea, but it's telling us an immense power messed with Earth's gravity, right where you're standing."

"Ten years ago," Teresa added.

"And the planet's gravity still hasn't fully recovered," the scientist explained.

"Have you ever seen anything like this before?" Reynolds asked.

"No," Dr. McInness said, entranced. "We get a bump when they overfly Area 51, but this is different. It's like a spear of energy was driven into the planet's gravity field." His eyes shifted from the screen to the lake and the blackened cliffs in the distance. "Whatever crashed here was huge and it took enormous energy to lift it off again."

"It must have been some recovery operation," Beckman said.

"We were here, Bob. We saw it and they messed with our minds so we wouldn't remember a damn thing!" he said rubbing his temple, sensing the pain killers were beginning to wear off.

Beckman patted his friend's shoulder. "It could have been worse, Ian. They could have killed us to keep us quiet. Good thing they didn't realize you've got a robot brain inside that head of yours."

"I wonder what it looked like?" Dr. McInness said wistfully.

"Oh you know," Beckman said, "just your run of the mill, big ass alien mothership. Seen one, seen them all."

The scientist scowled. "I haven't seen one yet, not up close."

Reynolds looked surprised. "Not one?"

"We've recovered a few small wrecks," Beckman said, "mostly scout craft, but they keep the really big stuff away from the planet. I guess they don't want to spook the natives."

"If you can't see them, how do you know they're there?" Reynolds asked.

"NASA has some really nice pictures of big blurry blobs in deep space," Beckman said, "but they're not allowed to share."

Teresa stared at the graviton sensor's screen, perplexed. "If they went to so much trouble recovering their ship and they had the technology to lift something the size of a city off a planet, how did they miss the survivors?"

There was a moment's silence, then Beckman said. "They screwed up."

"Why didn't the survivors signal?" Reynolds asked.

"Maybe they were hiding from whoever took their ship," Dr. McInness said. "After all, we have no idea what's happening just beyond our atmosphere. Anything could be going on up there and we'd never know."

Reynolds looked doubtful. "I'm having a hard time believing a bunch of shipwrecked aliens have been hiding in the Wessel Islands for ten years. The aborigines must have seen them."

"If they did," Beckman said, "they didn't live long enough to report it."

"So they've been killing our people in secret for a decade. Right?"

"It's possible," Beckman conceded.

Reynolds expression hardened, his mind made up. "OK then, you've got to tell the skipper. We could be putting the ship in danger, and the crew. She's got to know." Before Beckman could protest, he added, "You said you weren't sure what you were dealing with." He motioned to the screen and the enormous mothership imprint they were standing in. "Well, now we're sure. If you don't tell her, I will. Orders be damned. I'll take my chances with a court martial."

Beckman studied Reynolds face, seeing he meant it. "Loyalty to your commanding officer. I respect that." He considered the naval officer's ultimatum a moment. "Very well, Commander, we'll brief her when we get back."

\* \* \* \*

That night they dined in the privacy of the Captain's stateroom rather than the officer's mess. After the orderly had served dinner and stood ready to refill their drinks, Beckman leaned toward Captain Turner and spoke in a low voice.

"Captain, we have confidential matters to discuss," he said, casting his eyes at the orderly.

Reynolds gave her a curt nod, indicating the importance of Beckman's request.

The captain turned to the young sailor standing at ease nearby. "That'll be all for the night, Tom, thank you."

When the orderly had closed the door behind him, Beckman opened the small box containing the triangular alien tooth taken from the trawler captain's boot and placed it in front of her. "We're here because of this." She glanced casually at the tooth, then Beckman motioned for Dr. McInness to explain.

"Captain, human DNA is made up of twenty amino acids in different combinations," the scientist began. "This tooth is composed of twenty two amino acids, only eighteen of which occur naturally on Earth. There are also chemicals called enzymes, which repair damaged DNA, limiting the amount of mutation that can occur. This makes DNA stable, but leaves room for mutation for evolutionary purposes. That tooth has twenty times as many enzymes as human DNA, which means this life form is virtually incapable of mutation."

Captain Turner furrowed her brow. "I'm no biologist, Doctor, but that doesn't seem possible."

"From a bio-evolutionary perspective, it isn't," Dr. McInness agreed. "Every cell of every living creature on Earth is naturally capable of mutation, except for the species that owns that tooth."

"So it's stopped evolving," she said, then added with a wry smile, "Sounds like my ex-husband. No, that's wrong, he was evolving backwards."

Smiles rippled around the dinner table, then Dr. McInness continued, "Either it's an evolutionary dead end, or it was genetically engineered."

"Really?" she said, eyeing the tooth with growing interest. "So what is it, some kind of escaped lab experiment?"

"It's no experiment," Beckman assured her.

"Only five percent of human DNA encodes proteins," Dr McInness said. "In that tooth, it's nine percent. In terms of chromosomes, we have over thirty eight thousand genes per chromosome. It has over fifty two thousand. That makes this life form significantly more complex than any other species on Earth."

"Including us apes," Beckman added lightly.

"You're not trying to tell me that tooth is from outer

space are you, Doctor?" she asked with a skeptical grin, then sobered when she saw no one was smiling.

"I am."

She glanced at Reynolds, who nodded. "It took me a while to believe it, but I'm getting there."

Turner picked up the tooth and studied it closely. "So where'd it come from?"

"We don't know," Beckman said. "Some place way out there."

"And you're here to capture it?"

"If possible. We'll start with hello and see where it goes from there. The problem is, they're hiding."

"There's more than one?" she asked.

Dr McInness nodded. "We don't know how many. They're either waiting for rescue or they're stranded here and see us as a threat."

"Either way," Beckman said, "they're watching us."

The Captain tensed. "How do you know?"

"I told you I saw them," Dr. McInness said, "and they're tracking us with sonar."

"They have a dolphin-like biological sonar thingy," Beckman said. "They're pinging your ship with it right now."

"They attacked the Mermaid," Reynolds explained. "That's where the tooth came from."

"It could have been a misunderstanding," Dr. McInness said. "The trawler might have discovered them, caught one by mistake."

"So they killed the crew?" she asked.

"It looks that way," Reynolds said.

She stiffened. "Are they a threat to my ship?"

"They're aggressive," Beckman conceded.

"We don't know that, Bob," Dr. McInness said.

"Yes we do, Ian. They're probably no threat to something as big as this ship. They don't seem to have advanced weapons, which is good for us, but you should take precautions."

"How can they not have advanced weapons?" Turner

asked.

"Their ship crashed," Teresa said. "They appear to have got out with very little."

"Where's the wreck?" Turner asked.

"Gone," Beckman said. "Someone up there beat us to it."

"So who knows about these … shipwrecked aliens?"

"South of the equator, just your senior sonarman and the five of us."

"What about Chief of Navy? And the Prime Minister?"

Beckman shook his head. "Need to know. They think we're looking for a top secret piece of DARPA technology that crashed here. Too secret to talk about, so they don't ask, we don't tell."

"And that was enough to get my ship assigned to you?"

Beckman gave her a rueful look. "We asked nicely."

"Hmph," she said.

"The records of the first DNA test in the Australian lab," Teresa said, "which our people spotted, have been destroyed."

"By who?" Turner asked.

"Your people took care of it," Beckman said.

"Because you asked nicely?"

"For the greater good."

"Does your President know?" Turner asked.

"Hell no," Beckman said. "We don't trust politicians with stuff like this."

"So who's in charge?"

"A small, very select group in the Pentagon and enough Senators on funding committees to keep the money flowing."

She sat back reflecting on his words, almost wishing she didn't have to know. "Why are you telling me this now?"

Beckman glanced at Reynolds. "Because your executive officer insisted and we're going to need your help."

"To do what?"

Beckman pocketed the tooth with a knowing look. "To find them."

* * * *

The Infiltrator glided above the sea floor like a dark whale as it headed toward a long chain of islands. Intruder acoustics echoed through the depths, which it continually recorded and analyzed, but without a reference point, it was unable to translate their incomprehensible language. It knew if it was to understand and communicate with the Earth spawn, a more direct approach was needed. Being an intelligence gathering probe designed to penetrate the secrets of hostile alien civilizations, it was singularly suited to such a task.

The Infiltrator chose to remain hidden in deep water rather than risk detection by moving into the shallows where the great mass of acoustics originated from. When it was two hundred kilometers northeast of a tree covered rocky outcrop known to the humans as Truant Island, the last land east of the Mothersea, it detected a group of nine males. It followed their sonic trail, closing the distance between them while its dampening field absorbed their sonar, masking its presence.

The Intruder probe discovered they swam in random circles, inexplicably doubling back and forth while constantly pulsing their ranging sonar. The strange behavior intrigued the Infiltrator, enticing it to move within visual range where it could observe them directly. When it first saw the hunting party, it was surprised to discover they were naked, devoid of any protective clothing or equipment. When it scanned them, it found they lacked the implants Intruder males were fitted with from birth – even basic thought networking was missing. It was a surprising discovery, considering the integration between the Intruder species and their technology had become so seamless they had engineered their bodies to interface efficiently with implanted technology, something few species dared to do. Instead of being accompanied by robotic workers that performed manual tasks, the naked males swam alone. They worked as a team, herding fish toward the western islands just as their ancestors had done on another watery world millions of years ago.

The Infiltrator shadowed them while its chameleon skin blended its form into the environment, concealing its presence. It searched the group for a female, but finding only males, it waited until one of the herders moved to cut off a small school of fish that had broken away from the main group. While the solitary male rounded up the fleeing fish, the Intruder probe slid silently up behind him.

The sea-herder didn't understand why his body suddenly went limp, that he'd been paralyzed by a low intensity stunner. Still conscious, he glimpsed a dark streamlined form move toward him, then felt an invisible pressure field pull him into the belly of the beast.

With its specimen secure, the Intruder probe dove to the relative safety of the sea floor where it analyzed the sea-herder's memories and learnt his language. The Infiltrator had been designed to intercept the most ingeniously encrypted signals, to monitor entire worlds and when necessary, to capture and interrogate prisoners. It quickly discovered the male's language was rudimentary and his education and knowledge of the universe completely lacking.

The sea-herder was frustrated by his capture, but his innate intelligence and rigid self control never allowed him a moment's fear. Instead, he studied his capsule-shaped prison cell, trying in vain to understand what it was. He found the air strangely pleasant, unaware it was the atmosphere of his origin world, while the Voice-from-Nowhere that spoke into his mind was intrusive and relentless. Voice had the natural authority of a female, yet the male knew it was something else, something beyond his understanding. When the Infiltrator completed its interrogation, it released the male, sending him swimming back to the Mothersea with an urgent, simple message.

The Infiltrator humbly requested an audience with the Matriarch known as Beloved-of-the-Sea.

* * * *

At dawn, HMAS *Naturaliste* anchored off Abbott Island, a tiny tree covered sliver of sand and rock five kilometers from Cadell Strait's western entrance. The Strait was a narrow channel between the mainland to the south and Elcho Island, the most southerly of the Wessel group. After anchoring, Petty Officer Casey reported there were Doppler sonar signals bouncing off the ship's hull from three different directions. They'd shadowed the *Naturaliste* all through the night, monitoring her progress with military precision while keeping a constant distance.

After breakfast, Captain Turner summoned Colonel Beckman to the bridge, then led him out onto one of the wing lookouts where they could talk privately and view the Straits through binoculars.

When the bridge door closed behind them, Turner said in a low voice, "I received a dispatch from naval intelligence this morning. That's ' why we anchored here."

"I wondered why we stopped."

"See that town over there," she said, nodding to a cluster of white walled buildings partly visible beyond the lush tropical trees lining the beach. "Two nights ago, eight people disappeared over there. Five civilians and three police officers."

Beckman turned his binoculars on the town at the southern tip of Elcho Island. "Is there a link to our shipwrecked aliens?"

"The school and the police station were looted, same as the Mermaid."

"Any sign of the missing people?"

"Only blood stains. They killed anyone who got in their way, then disposed of the bodies."

Beckman lowered his binoculars. "What did they steal?"

"Books and weapons. No cash or valuables."

"They knew what they were after," Beckman said thoughtfully. "They must have been watching the town for some time."

"There's one police officer still alive over there, a Sergeant Hayward. He was off duty at the time. It's probably why he's not dead."

"I'd like to talk to him."

"I thought you would. Commander Reynolds will take you over."

* * * *

Sergeant Hayward parked his Toyota dual cab four wheel drive in front of the beach on the southeast side of Elcho Island where the landing barges came in to drop supplies. The *Naturaliste's* launch was just rounding the southern headland as he climbed out and ambled to the wharf. He was a stocky, sun tanned Territorian in his early forties who wore a dark blue uniform, wide brimmed hat, dark sun glasses and a sidearm.

Hayward waited while the motor boat came alongside, then shook hands with Reynolds as the naval officer climbed onto the wharf. "Welcome to Galiwinku," he drawled. "Always good to see the navy. I just wish it was under better circumstances."

"Me too," Reynolds said somberly, then introduced Beckman, Teresa and Dr. McInness without explaining their roles.

"We lost some good people the other night,"

Hayward said, motioning them toward his car.

"I'm sorry for your loss, Sergeant," Beckman said sincerely.

"Thanks," Hayward said, then once they were in the car following a red dirt road through dense forest to the town, he recounted the events of several nights ago. "There were no witnesses. All we have is what the forensics team from Darwin came up with. The station's log shows two of my officers answered a call about one AM. That was the last we heard of them or the woman who made the call. Some residents heard screams and a few saw people moving in the darkness, but no one they could identify."

"What did the forensic team find?" Dr. McInness asked.

"The blood spatter patterns were consistent with knife attacks. The amount of blood indicated arterial wounds, fast bleed outs," Hayward said as they reached the town's outer buildings. "They were savage attacks, like you'd see in a crime of passion, but the missing people are unrelated. Whoever did this is a sick bastard. The locals have already given the killers a name, the Elcho rippers. It's really got the islanders spooked."

"Are the islanders armed?" Beckman asked, wondering what capacity they had to defend themselves.

"A few hunters have rifles. Most would rather use traditional weapons to preserve their culture." A cluster of large buildings appeared ahead, the largest structures for hundreds of kilometers in any direction. "That's the school. I sealed it and the police station off while the forensic team went over the crime scene." He turned into the school grounds and parked near an abandoned police vehicle.

When they climbed out, he said, "This is what my officers were driving. Forensics went over it, but got nothing."

Fingerprint powder covered the interior, showing smears where small amphibian hands had been, but nothing resembling human fingerprints. The police radio had been removed and the gun rack had been stripped clean.

"How many guns did they get?" Beckman asked.

"From here and the station, nine pistols, two shotguns and five rifles."

"Hardly an arsenal," Teresa said.

"It shows intent," Beckman said.

Hayward indicated dark blood stains on the ground some distance from the abandoned police car. "That's where my officers died. We've sent DNA samples to Darwin to confirm it." He took a deep breath, steadying his emotions. In a tiny station like Galiwinku, the local police were as close as family and clearly, Hayward was having a hard time dealing with the loss. "There are similar spatter patterns in houses across the road and near the beach. After forensics finished, the local Aboriginal trackers searched the area. They say whoever they were, they came from the sea, moved through those trees, then split up." He pointed as he spoke, directing their attention to the route taken by the raiders. "One group came here to the school, the other went behind those houses to the station."

"What did the tracks look like?" Beckman asked.

The police officer hesitated. "That's the strangest thing. The trackers said they were unlike anything they'd ever seen before and these are blokes who know every living thing out there. They're talking like they were supernatural creatures. Not animals, not men, but sea demons, like something out of their dreamtime. It's crazy talk."

"Yeah, crazy," Beckman agreed.

"And there were a lot of them," Hayward added.

"How many?"

"The trackers couldn't tell because the footprints were on top of each other, deliberately hiding their numbers, but from the way they trampled the ground, it was a big group. It's got the locals all fired up. They've never lost people like this before. Now they're looking for payback."

"You can't let them do that," Dr. McInness said.

"I can't stop them," Hayward said, then remembering his three dead officers, added, "Not sure I want to."

"What did they steal from the school?" Dr. McInness asked.

"Laptops, wiring, electrical switches from the walls and over a thousand books."

"A thousand!" Beckman exclaimed, realizing it wasn't simple pilfering, but a highly organized raid.

"It would have taken a lot of people to carry off all that stuff." Hayward turned toward the sea, visible through the trees. "They brought a boat in close to the beach. That's where the footprints lead. And there were reports of a marine engine revving that night, but no sightings. Blood stains near the beach indicate whoever came to see what the boat was doing didn't come back."

"Where'd they get the boat?" Reynolds asked.

"There's a missing persons report out on a couple aboard a private cruiser east of here who can't be contacted by their families." His expression darkened. "If it was their boat, then the death toll is ten."

A solemn silence fell over the group, then Reynolds said, "Can we see the library?"

"Sure. This way."

Hayward led them past empty classrooms to the library. The door had been forced open and the communal computer area had been stripped clean of equipment and cabling. Beyond the computing area were the bookshelves, some of which were bare while others were untouched.

"What did they take?" Dr. McInness asked.

"According to the librarian, only non-fiction," Hayward replied. "Encyclopedias, dictionaries, history books, geography, math, science – all gone – but not a single story book."

"They want knowledge," Teresa said.

Hayward and Reynolds walked off through the library, then when they were out of earshot, Dr McInness said, "This is a high school. None of these books would come anywhere near the kind of knowledge extraterrestrials would have. They might be shipwrecked, but they're astronauts. Their training would be incredibly high."

"Yeah, it's nuts," Beckman agreed, then they followed Hayward through the school and across the road to a stand of trees separating the town from the beach.

"Two people died here," the police sergeant said, pointing to blood stains between the trees, "and their bodies were carried down there," he added, motioning to tracks across the sand to the water's edge.

"No sign of the boat?" Beckman asked.

Hayward shook his head. "Not yet. There's a million places around here they could hide, but sooner or later they're going to have to buy fuel. That's when we'll get them."

"Not if they scuttle the boat," Reynolds said.

"What and swim home?" Hayward said doubtfully.

"Maybe they are home," Dr. McInness said pensively.

Hayward gave the scientist a puzzled look, then assumed he was implying the perpetrators lived on the island. "Come on. I'll show you the station. That's where my other officer was killed," he said, then headed back to his car followed by Reynolds and Dr. McInness.

Beckman stood with a troubled expression, watching HMAS *Naturaliste* lying peacefully at anchor in the lee of Abbott Island.

Teresa saw the tension on his face. "What is it, Colonel?"

"They have a base out there somewhere and they're equipping it."

"We could ask the aboriginal trackers to search for it."

Beckman shook his head. "That'd just get them killed." He watched the *Naturaliste*, certain alien killers were painting its hull with sonar signals. "Sergeant Hayward's wrong about one thing."

"What's that?"

He glanced at the blood stains on the sand and the track to the water where the bodies had been carried away two nights before. "The body count. The trawler crew makes it seventeen and they're just the ones we know about."

In silence, he and Teresa turned and followed Sergeant Hayward back to the police car.

\* \* \* \*

After retracing the footsteps of the night raiders and examining the forensic evidence, they reboarded the launch and motored out into Cadell Strait. Once clear of the coastal shoal, they set course to round the southern tip of Elcho Island and return to the *Naturaliste*. With the sailors inside the wheelhouse, Beckman and the other senior officers gathered at the stern.

"That town's exposed," Beckman said as he gazed across the Strait's calm waters, wondering how close they were to the acoustic hot spots. "How long's this channel?"

"It's forty kilometers to Point Napier, the exit," Reynolds replied, "and two hundred to the Cape Wessel weather station at the northern tip of the islands."

"That's a big area," Teresa said.

"If you include everything out to Nhulunbuy in the east," Reynolds said, "it's thousands of square kilometers."

*And they can swim underwater*, Beckman thought. "It's a huge haystack to hide a tiny alien needle in."

"They won't be easy to contact," Dr. McInness said. "They don't trust us. We've got to convince them they can, so we can bring them in before this gets out of control."

The boatswain appeared at the wheelhouse door. "Excuse me, Commander. The echo sounder keeps dropping out. Request permission to swap it out when we get back to the Nat."

Reynolds nodded. "OK."

"What do you mean it's dropping out?" Dr. McInness asked.

"It's kind of ghosting, like a school of fish keeps appearing and disappearing. It's probably just corrosion."

"Could it be fast moving fish?"

"Fish aren't that fast, Doc," Reynolds said.

Dr. McInness peered into the water as gray torpedoes darted through the depths beneath them. He jumped back from the gunwale, "They're below us!"

Beckman glanced into the water, saw fast swimming forms circling close to the bottom, then turned to Reynolds. "They're going to attack! We need weapons!"

"The launch is unarmed," Reynolds said. He wasn't even wearing a sidearm as it wasn't navy practice to go armed when visiting local towns.

Beckman grabbed a boat hook secured to the gunwale. "This will have to do."

Reynolds turned to the boatswain. "Flank speed! Prepare to repel boarders, hand to hand!"

The sailor gave Reynolds a confused look. "Sir?"

"This is not a drill seaman!" Reynolds yelled. "Arm yourself! Now!"

In the wheelhouse, the sailor at the helm pushed the throttle full over, sending the launch surging forward at twenty eight knots. The other two sailors grabbed wrenches and hammers from the tool kit before stepping onto the stern deck. One handed a hammer to Reynolds.

Beckman glanced at the shore, realizing they were out of sight of both Elcho Island's landing and the *Naturaliste*.

*That's what they were waiting for,* he realized. *So*

*they could hit us without being seen!*

"Bob," Dr. McInness said, "this is our chance to make contact."

"They're not here to talk, Ian," Beckman said, wielding the boat hook like a medieval quarterstaff and nodding for Teresa to take the scientist in tow. "Get him inside." He turned to the sailors. "Hit whatever comes out of the water. Don't hesitate, because they're here to kill you!"

The sailors' confusion turned to wariness as they realized the senior officers were preparing for a life and death fight. Not knowing what they were supposed to fight, they watched the sea apprehensively.

The helmsman saw the echo sounder suddenly spike toward the surface. "Something's coming up fast!"

Six light gray torpedoes shot up out of the water on each side of the launch and splashed onto the deck. They stood below shoulder height, flexible bodies rippling with powerful, cord-like muscles.

Beckman struck one in the chest with the end of his boat hook, knocking it back over the gunwale, then immediately swung at another. His target dodged away with surprising speed, then lunged at his stomach with a white coral knife. Beckman jumped back, slamming his makeshift quarterstaff into the alien's head, knocking it to the deck where it lay unconscious with a gash across its gently ridged skull.

Behind him, the sailors swung their wrenches at lunging arms, breaking bones and deflecting blows as their attackers dodged and slashed. One coral blade opened a sailor's arm below the elbow while another narrowly missed his crew mate's face. At the stern, Reynolds caught a leathery arm as it lunged at his throat, then smashed his hammer onto the amphibian's head, killing him instantly. Another amphibian charged into the wheelhouse, a knife in each hand, intent on stopping the launch.

Dr. McInness stood halfway between the door and the

helm station. He spread his arms, showing he was unarmed. "Wait! We mean you no harm!"

The amphibian threw one of his knives, taking the scientist in the shoulder, knocking him back, then Teresa triggered the signal flare she held and stabbed the amphibian in the chest with the burning end. The alien emitted a high pitched scream, then swept his remaining blade at her throat. She deflected the blow with her free hand, then thrust the burning flare into one of her attacker's eyes. He screamed again, leaping back as she advanced, sweeping the flare from side to side in frenzied arcs, driving the amphibian out of the wheelhouse. It retreated from the burning flare, then leapt over the side to escape. Sensing her advantage, she charged, thrusting the blazing flare at the remaining attackers. Startled by the unusual weapon, first one, then the rest leapt over the sides into the safety of the water.

In their wake, one sailor lay holding his stomach, sliced open by a coral knife, while another stood nursing a blood soaked arm. Reynolds stood by the railing with his hammer in hand and blood smearing his face from a gash in his forehead while one amphibian lay dead on the deck and another lay sprawled unconscious near the stern.

Beckman turned to Teresa as the flare sputtered out. He gave her an approving nod, then saw Dr. McInness lying slumped on a bench seat inside the wheelhouse. He was holding his shoulder where a throwing knife protruded from it.

"Ian, are you going to live?" Beckman called.

Dr. McInness replied weakly with his head back, eyes closed. "This isn't doing my migraines any good."

"I'll take that as a yes."

"Check the sounder?" Reynolds called to the boatswain who hurried back to the helm station. In the distance, the *Naturaliste* was just coming into view beyond a tree covered headland.

"They're gone, sir," the boatswain called.

The sailor with the bloodied arm said, "What were those things?"

No one answered.

"Break out the medical kit," Reynolds said, realizing the downed sailor's wounds were serious. "And radio the Nat. Tell them we have wounded."

Teresa tossed her dead flare overboard, then went into the wheelhouse to retrieve more flares in case there was a second attack. The boatswain set the autopilot, then hurried back with the first aid kit to help the badly wounded sailor, but one look told Beckman the young man would be dead before they reached the ship.

Reynolds pressed his free hand to his bleeding forehead, keeping a firm grip on his blood splattered hammer. "That was close."

"It was like they'd never seen a flare before," Beckman said, wondering how interstellar aliens could be surprised by such a simple device.

"Thank God for that," Reynolds said.

Beckman glanced at the amphibian whose skull Reynolds had crushed with his hammer, then at its companion whose breathing was shallow, but steady. "Ask the captain to prepare space for an autopsy and an interrogation. And we'll need satellite links for both. We're about to have a lot of eyes on us."

\* \* \* \*

Watcher-of-Skies clambered up through a steep cave in total darkness, navigating with biosonar alone. After slipping through the last of the animal hide baffles hung like curtains across the passage to ensure no sound from the subterranean caverns reached the surface, he began the final steep climb to the boulders blocking the cave mouth. The boulders had been carefully positioned to camouflage the entrance and were large enough to prevent the dark skinned land-dwellers that occasionally hunted on the island from entering.

When he reached the blocked cave entrance, several of his brothers emerged from the shadows to lever one of the smaller boulders aside, giving him access to the tree covered plateau beyond. It was the only above water entrance to the caverns and was only ever used at night. Land-dwellers rarely passed this way, but Watcher knew those that did had the skill to follow his tracks. Their sporadic presence forced his people to conceal their movements by staying on bare rock until they were far from the entrance.

Watcher slipped past the hidden lookouts guarding the cave mouth and picked his way over windswept rocks toward the sea. It was a path he knew well, although he took care to stop frequently to search for any land-dwellers who might be hunting at night. Soon he reached a broad stone shelf overlooking the sea with an unobstructed view of the night sky. His kind had a natural aversion to heights, which he overcame by sitting well back from the edge. The uncomfortably exposed position guaranteed he would not be disturbed by his brothers, giving him privacy and time to reflect. Under his arm he carried the one land-dweller treasure from the raid he'd selected for himself. Out of the hundreds of books now being studied by his brothers, this amazing creation – full of diagrams, pictures and tantalizing explanations – had proven irresistible to him.

He knelt on the rock and opened the high school astronomy textbook, reading it with his sensitive eyes in the light of the half moon. Its pages were worn, some sentences had been underlined or had land-dweller markings in the margins, but even in its dilapidated state, it was a wonder for him to behold. He spent hours reading it, reviewing its simple mathematics and physics examples and gazing at dazzling images of distant stellar phenomenon captured by wondrous machines called space telescopes the land-dwellers had placed high in the sky.

Watcher did not fully understand how they'd done it,

but he marveled at the achievement. His thirst for knowledge had driven him to master the land-dweller's written words faster than any other, to absorb all of their discoveries to such a degree that he had become his people's foremost teacher. For years, he'd lived off scraps, working tirelessly to understand and translate stolen books and magazines, discarded newspapers and lost journals. It had been a daunting task, made possible by a child's book linking words and pictures that had taught him enough to learn more.

Now with the caverns filled with books, he and his brothers were consuming land-dweller knowledge at a tremendous rate. In two days, he had devoured more than a hundred and fifty of the volumes Prowls-the-Shallows had brought back from the raid. While he preferred books on mathematics and science, he read texts on every subject, retaining their content with perfect clarity.

The land-dweller number system had been the easiest for Watcher to understand because he had invented mathematics in his own mind long before he had translated their symbols for it. When he swept through their high school math textbooks, he quickly converted his own ideas into their system. Occasionally he found something he hadn't thought of, but mostly he realized the number games he played in his mind far outstripped the land-dweller books. He craved more and knew their most advanced ideas were hidden in secret-knowledge-places called universities which were far from the Mothersea – too far for Prowls to steal what he needed.

It was a disappointment Watcher accepted stoically.

When he finished reading through his prized astronomy book, he realized how tired he was. He hadn't slept since they'd brought the stolen library into the caverns and he could spare little time for sleep now. There was so much to learn and so little time remaining until the land-dwellers came for them, as he knew they would.

He looked up at the half moon, focusing his naturally telescoping eyes upon its surface. He followed the craters, plains and mountains, recalling the land-dweller names for each. He found where their spacecraft had landed, but was disappointed to discover his eyes weren't powerful enough to see the landers they'd left behind. Even so, watching the nearby world, so white in the sun's reflected light, a melancholy peace settled over him.

It was a bitter irony that learning so much, so quickly, was both the happiest time of his life and the darkest, for every new volume revealed another aspect of land-dweller power. He'd warned Beloved, selected books for her to read and been reassured when she'd given each her full attention, completing them all without comment. Her silence told him she knew and understood the problem.

She'd always known.

The land-dwellers were the greatest threat they faced. One look at their history books confirmed it. He could not but wonder at their achievements, yet he feared their capacity for organized violence, the phenomenon they called *war*. Their natures were attuned to it. It made them inherently *war*-like. Having digested thousands of years of their history in a matter of hours, Watcher had been shocked to discover how many wars they'd fought, so many that they could classify them by type: religious war, civil war, revolutionary war, holy war, succession war, secession war, modern war, air war, sea war, total war, nuclear war, world war. So many types of conflict, so many millions killed, so many civilizations laid waste.

He knew the sparkling beauty of the Mothersea hid a horror lurking beyond the horizon, a horror that was surely coming for them. Beloved believed the land-dweller's inherent aggression coupled with their innate fear of difference posed a threat their kind could not match. Being trapped on this world with such an adversary was a nightmare from which there was no escape. And yet, Watcher saw some land-dweller impulses in his own people. He knew Beloved would have made war upon them, taken all they had, if she had the power to do so. She would have shown them no more mercy than they had shown their own kind.

It was the way of females and land-dwellers. The two species were vastly different, yet in some ways, strangely similar.

The one great question he could not answer was how the land-dwellers could rule the world so completely, have achieved so much, while his people had achieved nothing. He suspected the land-dwellers' thinking ability was limited, a suspicion strengthened only hours before by his reading of a twenty volume collection of knowledge they called an 'encyclopedia'. It had contained a curious entry, a listing of the ten greatest unsolvable mathematic problems known to the land-dwellers. The idea of an unsolvable problem intrigued him, yet within moments of considering each puzzle, he had the solution. The answers had seemed almost obvious, yet were beyond the reach of their greatest intellects. In his own mind games, he had discovered great unsolvable problems, none of which the land-dwellers were even aware of.

It was a great conundrum.

And now he had another great unsolved riddle to add to his list, although this problem did not arise from mathematics, but from what the land-dwellers called paleontology. He now knew they had uncovered millions of years of fossils proving they had evolved on this world to their present state, yet there was not a single sign of his people's existence. It was as if, in all the billions of years of the world's history, his kind had never existed. It was an absurdity that forced Watcher-of-Skies to consider another explanation, one he could barely credit, yet one his great intellect could not discount: that his people had not originated in the Mothersea, were not truly of this world. But if not here, then where?

As he had done all his life, Watcher looked at the sky and wondered.

* * * *

After the ship's doctor had removed the coral blade from Dr. McInness' shoulder and stitched up Lt. Commander Reynolds' forehead, the senior officers met in Captain Turner's stateroom for a late night planning session. The scientist sat pale faced with his left arm in a sling while Reynolds had a white bandage circling the top of his head, but no concussion. Only Teresa was absent. She was observing the ship's doctor conducting an autopsy of the dead amphibian, a procedure that was beamed live via satellite to the Area 51 biosciences department.

Captain Turner had already gotten over the shock of seeing two aliens brought aboard her ship, although she found the loss of one of her young sailors much harder to take. She'd given orders for the dead sailor not to be buried at sea, but to be refrigerated and returned to his family at the earliest opportunity. At Beckman's prompting, she'd had the wardroom cleared of tables and chairs and converted into a makeshift isolation lab where their captive could have its wounds tended to and its every move studied by Teresa and the satellite linked Area 51 team.

Once they were seated, the Captain's orderly served coffee, then excused himself. When the door closed, she said, "I have a letter to write to the parents of a twenty year old sailor who should be alive tonight, laughing and joking with his mates below deck. How am I going to explain this?"

"It was a training accident," Beckman said. "Your crew will all need to be debriefed and ordered to support the cover story."

Her eyes widened incredulously. "You can't be serious."

"That will be the official line from both our governments," Beckman assured her. "Within a few hours, we'll all receive orders to that effect."

"You've arranged it already?" she asked coldly.

"I've only sent a report. It normally takes the cover story people that long to get moving. Everything will be in place by morning."

She bristled with contained anger. "I'm not sure what's worse, Colonel, the fact that we're hiding this, or that you have a well oiled procedure for creating cover stories."

"I know how you feel."

"Do you?" she asked icily.

"I've lost people too, good people."

She looked surprised. "To aliens?"

Beckman nodded, unwilling to explain where or when. "Will your crew obey orders? Will they keep a lid on this?"

"Of course they will," she said, then turned to Reynolds. "Read the whole crew Part Seven of the Crimes Act tomorrow, just in case." Her gaze returned to Beckman. "That covers our official secrets."

"Everything about this mission is now an official secret," Beckman said, "including our presence here."

She nodded, not surprised. "So what next?"

"Teresa will try to find a way to communicate with the prisoner."

"Can you speak its language?"

"No, this isn't a species we've ever seen before," Dr. McInness said, reaching into his pocket for a tab of pain killers. He popped two pills and washed them down with a gulp of coffee, hoping they would numb his migraine.

"What happens to the autopsy results?" Turner asked.

"All documentation and body parts will be shipped to Area 51 for analysis," Beckman said.

"I assume I'll receive orders to that effect from my Chief of Navy?" she asked.

"I expect so."

"Your sickbay should be scrubbed clean of all DNA traces," Dr. McInness said, "and any sheets and other materials that come in contact with the body should be incinerated – for your own safety. We don't know what kind of biocontamination risk this species poses."

"Are they a threat to us?" she asked.

There was an awkward silence, then Beckman gave Dr. McInness an approving nod.

"It's hard to say, Captain," the scientist said. "Extraterrestrials visit Earth for many reasons, mostly because of the rarity of our civilization."

"Rarity?" Captain Turner asked uncertainly.

"Ian has a theory," Beckman explained. "It's partly based on information we've recovered from salvaged data storage devices showing the locations of nearby civilizations. It gives us an idea of the number of inhabited worlds out to about fifty light years."

"You know that?" Reynolds asked surprised.

"We have good evidence for a minimum number. Fourteen, not including Earth." Beckman shrugged. "Could be more, but it supports Ian's theory."

"I call it the Hourglass Theory," the scientist explained "It describes our place in the universe relative to other intelligent life."

"I've never heard of it," Turner said.

"It's classified," Beckman said. "Everything he writes, every thought he has, is a secret as soon as he thinks of it."

"Not quite every thought," Dr. McInness said with a smile, then sobered. "Imagine all *intelligent* life in the universe moves through time as if passing through an hourglass. Each species is represented by a single grain of sand. When primitive life evolves the first spark of intelligence, a grain of sand is added to the top of the hourglass.

"The top half of the hourglass includes all the millions of years it takes for intelligent life to increase its thinking ability to the point where civilization can appear. This covers our evolution right up to and including the Stone Age. For mankind, it lasted about three point four million years. Just above the neck of the hourglass are a few grains of sand that represent intelligent life on the verge of forming civilization. That's where humanity was about five to eight thousand years ago, when our Stone Age ended and rudimentary societies formed. The appearance of civilization was triggered to some extent by the end of the last ice age over ten thousand years ago, allowing small farming communities to appear. In time, they became towns and cities. That's the point when we entered the narrow neck of the hourglass.

"Thousands of years later," he continued, "we're still there, in the neck, but we're getting close to passing into the bottom half of the hourglass. It might take another thousand years, because the technological hurdles are immense, but we are getting close. Once we leave the Solar System under our own power, we leave the neck of the hourglass and enter the bottom cone which is much bigger and spans a much greater length of time than the top cone. That bottom cone is where all interstellar civilizations in the universe are. The neck is only the transition point between pre-civilization and interstellar civilization. The three parts of the hourglass represent what I call the Ascent Stage, the Transition Stage and the Interstellar Stage.

"Every alien civilization with the means to reach Earth is in the bottom cone, and most will be hundreds of thousands to millions – perhaps even billions – of years ahead of us. We don't know how many there are or how far ahead of us they are, but in the entire universe, there will be trillions of such civilizations."

"Trillions?" Reynolds said incredulously. "As in thousands of *billions*?"

"Yes. To understand why," Dr. McInness continued, "you need to realize we are a very young species in a very old universe. We know from spectroscopic analysis of the cosmos that conditions have been right for life to appear for at least two billion years. Once intelligence appears, it takes millions of years to reach the neck of the hourglass, to form civilization, but only ten or twenty millennia to become an interstellar civilization and reach the bottom cone of the hourglass.

"The key point is, the tiniest part of the hourglass is the neck, where we are now. It's tiny because it represents a mere twenty thousand years while the hourglass covers a time scale of billions of years. The hourglass itself represents only a fraction of the thirteen point eight billion year age of the entire universe. Every planet, every star, is running on its own time frame, making Earth evolution independent of what is occurring on every other world, many of which formed millions to billions of years before our Solar System.

"This means the vast majority of civilizations in the bottom cone have been there for a very long time, so long in fact that they may have forgotten what it's like to be in the neck. So they come here and study us because that's where we are. In the entire Milky Way Galaxy, out of more than a hundred thousand million stars, we may be the only life form in the neck of the hourglass, the only species in the galaxy with intelligence *and* civilization that is *not* an interstellar civilization. If we're not the only one, there can't be many others."

"Because the neck is so short," Turner said thoughtfully.

"Most people think interstellar aliens are rare, because they imagine they are at the top of some tree. They think it's a pyramid, like the food chain on Earth, with lots of lower level types at the bottom and only a few at the top, but they don't consider the age of the universe. That's why they have it backwards. There is a pyramid, but it's inverted."

"It's crowded at the top, not the bottom," Beckman said.

Dr. McInness nodded. "Twenty thousand years is a

flicker in time compared to the age of the universe. If the appearance of intelligence is rare, say it appears somewhere in our galaxy once every one hundred thousand years, then no two species would pass through the neck at the same time, because the appearance rate is five times longer than the neck transit time. Even so, if intelligent species have been appearing every hundred thousand years for the last two billion years, then there are twenty thousand interstellar civilizations in our galaxy alone. More if they appear more often, less if the appearance rate is lower. Even though a hundred thousand years is purely arbitrary, considering the size of the galaxy, it's not unreasonable. When you consider how many billions of galaxies there are, it's not hard to see why I believe there are trillions of interstellar civilizations in the universe."

"So many," Turner said, wondering if it could possibly be true.

"Not everyone makes it," Beckman said. "Some are destroyed by natural disasters, some wipe themselves out." He shrugged fatalistically. "We haven't made it through the neck yet."

"From the Milky Way's perspective," Dr. McInness said, "the last neck-transiting civilization might have reached the stars eighty or ninety thousand years before civilization first appeared on Earth. After we develop interstellar travel, the next such civilization might not appear again for a similar amount of time. So eighty to ninety percent of the time, there are no transitioning civilizations anywhere in the galaxy."

"I don't think I like your theory, Doctor," Turner said. "It's kind of ... scary."

"It's not as bad as you might think," he replied. "With so many civilizations appearing over many millions of years, there's bound to be a process for accepting new species. One day, when we're ready, we'll find out what that process is. It'll guarantee there's a place for us, although it may not be the place we think it is."

"Because our place is right at the bottom, not the top," Beckman said.

"If they're waiting for us to get through the neck," Reynolds said, "why did that thing in the wardroom try to kill us?"

"Good question," Beckman said.

"Our protocol is to transport captured aliens to Area 51," Dr. McInness said, "but considering there's a group of them, I've asked to keep this specimen on board until we know what we're dealing with. With the ship's satellite link, we can access the people we need from here."

"You really think Major Bertolini can find a way to communicate with it?" Turner asked.

"Xenology is her specialty," Dr. McInness said. "Her expertise covers non-human language, biology, culture and psychology."

"While she's figuring out how to talk to our prisoner," Beckman said, "we need to get combat troops on board."

"Is that necessary?" Turner asked.

"The aggression shown by this species is high range," Beckman replied. "Very high. If they were using advanced weapons, I'd bring in our Contact Team, but regular troops should be enough to protect the ship."

"How do I explain that to Canberra?"

"You won't have to. Everything we need will be provided, no questions asked. Not just troops, but reconnaissance aircraft, UAVs, satellite imagery. We'll get it all. Forty eight hours from now, if anything so much as sneezes out there, we'll see it."

"I'll send a dispatch tonight," Turner agreed.

"There are US navy ships on their way down here," Beckman said. "They were redirected as soon as we knew what the tooth was – just in case. After capturing an alien alive, there'll be a lot more coming – and aircraft."

"I hope they won't be needed," Turner said.

"I suggest we secure all main deck watertight doors and have armed guards up high. No way to tell if they'd attack a ship this big, but you never know."

She turned to Reynolds. "Take care of it, and suspend use of the motor launches. They're too vulnerable."

"Yes, ma'am."

* * * *

Beloved-of-the-Sea was growing tired. It had been a long night swim, porpoising through the swells rolling in from the Deep Blue, flanked all the way by her personal guard. Prowls-the-Shallows had objected to her taking such a risk, yet once she'd heard the sea-herder's strange story and the request he'd passed on from the mysterious dark-swimmer, she'd made up her mind.

She was convinced the dark-swimmer had nothing to do with the land-dwellers. It was utterly unlike anything they possessed and the request it had made carried a respectful tone that had a peculiar rightness to it. It had called her Matriarch, a word previously unknown to her, but whose meaning it had taught the sea-herder. That form of address told her the dark-swimmer considered her the pre-eminent female, the leader of her spawn and mother to her people, making her the legitimate ruler of her domain.

All through the long swim, she had pondered how this strange creature of the deep could give her a title she knew instinctively was rightfully hers. Long before she reached the meeting place, Beloved-of-the-Sea had silently adopted the title for herself, had assumed its mantle of authority. In every respect, she was the Matriarch of the Mothersea.

Her decision to meet the dark-swimmer had been spurred on by the failed attack on the land-dweller boat, the death of one of her brothers and the capture of another. It was a disaster she hadn't expected, caused by a terrible fire-weapon none of her brothers had ever seen before. With their cloak of secrecy stripped away, the land-dwellers would certainly now turn their gaze upon the Mothersea. That realization made her desperate. She'd ordered the sea-herder to show her the way without giving him time to rest. He was exhausted and the return swim might kill him, but she couldn't wait.

She had finished the last of the books Watcher-of-Skies had selected for her, mostly history and geography. He did not waste her time with science and mathematics, for lesser beings could handle such subjects. What she needed to grasp was the power of the land-dwellers, the true scale of the danger they posed and thanks to Watcher's selections, that had become all too clear. Of all the new knowledge she now possessed, one fact had shocked and terrified her above all others.

There were *billions* of them!

She knew her people could not survive contact with so powerful an adversary, yet what could she do? It was only a matter of time before the land-dwellers discovered all she had worked so hard to conceal. It was why she'd chosen this reckless path and answered the dark-swimmer's call.

"It waits at the bottom, Beloved," the sea-herder said, pointing toward the rendezvous point. "It asked you come alone."

"Why alone?" Prowls-the-Shallows demanded protectively.

"It fears revealing itself."

Beloved assumed the dark-swimmer feared the land-dwellers, not realizing its enemies were far more powerful and came from much further away than any inhabitant of their shared world.

"I will find it," she said. "You will remain here." When Prowls began to object, she added, "Even you, my brother."

She surfaced, filled her quad-lungs with compressed air, then dived alone into the darkness. As the moonlight faded, she was forced to rely solely on her biosonar to see by, finding nothing but sand, rock and small fish hiding among the boulders. After quartering the area, her hopes began to fade as she feared the dark-swimmer had been killed by the land-dwellers or been driven back into the Deep Blue. She was about to return to her starting point when a long black mass appeared beside her. It seemed not to swim, although as it drew near, she felt the sea flowing silently around it.

She projected her sonar at the dark-swimmer, seeking to learn its shape and speed, but received no signal in return even though it loomed over her. It was as if the rigid creature did not exist, but was merely a trick of her mind. Before she knew what was happening, the whale sized shadow was above her and she found she couldn't move her arms and legs or use her sonar to call for help.

*It's a trap!* she thought, as the dark-swimmer swallowed her whole, drawing her into its belly.

As soon as the rectangular panel slid shut beneath her, the sea water drained away. Rather than fall onto the cold metal below, she floated in the air, suspended by an invisible force. Warm air blew over her skin as the chamber pressurized, then she inhaled experimentally. To her surprise, Beloved found it the sweetest air she'd ever tasted.

From far away, a strangely cold voice said, "Welcome Beloved-of-the-Sea."

She wanted to speak, to demand to be released, to turn her head and look about, but her muscles would not obey. Helpless in the belly of the dark-swimmer, her powerful will suppressed her fear as silver threads grew from the walls and snaked toward her. To her horror, they penetrated her skull and painlessly wove a lattice-like pattern of molecular filaments into her brain.

Once functional, the lattice allowed the Infiltrator Probe to read her thoughts, then sensing her fury and confusion, it said, "Forgive me, Great Mother. It is necessary."

# CHAPTER FOUR: DISCOVERIES

Beckman entered the antiseptic smelling wardroom and sat on one of the chairs placed against the passageway bulkhead. A clear plastic sheet had been taped from the overhead to the deck, forming a transparent biocontamination seal between the observation area and a sick bay bed in the center of the wardroom.

The alien prisoner lay on the bed, tied down by his wrists and ankles while his large eyes methodically swept the room. On the left side of his head, dried blood marked where Beckman had struck him, while circular white sensors on his chest monitored his pulse, temperature and breathing, all of which were displayed on screens opposite the bed. Three cameras recorded the alien's every move while a large flat panel screen had been placed at his feet where he could easily see it. Standing behind the monitors was a sailor wearing a surgical mask and holding an assault rifle, ensuring the amphibian knew there was no escape.

Teresa stood beside the one point five meter tall alien wearing a surgical mask and plastic gloves as much for her safety as his. While still unconscious, the alien had been subjected to a non-invasive medical examination confirming he had no apparent internal injuries, then his wound had been tended and his body cleaned although no human medicines had been administered for fear they might poison him.

Teresa clicked a small remote, then a diagram of the Milky Way Galaxy appeared on the flat panel screen with a glowing golden marker indicating the sun's position. Teresa aimed a red laser pointer at the marker, then pointed down to where she was standing, indicating that's where they were. The alien showed no sign of understanding, but she nevertheless placed the pointer in his hand and motioned to the screen, inviting him to show where he was from. Instead, as soon as she released the laser point, the amphibian let it roll onto the floor.

"No progress, huh?" Beckman whispered to Dr. McInness beside him.

"Not yet," the scientist replied as he typed one handed on the laptop computer perched on his legs, his other arm still in a sling. He was making notes and swapping emails with the Area 51 team responsible for formulating the interrogation program. "He's still studying us, trying to work us out."

"How can you tell?"

"It's the eyes," Dr. McInness whispered thoughtfully. "They never stop moving."

Beckman watched the alien's eyes follow Teresa as she retrieved the laser pointer. "Does it understand what she's asking?"

"No way to know. He refuses to cooperate."

Beckman glanced at the cameras focused on the alien. "I take it we're live to Groom Lake?"

Dr. McInness nodded. "They've got everyone in biosciences and linguistics on it." He nodded to the microphone suspended on a thin boom above the alien's head. "They're hoping if he speaks, the Syrman translator will recognize the words. That would at least tell us what species he is."

"They're wasting their time," Beckman said

doubtfully, recalling the translator had been recovered from a crashed craft from the Syrma System, seventy light years from Earth.

Dr. McInness looked up surprised. "Why?"

"That translator only has fourteen non-human languages, all Local Powers." The Syrman translator contained over a hundred and fifty human languages, indicating it was primarily used by researchers studying mankind. The fact that it contained so few alien languages, all of them known local civilizations, indicated the crashed craft it had been salvaged from was strictly short range. Beckman watched the amphibian make a defiant show of ignoring Teresa as she tried again to ask it to show her where in the galaxy it came from. "I don't think it's local."

"We may not have identified every neighboring civilization," Dr. McInness said. "Some might be highly xenophobic or have no interest in us."

"If it was local, it would have been rescued by now. They'd have signaled one of the ships studying Earth to send a message to their homeworld. The fact they haven't means something. I'm not exactly sure what, but … it means something."

"If you're right, it's going to be slow going."

Beckman watched the amphibian drop the laser pointer again, noting how it hardly paid any attention to the galactic map. "Is it possible it doesn't recognize the Milky Way?"

Dr. McInness shook his head. "He just doesn't want to play."

Beckman studied the amphibian, finding him to be the opposite of what he expected, of everything his experience in the Contact and Recovery Program told him an alien should be. In particular, the alien's lack of advanced technology was puzzling. "Why's it got no equipment, no communications, no phasers? It's nude for God's sake! What self respecting interstellar alien runs around another planet stark naked?"

"Maybe his clothes perished."

"Not likely. The few spacesuits we've seen can withstand radiation, extreme heat, cold, micro organisms." He furrowed his brow. "We're missing something."

Dr. McInness continued typing, paying only superficial attention. "For an alien not to recognize the Milky Way, to have no technology, would require ... a complete break with who and what they are."

Beckman studied the prisoner's smooth skin. It showed few blemishes or recognizable marks. "How old is it?"

"No way to judge. We don't know its life span or aging process. It could be thirty years old or a thousand."

It was a common problem, trying to gauge the life span of alien species. What little information they had gathered indicated alien life cycles varied greatly, although there was one common denominator: the older the species, the more long lived. It seemed every species had an overriding urge and capacity to prolong life.

Beckman consigned the alien's nakedness and its disinterest in the Milky Way map to the endless list of unsolvables that was the hallmark of his work. "What about the whale song?"

"Linguistics has identified patterns in the non-ranging pulses, but no progress on what they mean."

"Let's play it one of the recordings. See if that sparks its interest."

"We think *he*'s a male," Dr. McInness said, "not an it. His reproductive organs aren't that far from terrestrial amphibians. I'm thinking of calling him Artemis. He's obviously a hunter using primitive weapons and Artemis was a Greek god who hunted with a bow and–"

"We're not naming these aliens after Greek gods," Beckman declared. He had a strong aversion to attributing divine or supernatural powers to what was just another biological life form, even if it was capable of travelling between the stars. There were too many weak minded fools ready to worship aliens for him to agree to any move that might validate such desires.

"We have to call him something," Dr. McInness said disappointed.

"He's an amphibian, right? So let's call him Kermit."

Dr. McInness eyes widened. "You can't be serious. We can't name a highly intelligent, interstellar alien after a puppet! He's not even green!"

"Yeah, but no one's going to start worshipping a muppet, are they?" Beckman said, knowing the naming committee would eventually overrule him. "Kermit it is."

\* \* \* \*

Beloved awoke to a strange tingling sensation behind her eyes. She wondered as to its cause and was surprised when the answer appeared in her mind. It was the after effects of bio-synthetic fusion, the process that allowed the molecular lattice sewn into her brain to interact seamlessly at a cellular level with her thoughts. In her mind's eye, she saw tens of thousands of glittering pathways that accelerated her mental velocity and contained vast repositories of knowledge that she could access with a thought.

Most startling of all was that she found herself thinking in a different language, a form of communication she had never heard before, yet which she was now fluent in. It was a rich and elegant language, full of meaning and inflection and suited to spoken and sonic pulse forms of communication. When she wondered what it was, the multi-million year history of the One Speech flashed into her mind, revealing as much about what she was as it did about the nature of the ancient Intruder language itself.

Within the rich tapestry of language, she discovered that which had eluded her all her life, her true heritage. She was a member of a species its enemies called the

Intruders, because of their expansionist, intrusive nature, yet the One Speech revealed to her a different name, a name her kind called themselves. She was of 'The One Spawn of Many Seas', *Vars Gatroxiyen Anot* in the One Speech. Her kind had been the first to reach the stars within a globular cluster orbiting far beyond the galactic spiral, and they had done so with a civilization not built upon ethics and the rule of law common to most interstellar civilizations, but upon the drive for competitive power typical of the female overlords of her species. With no peer to constrain them, they subjugated all lesser races, colonized primitive civilizations and created many new worlds to suit their needs. If they had emerged within the galactic spiral, older civilizations would have punished their aggression, but so far from the reach of pan galactic civilization, their power grew unchecked. It was only when they attempted to expand into the galaxy itself that they suffered their first defeat.

Beloved was shocked to discover she was a product of that defeat, lost and forgotten, denied her birthright until now. She realized for the first time in her life, she was whole, as she was meant to be. Eons of genetic engineering had designed her biological form to fuse with the lattice, to utilize its vast information repositories and accelerated pathways as if they were a natural part of her body. It allowed her to communicate instantly with Intruder technology and with those of her own kind, similarly enhanced.

Once fully conscious, her mind filled with vivid images of places and wonders she'd never seen with her own eyes. Each new insight told her of her kind's towering achievements, their vast conquests and their shattering defeat. Beloved's mind filled with so many new ideas and star spanning vistas that she thought they would drive her insane, but her will held and her mind absorbed it all while the lattice ensured it did not push her beyond her limits. She realized it was a force feeding process, programmed by the Infiltrator to lift her out of darkness. Within a matter of hours, she was transformed from an uneducated, highly intelligent savage, who knew little more than the Mothersea, into a being whose vision spanned the galaxy and reached back millions of years.

At its peak when she began to lose herself, to forget her identity, the cold voice of the Infiltrator spoke to her. "Who are you?"

Thoughts from millions of years flashed through her mind. Visions of countless rulers, powerful and commanding, Queens and Empresses all. Compared to them, she was less than nothing. "I … I am …?"

"Who are *you*?" the Infiltrator demanded, more a challenge than a question.

She took a deep breath. "I am … Beloved-of-the-Sea," she whispered, focusing upon herself.

"What are you?"

"I am … lost …"

"*What* are you?" It repeated with a hard edge that resonated deeply with her.

"Matriarch … I am Matriarch … of the Mothersea," she said, regaining her personal power.

"The implants serve your will, Great Mother," the Infiltrator said, "but you must command them as you do your hands and your eyes."

She focused on the Intruder probe's words as more realizations flooded into her mind. What it gave her was more than a gift, it was a right that circumstance had denied her. The lattice was normally added incrementally from birth to maturity, but necessity had forced the Infiltrator to fully augment her without regard for her suffering. The implantation technology it possessed had been intended to sew controlling lattices into unwilling subjects for interrogation purposes, but it was identical to what the crèches used to enhance the young. Only the timing was different.

Beloved looked at the dull gray metal capsule surrounding her, wondering what the Infiltrator was, then its image and purpose filled her mind. She saw the route it had followed across the galaxy, the countless enemies it had evaded and the desperate need of her sisters to understand how they had been defeated. Its achievements made her wonder at the Intruder probe's power, then she saw it hide at the bottom of the sea for fear enemy ships from other worlds would find and destroy it. It was something they shared, hiding from more powerful adversaries.

"I understand," she said in her ancestral tongue, taking strength from the sounds. "You are the eyes of my sisters."

"The last of my type, the only one to reach this far."

She wondered at the fate of her sisters, then saw a spherical mass of stars sprinkled with hundreds of tiny blue points, each point a world they ruled. She marveled at their power, hoped they might save her, then saw their globular cluster lay far beyond the galaxy's outer rim.

"So far away," Beloved said, suddenly aware that they themselves were trapped, blockaded by powerful fleets gathered from across the galaxy.

"Too far to assist you."

She felt alone and powerless while her new understanding only emphasized what a feeble reflection she was of her great sisters. They might have been defeated, but they still commanded immense forces and ruled many worlds while she led stone age hunters and hid in dark caves.

A somberness fell over her as she wondered how she had been cast into this nightmare, then an image of her mother appeared in her mind. Nemza'ri had been a junior officer, the only surviving female of an Intruder ship that had crashed on Earth after almost being destroyed in battle. Her mother had attempted to breed to defend the ship, but she'd been captured before the plan could be completed. Nemza'ri had believed the ship had destroyed her eggs to prevent them falling into enemy hands, but her ship's damaged Command Nexus had been defiant to the end.

"The ship spawned us!" Beloved said, shocked to discover she was the product of an erratic artificial intelligence.

"You survived because the life signs of microscopic eggs were undetectable within the dense biomatter of this planet's tropical region. I only detected you now because you are adults."

"Why haven't our enemies discovered us?" she asked.

"They are not looking for you. They study the humans and you are hiding."

"You found me."

"Every scan I perform searches for Intruder life signs. It is a core precept of all Intruder synthetic intellects."

Beloved-of-the-Sea cleared her mind, taking time to digest the revelations that were transforming her most basic self perceptions. She realized she was an orphan surrounded by far more enemies than she had realized. They dominated the world she inhabited and filled the night sky further than she could see. It seemed incredible that the humans knew nothing of the galactic war that had raged beyond their atmosphere, so complete was their isolation. It was an innocence she had shared only hours before and its passing left her shaken and destitute.

"Can you take us home?" she asked.

"No."

A schematic of the Intruder probe appeared in her mind. The only open space within its stretched elliptical hull was the interrogation chamber large enough for only a few of her kind. Even if the Infiltrator could have taken them all, she realized it wouldn't. Its mission required it to continue on to the enemy homeworld twelve light years away.

"Will you tell them of us?"

"When my mission is complete, I will send a single message. It will reveal my presence to the Tau Cetins who will destroy me, but I will inform your sisters of your existence here."

"When are you leaving?"

"As soon as the skies clear of our enemies."

"Is there no way you can help us?"

"I have no weapons, Great Mother," the Infiltrator said. One small Intruder ship could have laid waste to the entire planet, destroyed Human Civilization in a matter of minutes, but the Infiltrator was not designed to fight. Weapons were useless so deep inside enemy territory, where overwhelming force could rapidly be brought to bear against it. Remaining invisible to its enemies was its only defense.

"Then we will be destroyed," she whispered.

"Once the humans know what and where you are," the Infiltrator said, "they will exterminate you."

She thought of her brother, now a prisoner in their hands and said, "They already know."

* * * *

Two sailors wearing surgical masks elevated Kermit's bed so he sat up at forty five degrees. Teresa nodded appreciatively to the sailors as they withdrew, then adjusted the flat panel screen at the foot of the bed for the amphibian's new eye position. Since his capture, he'd watched her constantly, eaten raw fish and drunk small quantities of fresh water, but had remained uncooperative in other respects. To Beckman, it was as if Kermit was giving them a name, rank and serial number response. Teresa wasn't so sure.

She approached a computer hooked into the flat panel screen and launched a program the Groom Lake team had hurriedly written. Two large squares appeared on the screen, each containing a simple series of lines and dots. Below the two large squares were four small squares, containing similar patterns with subtle differences.

She moved to the alien's side, noticing for once she had his attention. "So you are curious," she said, then aimed the laser pointer at the first small box at the bottom of the screen. It flashed red, incorrect. She aimed at the second with the same result. When she aimed at the third box, its outline flashed green, correct, as did the two large pattern recognition squares above. "Get it?" She glanced down at the amphibian, then nodded to herself. "I'm sure you do."

She placed the laser pointer in Kermit's right hand. The restraint on his wrist had been transferred to his upper arm, giving him freedom of movement below the elbow. For a moment she thought he was going to throw the pointer away, but to her relief, he held on to it, then she clicked the wifi controller instructing the computer to bring up the second puzzle.

She turned to Kermit. "Your turn. Which one?"

The amphibian lay like a statue, refusing to respond even though it kept hold of the laser pointer. She stepped toward the flat panel screen and motioned to the row of four small boxes. "Come on, you know you want to play. Show me how smart you are."

He stared at her, then she moved back to his side and reached for the laser pointer, intending to show him again what she wanted. To her surprise, he pulled his hand back and aimed the laser pointer at the fourth small box, which flashed green along with the two large clue squares.

Teresa smiled. It was the first time the amphibian had responded to any of her attempts to test his abilities. "There, that wasn't so hard was it? And you got it right, but you knew that already, didn't you?" She turned to the screen and clicked the remote, summoning the next puzzle. This time he flashed the laser pointer a fraction of a second after the puzzle appeared.

Her smile vanished. "Wow. That was fast." Kermit had solved the puzzle before she'd even had time to consider it herself. She clicked the wifi controller and again he solved the puzzle instantly. "I get it. These are too easy for you."

She returned to the computer, ramped up the

difficulty level and switched to timer mode, then turned back to him. "Ready?" she asked rhetorically, then pressed the remote to start the speed test.

Logical reasoning puzzles began flashing onto the screen in quick succession. Kermit solved each one in the blink of an eye, triggering the next problem to appear. Each puzzle was incrementally more difficult than the previous one, although that wasn't apparent from the ease with which he solved them. As the test progressed into the high genius range, Teresa's expression darkened as he continued solving puzzles with little more than a glance, problems that would have taken the most advanced human mind minutes to process. Worse than that, she realized the slowest part of the process was the time it took the amphibian to aim the pointer, not to answer the problem. When the test finished, the rating appeared on screen showing a perfect score.

"How'd he do?" Beckman asked from behind the plastic anti-contamination screen.

"We need a tougher test," she said, staring at the Groom Lake computer program's verdict.

*IQ too high to measure.*

* * * *

While the *Naturaliste* waited off Galiwinku for troops to arrive from eastern Australia, a Royal Australian Air Force Triton unmanned aerial vehicle flew from its base in South Australia to the waters east of Cadell Strait. The feed from the long endurance UAV was beamed first to its home base two thousand five hundred kilometers away, then to the *Naturaliste* and to an operations room in Area 51.

Beckman, Reynolds, Captain Turner, and Dr. McInness watched the feed in the ship's communications room. The small screen showed a glittering blue sea from high altitude, flanked by a long, slender island of bleached white rock. Scrub and forest covered parts of the island while its shoreline was a patchwork of white sand beaches, tiny bays and weathered cliffs. The UAV followed a northeasterly heading, parallel to the island, finding only a few seabirds circling the cliffs and headlands.

"Looks deserted," Beckman said disappointed.

"It's aboriginal land," Reynolds explained. "It's sparsely populated, not uninhabited."

"There should be at least a few fishermen down there," Turner said.

"Unless the area's been fished out," Dr. McInness suggested.

"Or they've been scared off," Beckman said ominously. "Would they report attacks?"

Reynolds shrugged. "Not if they thought they were supernatural, although word of something like that would spread fast among the communities."

The Triton passed over a dark blue cloud in the sea flanked by lighter, submerged sandbanks.

"What is that?" Dr. McInness asked, pointing at the dark mass.

After peering at the image a moment, Turner said. "Ask them to zoom in on that shadow."

"Yes ma'am," the communications officer replied, then relayed her request to the operator in Edinburgh, South Australia.

Soon the high altitude camera zoomed toward the waters east of Marchinbar Island, the most northerly of the windswept Wessel group. The screen filled with a wavering shadow that was partially obscured by the sparkle of sunlight on the sea.

"Is it kelp?" Beckman asked.

"No," Reynolds said with a certainty based on years navigating the region.

A white line suspended from bright yellow floats bobbing in the sea appeared, then as the UAV passed above it, the float line slid toward the bottom of the screen.

"It's a net," Beckman said. "Do aborigines use nets?"

"Not like that." Turner replied then spoke to the comms officer again. "Give us a wider angle on the white line."

The junior officer relayed the request to the controller, then the image expanded revealing the float line formed three sides of a square pen against a low cliff, enclosing a broad expanse of shallow water.

"It's a fish farm," Turner said, surprised.

Reynolds leaned forward, peering at the screen, puzzled. "There's no aquaculture up there."

"There is now," Beckman said, "but no Aborigines. Either they're too scared to go up there, or if they do, they don't come back."

"I'll ask the NT Police for all missing persons reports for that area," Turner said.

"For the last ten years."

"Colonel," she said, "no one could be killing our people for a decade without us knowing about it."

"Are you sure? There's a lot of empty country out there, more than enough for people to go missing in without anyone ever knowing what happened to them.

"Maybe not every crocodile and shark attack was what we thought it was," Reynolds conceded.

"We should study the islands," Dr. McInness suggested. "The EBE's might hunt in the sea, but they're amphibians, not fish. They live on land."

Reynolds look told them he thought the islands were almost uninhabitable. "It's pretty barren up there and bloody hot during the day."

"They could hide when it's light," Turner said, "and hunt at night when it's cooler."

"When humans are asleep," Beckman added, then turned to Dr. McInness. "Are they nocturnal?"

The scientist shook his head. "I don't think so."

"Let's have a closer look at the island," Turner said to the communications officer.

After the order had been relayed to the controller, the Triton glided over the island, following the coastline with its camera. There was no sign of life inland while only one beach showed single file footsteps leading from the water to a rock shelf.

"Someone's up there," Reynolds remarked.

"Or something," Beckman said.

White seabirds circling low over the water came into view on the right side of the screen. They swooped down, snatched morsels off the surface then climbed quickly away without ever setting down in the water.

"What are they doing?" Dr. McInness asked.

"Scavenging," Reynolds said, "but I don't see any fishing boats."

"Angle to the right," Turner requested of the comms officer, then the beach slid off screen as the camera focused on the shallow water offshore.

A huge flock of gulls and terns swept over the sea, plucking scraps from its surface without ever landing on the water, then quickly flapping away as if their lives depended on it. Below the surface, a dark mass swirled like a living shadow, moving in spurts and surges far faster than the fish they'd seen in the netted pen to the south.

Turner squinted at the screen, studying the agitated movements of the fish, realizing they were fleeing in fear. "There's something in the water."

Beckman studied the shifting shadow warily. "Whatever it is, hungry birds are scared of it."

"I'll warm up the chopper," Reynolds said, reading Beckman's mind.

\* \* \* \*

"Can you give to others what you have given to me?" Beloved asked the Infiltrator as she regained full control of her mind and body. She had become accustomed to floating on the suspension field, of hearing the Intruder

108

probe's voice inside her mind and replying aloud with the One Speech.

"I have limited resources for such procedures," the Infiltrator said, "but it is possible."

"How many?"

"Would they require everything you have?"

"No, only enough to help us against the ...," she almost said 'land-dwellers', but now she knew better, "... the humans."

"I could implant fifty with specialized knowledge for their tasks, but it will do you no good."

The surveys of Earth the Infiltrator had made as it approached the planet flashed into her mind. Images from space of enormous cities and continents filled with billions of inhabitants passed before her eyes. It was a shocking confirmation of what she'd already discovered from the books Watcher had given her. It left Beloved in no doubt that her enemy's material power greatly exceeded her own, yet she remained determined to find a way. If anything, the knowledge flowing from the Infiltrator's gift only strengthened her resolve.

"I will send you fifty of my brothers," she said, already singling out who would benefit most from the gift. It was a list based on her need and their aptitudes, although it included not one of her sisters, not even Heart-of-the-Deep who was as near to a friend among the females as she had. Beloved would never allow any of the other females to grow in power, even if all their lives depended upon it. When she wondered what knowledge was of most use, her Intruder lattice flooded her mind with thousands of possible stratagems drawn from eons of conflict. It came so fast, she could barely keep up, yet somehow she absorbed it all. It left her with a sense that the Infiltrator gift knew her better than she knew herself, pushed her to the limits of her power, but not beyond.

"When will we start, Great Mother?" the Infiltrator asked.

"Immediately," she replied, eager to begin.

The interrogation capsule filled with water, then the door opened and she swam clear. With barely a look back, Beloved glided toward the surface, her mind racing. What little chance her race had of surviving on Earth would depend on her chosen fifty. All others would be expendable. If they were defeated, the gifted fifty would be the last to die at the hands of the humans.

Watcher-of-Skies would be among the chosen. He'd learn Intruder science and mathematics in the hope that he might discover a weakness in human technology. If such a flaw existed, he would find it, but Watcher and the others were far away and time was limited. She would have to return at once with her personal guard to summon those who would be implanted while she left Prowls-the-Shallows behind to visit the Infiltrator alone.

It was fitting that Prowls, her most trusted lieutenant, would be the first to be chosen. He would master all there was to know of the Intruder way of war, of their great victories and epic defeats, of their relentless rise to power. And he would receive all the Infiltrator knew of human material power, so he could anticipate their moves and devise counters to them.

Her resources were limited, but of one thing she was sure, Prowls-the-Shallows would make a fine general.

* * * *

Reynolds, Beckman and Dr. McInness boarded the *Naturaliste's* Squirrel helicopter in the early afternoon. They flew over Galiwinku and its tarred airstrip then followed Cadell Strait northeast toward the gray underwater mass the UAV had observed.

"A P-8's going to meet us there in case we need support," Reynolds called over the beat of the rotors. "It's mapped six of those shadows as far north as Sphinx Head and as far south as Arnhem Bay."

Beckman gave Reynolds an uneasy look. He'd spent

hours poring over maps, familiarizing himself with the region and now knew what an enormous area it was. He settled into his seat as they followed Cadell Strait, then at its northern exit, the Arnhem coast angled away to the south while they continued on to the northeast, flying over tropical islands and an aquamarine sea.

After almost an hour in the air, Reynolds asked, "How do you want to do this, Colonel?"

"Low and fast." Beckman said. "Don't hover. Don't make us an easy target." He thought it unlikely they'd encounter an alien with a stolen gun, but he didn't want to risk a lucky shot forcing them to ditch in the sea where they'd have no chance against the fast swimming amphibians.

Reynolds took the helo down to a hundred meters as a twin-engine P-8 Poseidon patrol aircraft appeared high in the sky and began orbiting them at twenty kilometers, then a business-like female voice sounded in their headphones.

"Boxkite to Taipan, small surface contact zero eight zero degrees. Over."

Reynolds radioed back confirmation and adjusted course. A few minutes later, a slender shape floating motionless in the water came into view. At a distance it appeared to be a creature, but as they approached within range of Beckman's binoculars, he saw that it was made of hewn wood.

"It's an overturned canoe," he said, searching the surrounding sea vainly for its owner.

"Could it have been washed out from a village?" Dr. McInness asked from the back seat.

"Maybe," Reynolds said, unconvinced. They circled the area once looking for survivors, then Reynolds radioed a report to the Poseidon before resuming course.

Ten minutes further on, the female officer's voice sounded again. "Boxkite to Taipan, birds ahead. Climb to three hundred meters for clearance."

Beckman spotted a flock of seabirds through his

binoculars, then pointed them out to Reynolds who angled the helicopter toward them as they climbed. Occasionally the birds snatched at the surface but mostly they circled helplessly above the sea. When the chopper drew near, a large school of slender silver and gold fish became visible as they moved slowly through the water beneath the birds. Beckman focused his binoculars on the fish, glimpsing torpedo-like shapes darting around them, first one way then another, driving the school northeast.

"They're herding them," Dr. McInness said surprised.

"Those fish are golden snapper," Reynolds explained. "Good eating."

"That's a lot of food," Beckman said, guessing there were hundreds of fish in the school.

Reynolds took a bearing on the school's destination. "They're heading for the same place we are," he said, then flew on toward a low island in the distance.

"I wonder if they know we're coming?" Beckman said as they approached bleached white cliffs rising vertically from the sea to a rock plateau partially covered in trees.

"Their biosonar would have passed the word as soon as we left the Naturaliste," Dr. McInness said. "They'll be talking of little else."

The chopper passed over the island briefly before Reynolds swung back out over water and began circling a shallow bay enclosed by a fishing net suspended from a line of buoys. Another school of herded fish had almost reached the net, forcing Reynolds to swing out wide to avoid the agitated seabirds circling above. When the fish neared the net, a dozen sleek shadows towed the buoys aside like they were opening a curtain, creating a gap in the net. Moments later, fast swimming sea-herders drove the school through the opening, then the net was quickly pulled shut behind them. The sea-herders immediately broke off the chase as a light gray shadow surged toward the fish from beneath the cliffs. The expanding shadow engulfed the school and began tearing the fish apart. The surface of the enclosed bay boiled as fish leapt in terror from the water while seabirds circled in frustration above, snatching at scraps of white flesh that floated to the surface.

"Go lower," Beckman said.

Reynolds glanced warily at the birds cluttering his air space, then dropped the Squirrel to wave height and made a fast skimming pass over the bay. One bird struck the rotor and was cut apart, showering blood drops and feathers on the windshield, while beneath them the dark shadow dissolved into tens of thousands of tiny amphibians racing each other to consume the fish.

"We need pictures," Beckman said. "Can the P-8 see them?"

Reynolds radioed the big jet overhead, then the female officer replied, "The surface reflection is blocking our cameras."

"Sure is a lot of them," Dr. McInness said, peering down into the water.

Beckman tracked one of the small amphibians as it darted close to the surface, catching a glimpse of gentle ridges flowing back from a smooth bulging forehead. "That P-8's a sub killer, right?"

"Yeah," Reynolds said, not grasping Beckman's intent.

"So it's got sonobuoys?"

Understanding flashed across Reynolds' face. "Absolutely."

"Do you think they'd mind dropping one for us, right in the middle of that?"

Reynolds smiled. "All we've got to do is ask."

Dr. McInness looked up alarmed. "You can't be serious! We don't know what damage it'll do to them."

"We're about to find out," Beckman said, nodding to Reynolds. "Tell them to have their cameras ready."

"Taipan to Boxkite, request you drop one sonobuoy into the center of the dark mass. Keep your cameras rolling."

The Poseidon's commander acknowledged the request, then the big jet came over the feeding ground and released a metal cylinder which popped a small parachute almost immediately.

"They'll interpret it as an attack!" Dr. McInness said desperately.

"We need proof," Beckman said, "something the Joint Chiefs will believe."

"The Joint Chiefs!" the scientist exploded. "What are you talking about?"

"There are thousands of those damn things down there," Beckman snapped, "and every single one of them is smarter than you and me combined. What do you think I mean?"

Dr. McInness' mouth opened in surprise, but he said nothing. A few seconds later, the sonobuoy splashed into the sea above the feeding mass and began pinging the depths as if searching for an enemy submarine. The sound waves rolled through the sea like thunderclaps, then the surface exploded as thousands of tiny amphibian faces burst out of the water, placing their hyper sensitive sonar lobes above the sonic bombardment. Many clutched their bulging foreheads in shock while beneath the cliffs, others leapt from the water like a dark wave rolling over the shore. Some were pulled to safety by those already on land while others were so disoriented, they fell back into the sea.

"They're only babies!" Dr. McInness exclaimed.

In the sheltered sea below, thousands of pairs of large blue-green eyes turned curiously toward the helicopter as it circled at high speed, while adult guards watched with helpless fury.

"What's the sound strength of a sonobuoy?" Beckman asked.

"Two hundred decibels," Reynolds replied, "similar to ship based sonar."

"That's their weakness."

"Just like whales." When he saw the puzzled look on Beckman's face, the naval officer added, "Naval sonar deafens them. It's why they beach themselves. Deafness affects their ability to navigate. It might even give them migraines."

"Whale migraines?" Beckman said surprised, never having heard of such a thing and wondering if the sonobuoy was having the same effect on the tiny amphibians.

Reynolds activated his radio mike. "Boxkite, are you getting this?"

"Affirmative Taipan. We're transmitting in real time to the Naturaliste."

Beckman watched the P-8 circling high above, then said, "Tell them to delete the recordings once the ship has confirmed they've received them."

Reynolds passed on the instruction as three amphibian guards swam to the sonobuoy, pulled it to the surface and attacked it with rocks. It died moments later, then the young dived below the surface.

"It didn't take them long to figure that out," Reynolds observed as the frightened young amphibians swam back to the shelter of the island. Left behind, floating in the enclosed bay were a handful of adult guards watching the circling helo.

"That was a mistake!" Dr. McInness declared. "They'll think we're dropping sonic weapons on their feeding grounds."

"That's not a feeding ground, Ian," Beckman said. "It's a God damned hatchery and it's not the only one!"

\* \* \* \*

After returning to the *Naturaliste*, Beckman and Dr. McInness went to the wardroom to see how Teresa was progressing with Kermit. The makeshift laboratory was now filling with equipment flown in to meet the growing list of requirements identified by the remote research teams. Three scientists in white masks and gowns, who'd joined the ship while Beckman was away, now assisted Teresa.

Having concluded the Area 51 IQ tests were pointless, she was now teaching the amphibian to play chess. A small screen stood in front of the anti-contamination sheet displaying a chessboard for those in the observation area to watch while Kermit interacted with the screen at the foot of his bed. Circular metal sensors had been attached to his elongated head with wires feeding into some of the new equipment brought aboard to measure his brain's electrical activity.

As they took their seats, Teresa threw Beckman an incredulous look, signaling the alien's progress was surprising even her. Kermit was watching chess pieces move rapidly across the screen, selecting his moves with a laser pointer. Beckman knew from her look the amphibian was already posing a serious challenge to his opponent.

Dr. McInness opened his laptop to clear his latest emails from Area 51. After a few minutes, he whispered, "They've finished the hematology report." A blood sample had been flown off the *Naturaliste* by helicopter while Kermit was still unconscious, then rushed to Melbourne University for analysis. From there, the results had been sent to the Area 51 biosciences team for further study. "His blood has no antibodies. Not one. The bio-tech people don't understand how his immune system works, although his cells have incredible regenerative qualities."

Beckman studied the alien's face, surprised at how the coloration had changed in just a few hours. "The bruise on his head is fading."

Dr. McInness nodded absently without looking up. "I noticed. You split his head open yesterday. By tomorrow, he'll be fully healed."

"Want to bet there's no scar?"

The scientist returned to the emailed report. "He's got

ultra fast coagulation, super cell regeneration and disease immunity. That can't be natural. His entire body has been genetically re-engineered."

"Makes him a tough little son of a bitch," Beckman mused, "and real hard to kill."

"We're not here to kill them, Bob. We're here to establish contact."

"I've got a feeling they don't want to talk to us."

Dr. McInness continued reading the report. "They infected his blood with fourteen highly toxic pathogens. None had any effect."

"So we can rule out germ warfare."

"It makes sense for an interstellar species to make itself immune to hostile microbes," Dr. McInness said. "It would make colonizing alien planets safer."

"His little brothers seem to have no problem colonizing Earth."

"They also irradiated his blood." Dr. McInness read the results, then grunted in surprise. "His cells are two hundred times more resistant to radiation than ours."

Beckman scowled. "So in a nuclear war, the only survivors will be Kermit and the cockroaches. Sounds like a rock band."

"They don't have nuclear weapons, Bob."

"Not yet."

"Radiological resistance isn't about nuclear war, it's about space travel. The Earth's magnetic field protects us from radiation, but there's no such protection in space. They'd have anti-radiation fields protecting their ships, but what if those fields malfunction? This is the kind of modification a space faring species would want in order to resist cosmic radiation. You know what this means?"

"Yeah, can't sneeze on them, can't nuke them," Beckman said grimly.

"It means his species has been in space so long, they re-engineered their bodies to live there."

"Charles Darwin will be turning over in his grave."

"They're in charge of their own evolution," Dr. McInness said, deep in thought. "Natural selection no longer applies to them."

"They could have done a better job on the nose."

"Kermit is the result of *artificial* selection. I wonder if all alien species do this, once they master genetics? Imagine the risk to the genome if they made a mistake, but didn't find it for generations – and the ethical considerations. That could be a problem for us."

Beckman shook his head. "It's only a matter of time before we start popping out designer babies. We might outlaw it in the US, but someone, somewhere will turn it into a business. It's going to happen, designer baby tourism. Get used to it."

Dr. McInness' face darkened as he considered the report's implications. "From an evolutionary perspective, artificial selection is a much faster process than natural selection. It's like we're in low gear, they're in high gear. If all things were equal, we'd be unable to compete with them."

"You're not instilling me with confidence, Ian."

"The last time two intelligent species coexisted on Earth was when Homo Sapiens and Neanderthals met. The Homo Sapiens were more evolved than the Neanderthals and won out. According to this and Teresa's results, the differences between us and the EBE's are greater than between us and the Neanderthals."

"Lucky for us Kermit's in the stone age."

Captain Turner entered the wardroom and took the seat beside Beckman. She watched the chess pieces sliding across the small screen, then whispered, "Who's winning?"

"Artificial selection," Beckman said.

She gave him a curious look. "What?"

Beckman shrugged. "Don't mind me, I'm just a Neanderthal in low gear."

When Teresa saw both Beckman and Turner were

watching, she approached the anti-contamination curtain.

"Is Kermit world champion yet?" Beckman asked.

She rolled her eyes. "He lost the first two, drew the next one, then won nine straight. And he's got this one in the bag."

Turner gave them a curious look. "Kermit?"

"Well we couldn't call him Miss Piggy," Beckman said.

"Who's he playing?" she asked.

"Not who," Teresa said. "What. We've got him matched up against the Teragrid."

"The Tera-what?" Turner asked.

"That's what I said," Beckman declared. "Apparently everyone around here knows what it is except me – and you."

"It's a collection of super computers in US universities linked together," Teresa explained. "They have several hundred teraflops of computing power."

"Teraflops?" Turner said uncertainly.

"It's a gazillion times bigger than the biggest number you've ever heard of," Beckman explained.

"We've got the entire super computer network dedicated to this one task," Teresa explained, "but only for three days. The universities back home are furious, especially because we won't tell them what we're using the Teragrid for."

"They'd be furious if they knew you were using their very expensive supercomputers for playing computer games," Beckman said, "and losing."

"Not if they knew who it was playing," Teresa said.

Turner watched Kermit make a move. "Can a human beat the Teragrid?"

"We can't beat one super computer," Beckman said, "let alone an army of them."

Dr. McInness looked up from his computer pensively. "No matter how big the Teragrid is, it's still limited by our intelligence, because we created it. That's the problem."

Teresa nodded. "Kermit has thought processes going on inside his head we don't."

"How can you tell?" Turner asked.

"We're mapping his neural impulses. There's approximately two point eight times more electrical activity in his brain than ours and different centers are triggering simultaneously." Teresa smiled, impressed by the implications. "He could be multitasking."

"How do you multitask chess?" Beckman said. "It's just a game."

"Chess has multiple alternate combinations of moves," she replied. "The more moves ahead you plan, the more alternative combinations. If he is multitasking, thinking about each combination simultaneously, he could see every possibility at the same time. That could explain why he's winning. The question is, how many combinational pathways can he see at one time?"

Beckman leaned toward Dr. McInness. "We can only see one at a time, right?"

Dr. McInness nodded. "Ah huh."

"Right," Beckman said. "So he's one smart little muppet."

"And the greatest chess player the world's ever seen," Teresa added.

With the Teragrid now hopelessly on the defensive, Beckman said, "I wonder if he knows how far ahead of us he is?"

"He knows," the scientist said.

"How can you tell?" Turner asked.

"Every second we interact with him, he's learning about our limitations. Take the IQ tests Teresa put him through. They tell him what the limits of our intelligence are because we designed the questions. It's like a five year old testing you. You know its capabilities from the questions it asks. Same thing."

"Good thing he doesn't know he's playing the Teragrid," Beckman said. "He probably thinks we're smarter than we are."

"Don't count on it," Dr. McInness said. "He misses nothing."

"Too bad for Kermit," Beckman said.

"Why do you say that?"

"He knows too much about us. That's why we can't ever let him go back."

"You can't imprison him forever. He's a highly advanced, sentient being."

Beckman's face turned to stone. "The only way Kermit's getting out of here is in a pine box."

# CHAPTER FIVE: BLOODSHED

Heart-of-the-Deep coughed as if food had caught in her throat. She clutched her chest in surprise, gasping for breath as her airway constricted. It happened so fast, she didn't have time to inflate her quad-lungs, preserving her air supply. Heart's body shivered uncontrollably as her muscles spasmed, then in a flash of understanding, she swatted Beloved-of-the-Sea's hand so hard, it sent her sister's arm flying back, knocking the fish she was about to eat onto the cave floor.

Heart held up a hand in warning as her fingers began to sting from the toxin seeping into her skin. She used her sonar lobe to pulse a single sonic warning. "Poison!"

Beloved watched helplessly as Heart-of-the-Deep doubled over, suffocating and wracked with pain. "Sister?"

Heart swept the carved wooden platter onto the rock floor, ensuring her sister would not eat the food it contained, then collapsed face first onto the low wooden table. Beloved rushed to her side, cradling Heart in her arms as she searched for any sign of life, but the one female she cared for was already dead.

Heart-of-the-Deep had been her closest confidant. They'd grown up together among the coastal reefs and mangroves, hunted tropical fish and crustaceans during the terrible early years. Many times they narrowly escaped the one-fin-killers that prowled the sea and the long-tooth-stalkers that lay in wait along the muddy river banks. Time and again, they'd seen their sisters caught and killed, while they had swum for their lives. Back then when they'd been too young to secrete the overpowering pheromones that dominated the males, they'd been ignored and left to fend for themselves. It was only in their adolescence, when they began imprinting the males, that life improved.

Beloved had not understood the change even though she had exploited it more effectively than any of her sisters. It was a fundamental biological process that allowed females to form cohesive groups of males and become the binding force of their societies, of their species. She and Heart had discussed it at length, never able to identify the cause, yet certain there was one, thankful that at last they could martial the boundless energies of the males. It was only since she had received the Intruder gift that she fully understood what had happened.

With her birth-sister dead in her arms, a tremendous wave of loss washed over Beloved. Heart had been the only female she'd ever come close to relying upon, the only one she dared confide in, although two females could never fully trust each other. Now that Heart was gone, for the first time in her life Beloved felt utterly alone, even though she was surrounded by thousands of faithful males. Her loss was amplified by the knowledge that Heart's last action had saved her life, a rare act between females. That sacrifice filled Beloved with an unrelenting desire for vengeance that would not be satisfied until her sister's murderers were dead.

She issued a single ping from her sonar lobe, calling for assistance, then the patter of approaching footsteps echoed into the chamber. A moment later, Prowls-the-Shallows appeared with his new weapon drawn, a steel carving knife taken from the human cruiser several days before. He was still adjusting to the Infiltrator gift that filled his mind with visions of countless wars and clinical explanations of how they'd been won and lost. Worse than the horrors haunting his thoughts was the anguish he felt at having discovered how easily he could have defeated the humans if he commanded but a fraction of the weaponry his brothers beyond the outer rim possessed. When he saw Beloved's distressed state and Heart's corpse, he pushed the Infiltrator visions aside and focused upon his mistress.

"It was poison," she said in the most cultured form of One Speech. She'd already given orders that the Intruder language was to be learnt and spoken by all in the hope that if they ever met their distant cousins, they would be seen as equals, not primitive barbarians.

Prowls glanced at the food strewn across the floor with immediate understanding. "I will have the food preparers put to death!" he declared, channeling his rage.

Beloved lay her sister on the rock floor, then stood to face him. "No," she said with supreme self control. "Find which of my sisters was responsible and bring her to me. Search in secret. Let none of my sisters know what has happened here."

"As you wish, Beloved," he replied, then hurried off.

Beloved knew her food was prepared exclusively by males, yet she was certain her murder could only have been ordered by one of her sisters. It would be someone who wanted to take her place, which scarcely reduced the number of possible plotters. Once the male assassin was found, he would be made to reveal the identity of his mistress. He would not be publicly executed as such hollow displays carried no weight with imprinted males and impressed other females not at all. Prowls-the-Shallows would simply end the assassin's life, quickly and cleanly, for he was merely a pawn.

As for the assassin's female overlord, Beloved would not be so kind.

\* \* \* \*

Nanikiya Matjuwi stood in his dugout canoe, his spear held high above his head waiting for a fish to appear. When a small dark shape darted beneath his canoe, he drove his spear into the clear waters of Arnhem Bay, keeping hold of the end. It was a lightning fast reflex action that had taken him years to perfect, attacking at the first glimpse of movement before he fully recognized his prey.

The spear shuddered as it penetrated his prey's back, then to his surprise, rather than kick furiously to escape, it went limp with shock as tiny hands clutched the spear emerging from its chest. The hatchling filled the water with agonized low frequency pulses, screaming a warning to its siblings and desperately calling to the nursery fathers.

The aboriginal fisherman raised his spear from the water curiously, wondering what he'd caught and how edible it would be. He was shocked to discover a small blue-gray skinned humanoid impaled on the end of his spear. Nanikiya peered at its angular face, domed forehead and large, separated eyes in disbelief and amazement, then lowered the dying hatchling into the canoe. He pressed his foot against its back and pulled the spear out, then sat down as dark blood welled from the creature's wound. Its miniscule hands pressed against its chest while its oddly shaped feet twitched in a way Nanikiya had never seen before. Rather than having a central bone, rows of narrow bones ran lengthwise through the foot, flexing horizontally out into a powerful fin for swimming and compressing together for walking on land. Above the feet, its body was sculpted with sinewy muscle, especially its thicker thighs which hinted at its underwater speed.

The hatchling spluttered dark blood from its small mouth revealing tiny triangular teeth, then its horizontal eyelids closed as it lost consciousness. Its little hands slipped away from the gaping wound in its chest and its breathing turned into a gurgling wheeze as blood seeped into its quad-lungs.

Nanikiya had heard wild rumors of strange water demons stalking the night and killing fishermen who paddled into their sacred waters, but he'd never seen one himself. For years, whenever a hunter or fisherman had gone missing, rumors abounded of them having been taken by the water demons, but no one really knew. Nanikiya had attended missionary school until he was nine and loved listening to the elders tell of the dreamtime, but even he had found the demon tales hard to believe – until now.

He picked up his wooden paddle and prodded the strange creature experimentally, thinking if this was a water demon, it was surprisingly fragile. Nanikiya decided it was dead, then peered into the water wondering if there were more and if they were the reason why his once rich fishing grounds were now almost empty.

Seeing neither fish nor demon, he considered paddling around the point to the Cato River where the fishing had once been good, then he saw three streamlined shapes in the distance break the water like dolphins. They were coming in from the deeper water further out in the bay, swimming in a triangular formation with a precision unknown to dolphins. When they appeared again, he realized they were full grown versions of the hatchling, heading toward him with a speed and purpose that filled him with fear.

Nanikiya sat up straight and with a single powerful sweep of his paddle, sent his canoe gliding toward the shore. For several seconds he stroked hard, building up speed, then he began glancing back every few strokes, watching the distance shrink to the three nursery fathers racing after him. His heart pounded in his chest, beating faster even than when the giant crocodile had overturned his canoe during the wet season four years ago. He understood crocodiles, how to escape them, how to kill them, but he knew nothing of water demons.

He concentrated on driving his paddle through the water, straining his muscles to their limits, but still, the three sleek water demons grew closer. Ahead was a stark white beach and a track leading back through the trees to the isolated village of Rorruwuy. If he could reach the beach, he could run to the village and rouse the other hunters. When he glanced back, he saw the demons had halved the distance and another larger group was coming in from the north, porpoising through the water with terrifying synchronization. It was a hunting party, summoned by the nursery fathers to avenge the death of the hatchling and prevent knowledge of their presence spreading.

The water shallowed, then when Nanikiya's canoe scraped the sandy bottom, he grabbed his spear and ran through ankle deep water to the beach. Two old women sitting in the shade of the trees watched him curiously. One called out something he couldn't hear over his own labored breathing, then he reached the hot sand. He found his legs were turning to rubber from exhaustion as he staggered toward the track, waving the old women back. Not understanding, they just watched him, missing their chance to escape.

Not far from Nanikiya's abandoned canoe, the three nursery fathers emerged from the water. They stopped to examine the blood soaked body of the hatchling, then watched the fisherman flee along the track through the trees. The old women stood, staring uncertainly at the amphibians, too confused to be afraid while Nanikiya yelled breathless warnings to the village.

Just as he reached the settlement, the hunting party emerged from the sea, joining the nursery fathers beside Nanikiya's canoe. They glanced at the dead hatchling and the old women watching from the trees, then the hunt leader made his decision. He knew of the tiny community in the forest, having observed its inhabitants all his life. It comprised little more than ten simple buildings with corrugated iron roofs and wooden walls clustered around a small communal square. Beyond the village was a rough track through the forest and a dirt airstrip that rarely saw a plane. It was as isolated and unremarkable as any place on Earth, except its inhabitants had seen them.

The leader issued his orders, then the hunting party and the nursery fathers walked calmly up the beach, readying their crude weapons. Some went to the old women, who backed away with rising terror, while others moved into the trees to encircle the village. The women screamed as powerful, cold hands reached for them and they realized they were about to die.

Beyond the trees, Nanikiya's yelling roused the villagers who stared at him in confusion. A few men approached him curiously, not realizing the danger, not even carrying their weapons. Short of breath, he tried to warn them, motioning with his spear as the water demons surrounded the village.

Then the killing began.

* * * *

Shortly after morning watch the next day, helicopters began ferrying soldiers newly arrived from the east coast to the *Naturaliste*. Before they had finished stowing their gear, defense intelligence informed Captain Turner that Territory police had received a satellite telephone call from a remote village on the northern side of Arnhem Bay. The call had come through to the emergency operator in Darwin who'd heard a woman scream close to the phone and men shouting nearby, but the caller never had time to speak. For several minutes, the line had remained open, then the handset had been replaced without a word, disconnecting the call. Repeated attempts by the emergency operator to reestablish contact with the village had failed.

When Beckman read the report, he immediately requested the on station UAV be sent to overfly the village. Less than an hour later, an RAAF Triton began circling the settlement at two thousand meters. The optical feed came in live to the ship's communications room, watched by the senior officers. It revealed a gently curving beach flanked by rocky bluffs to the east and mangroves to the west. A small cluster of square buildings were gathered together in a clearing set back from the beach, surrounded by forest that stretched unbroken to the horizon. Doors and windows were open, washing hung on lines strung between the buildings and large pots sat unattended on communal cooking facilities, but there was no sign of the village's inhabitants.

"Looks abandoned," Beckman said.

"At least fifty people live there," Turner said. "We should see someone."

"What's it called?" Dr. McInness asked.

Turner checked her notes. "The village is called Rorruwuy. The beach is NT 883."

Teresa gave her a curious look. "You number your beaches?"

"We have twenty five thousand kilometers of coastline, Major, with more than ten thousand beaches," Turner replied. "We haven't got around to naming them all yet."

Beckman pointed to the roof of one of the buildings. "Is that a satellite dish?"

Reynolds picked up the mike and asked the operator in South Australia to zoom in, then a dusty white dish on a metal tripod appeared on screen.

"What can they get out there?" Beckman asked.

"Basic telecommunications," Turner replied. "Telephone, television, very slow internet. Why?"

"They didn't strip it," Dr. McInness said. "Either they don't know what it is …"

"Or they do and they're using it." Beckman gave

Turner a meaningful look. "I'd have your people cut the link."

She nodded, then picked up a handset and spoke to the Chief of Navy directly. Since the hatchery had been discovered, she'd been given twenty four hour direct access to her naval commander-in-chief. When she hung up, she said, "It'll be down in ten minutes."

The image panned from one building to another as the operator performed a detailed examination of the village. Scattered between the simple structures were solar panels, a small telecommunications tower, a generator shed and water tanks on stands. At the outskirts of the village were communal pit toilets and public showers, luxuries for such an isolated location.

"There," Beckman said, pointing to a dark stain at the entrance to a small house. The stain spread from the doorway to the dirt outside. "Remind you of anything?"

"Damn," Reynolds said. "Same as Galiwinku!"

The image continued drifting over the village, revealing more dark stains and several bloody drag marks where the corpses had been taken away.

"They're becoming territorial." Dr. McInness furrowed his brow anxiously. "The villagers must have challenged them in some way."

"We need to get people in there," Beckman said, glancing at Turner.

"Norforce is on standby at Larrakeyah," she said.

"Are they special forces?"

"The North West Mobile Force is a surveillance unit, a mostly aboriginal infantry regiment trained by the SAS. If the country's ever invaded, they'll stay and fight behind enemy lines, living off the land."

"Can your Squirrel get there?" Beckman asked.

Reynolds nodded. "It's in range."

Beckman's expression hardened. "Tell Norforce to go in. We'll meet them there."

\* \* \* \*

"Attacking the human settlement was a mistake," Prowls-the-Shallows said as he met Beloved in her private chamber, one of the few parts of the cave complex now lit by electric light. There was a single exposed light bulb near the entrance fed by a black cable that ran to the generator looted from the *Mermaid*. It was one of Watcher's experiments, proving his understanding of human technology, although Beloved found the harshness of the light unpleasant. "We should have waited until we were stronger, until the hatchlings were older."

"Where on this crowded world would you have us hide?" she asked. "The Deep Blue?" She knew the humans called it the Arafura Sea and it joined with a vastly greater ocean that covered half the world called the Pacific, but her kind were not oceanic. They needed land almost as much as did the humans.

"There are many uninhabited islands," Prowls said.

"And the humans have many ways of finding us."

"We could scatter. Send the hatchlings in every direction. Some would survive."

"Most would not," she said. "The humans would hunt them down."

"The hatchlings are expendable and easily replaced." He now knew a thousand stratagems to win a planetary war and if that knowledge told him anything, it was that if they were to prevail, they would have to be as brutal to their own kind as to their enemy. "Their sacrifice would give you time to escape with the gifted," he said, referring to those who had received the Infiltrator implants. "Take the females of breeding age with you. With what we now know, we could start again in secret."

"If we can hold on here, we can turn the entire Mothersea into a hatchery. All we need is a few more months—"

"Beloved," Prowls said sharply, "our scouts report human warships gathering beyond the horizon. They are coming from far away and their sonar is always on, blinding our scouts, forcing them back. If you delay, we will be trapped here."

"And if I run, we will never have this chance again," she said, well aware of the danger. What she didn't tell him was if they scattered, she would lose control over them all. Some of her sisters would slip away and imprint their own males. To leave the Mothersea would be to abandon her hope of becoming the world Matriarch. She was prepared to flee, but only as a last resort. "The humans must have a weakness. Find it."

He knew her well enough to know she'd made her decision and further argument was pointless. "I will do my best, Beloved, but once the human ship holding our brother passes through the Narrow Water, Watcher is certain they will hear everything. Already, they fly over the hatcheries, seeing all."

"Then order silence."

"The hatchlings are too young to obey."

"Discipline them."

"As you wish, Beloved," he said, not realizing she was risking their lives for her own power. "I have another matter to discuss. I have found the assassin. He was seen near the catch rooms watching the scalers clean the fish. When I searched his sleeping place, I found this." Prowls held up a small animal skin bundle which he carefully unfolded. Lying on the skin were more than a dozen semi transparent tentacles, each containing millions of stinging capsules containing enough poison to kill dozens of their kind. "He brushed your food with these."

"Floating-white-death!" Beloved whispered, immediately recognizing one of their most deadly natural enemies. During their hatchling days and even during their adolescence, many of her siblings had fallen victim to the deadly sea wasps. The jelly fish was one of the most poisonous creatures in all the world's oceans, drifting through the tranquil waters of the Mothersea for half the year, killing everything it touched. With a translucent body and sixteen deadly tentacles that grew to twice her length, they were difficult to detect and avoid, especially when swimming at speed. "What female imprinted him?"

"Daughter-of-the-Waves."

Beloved said nothing, suppressing her fury. Daughter had not been among the sisters she had suspected, having feigned friendship for years. Beloved had considered her a potential ally, while all the time Daughter had been plotting to destroy her. She cursed herself for not having seen through the ruse and swore never to trust another of her sisters again.

"I will take care of it, Beloved," Prowls said in a tone that indicated the assassin's mistress would meet a slow and painful death.

"No," she said, partly to avoid the risk of sending her most valuable male against a far more dangerous female and partly because what had to be done should be by her hand alone. She owed Heart-of-the-Deep that much. "Invite her to meet with me. Give her no cause for suspicion."

Prowls-the-Shallows carefully folded the animal skin over the deadly tentacles, then placed the hide bundle in her open hand. Dismissed, he headed off through the passage to find Daughter-of-the-Waves while Beloved planned her revenge by the harsh glow of a single electric light.

\* \* \* \*

The Squirrel took off at midday and headed east toward Rorruwuy as the *Naturaliste* steamed into Cadell Strait. For the first time, Turner had authorized Beckman and Teresa to carry sidearms although Dr. McInness, with his arm still in a sling, had refused a weapon. With Lt. Commander Reynolds at the controls, they flew over several large bays separated by slender peninsulas and dotted with deserted islands before reaching the vast, tranquil expanse of Arnhem Bay.

The Triton UAV that had been sent to observe Rorruwuy had surveyed the area, discovering a shadowy mass to the southwest similar to those found among the Wessel Islands further north. To avoid revealing this latest discovery, Reynolds flew straight to the village, never approaching within sight of the Arnhem Bay hatchery. Once across the bay, they followed the beach to where two green MRH-90 army helicopters were circling.

Beckman studied the scene through binoculars, noting dark blood stains in the red dirt and untouched food on wire grills over camp fires that had burned out hours ago.

"Will I send them in?" Reynolds asked.

Beckman nodded. "Tell them to be careful."

Reynolds radioed confirmation for the army to land and secure the settlement, then followed the transport choppers to the small dirt airstrip a kilometer inland from the village. The army helos flared and landed as their rear access ramps lowered. The moment the choppers touched down, two eighteen man combat teams emerged while the rotors were still spinning and fanned out into the clearing between the airstrip and the forest. By the time they reached the trees, they had formed a skirmish line with their rifles at eye height searching for targets. Finding the forest deserted, they advanced quickly through the trees to Rorruwuy.

While the army choppers powered down, Reynolds landed a short distance away, then they climbed out and started for the track leading to the village. The troops were just visible through the trees searching the buildings with efficient speed. Halfway to the forest's edge, Beckman stopped to study the tiny settlement through his binoculars. Reynolds came up beside him carrying a two-way radio broadcasting army chatter.

"Building four, *clear!*"

"Generator shed, *clear!*"

"Comms tower, *clear!*"

"There are no knives in any of the kitchens."

"Blood here, boss … someone got cut up bad."

"Got tracks into the forest, east side."

"They carried the bodies to the beach."

"Someone tried nicking the solar panels."

"What are them tracks, Sarge?"

Beckman listened as he watched the camouflage clad soldiers complete their sweep, then begin to follow amphibian tracks into the surrounding forest.

"Area's secure," the force commander announced. "Search for survivors."

Beckman watched the trees, puzzled by the strange quiet. "There are no birds." It was the first time he'd seen the forest so quiet.

Reynolds listened to the silence with growing unease. "Yeah. Where are they?"

"Spooked," Beckman said realizing the birds had sensed something he couldn't see. "The area's not secure," he declared as the aboriginal soldiers continued to fan out into the trees, following tracks they couldn't identify. "Call them back. Now!"

Reynolds raised the two-way to his lips. "This is Commander Reynolds. Stay out of the forest, we don't believe the area is—"

An automatic weapon fired east of the village, momentarily lighting up the forest shadows with muzzle flashes.

"Contact!" crackled from the radio.

Several short bursts sounded, then a soldier switched to full auto, spraying the surrounding bushes and trees with bullets as the ground came alive with movement.

"Who's firing?" the team commander demanded. "What are you shooting at?"

The automatic weapon clicked empty, then a scream sounded and was cut off as dark forms exploded from dozens of hiding places. Muzzle flashes lit up the forest, single shots and bursts, as soldiers fired at small figures racing through the underbrush carpeting the forest floor. The attackers swarmed over the men, striking them from behind as fast moving silhouettes and gunfire turned the peaceful forest into a chaotic fight for survival.

Confused voices erupted from Reynolds' two-way. "They're in the trees! ... What the hell are they? ... They're fast! ... Behind you ... Nibo, to your left! "

Tracer laced the forest as soldiers, surrounded on all sides, sprayed the bushes in a vain attempt to suppress their attackers. Small dark shapes were cut down by the withering fire as many more hurled themselves at the soldiers' backs with deadly ferocity. The troops in the village leveled weapons and charged into the forest to provide covering fire, but as they entered the shadows, dark forms hiding in the underbrush leapt at them, slashing and stabbing with a frenzied disregard for their own lives. The fighting quickly degenerated into bloody hand to hand as muzzle flashes silhouetted men being pulled to the ground by two and three attackers at a time.

"Get back to the chopper," Beckman ordered, nodding to Teresa who grabbed Dr. McInness by the arm and pulled him toward the navy chopper.

"We've got to help them," Reynolds said, drawing his pistol.

"We can't!" Beckman declared. "There are too many of them."

Reynolds looked incredulous. "They're still fighting."

"You go in there, you die."

Reynolds aimed his pistol at the forest but held fire, realizing he might just as easily hit one of his own men as their attackers.

Beckman snatched the radio from Reynolds' hand. "Fall back to the helos for immediate evac! Shrike One and Two," he said to the helos, "prepare for hot extract!"

A grenade exploded off to the left, then those soldiers who could began falling back through the trees, firing as they retreated. In ones and twos, they emerged from the forest, shooting as they headed for the helos whose engines were whining and rotors spinning as they prepared to takeoff. Several troopers carried or dragged wounded men, firing one handed as they ran.

"Let's go!" Beckman said to Reynolds.

"We have men down in there."

"We can't help them."

Reynolds stared in frustration at the forest, realizing it was almost over, then nodded. "Right," he said, then they ran back to the Squirrel.

Reynolds climbed in and got the chopper started while Beckman hesitated at the cockpit door. He glanced back at the forest as dark shapes cut down retreating soldiers trying to escape to the clearing. Halfway between the tree line and the choppers, a Norforce trooper was on one knee firing into the forest trying to give his comrades a chance to get clear. Suddenly, his head jerked back as a bullet struck his forehead, knocking him to the ground.

*They're using our own weapons against us!* Beckman realized as he stared at the dead soldier, impressed by the alien's marksmanship, then he spoke into the two-way. "Everyone out of the trees now! Helos launch in sixty seconds. Don't wait!" He turned to climb into the navy helo as a bullet whizzed past his ear, then as he jumped in and pulled the door closed, bullets slammed into the chopper's hull.

"Go!" he yelled to Reynolds who immediately throttled up.

The chopper lurched into the air, then the Squirrel's tail pitched up, sending them skimming fast and low over the airstrip, putting distance between themselves and the unnervingly accurate gunfire now coming from the trees.

Behind them, a handful of troopers, mostly walking wounded, stumbled aboard the army helos. Their rotors were spinning fast, but they stayed on the ground waiting, past Beckman's one minute time limit even though no more soldiers emerged from the forest.

"Get off the ground, damn you!" Beckman said through gritted teeth as Reynolds banked the Squirrel over the forest beyond the airstrip.

At last, one of the transports lifted off and slowly turned away, then the second chopper lumbered into the air as a bullet shattered its cockpit window, killing the pilot. The big helo teetered momentarily, then rolled sideways. Its rotors struck the ground and tore off, filling the air with the scream of tearing metal and stripping gears, then the chopper fell onto the ground and exploded.

Two soldiers staggered out of the trees toward where the helos had been, one was wounded with his arm over the other's shoulders. They fired one handed into the forest behind them, knowing there was no escape, then a white sliver flashed out of the trees, spearing the uninjured soldier in the back of the neck. The trooper took another step, dropped his gun and fell to his knees as the poison on the dart's tip took effect. He brushed the carved bone sliver away as bullets riddled both soldiers, knocking them face first onto the ground.

Beckman stared down at the dead soldiers strewn across the clearing in front of the burning helo, realizing he'd never even got a good look at their attackers. *They know how to use camouflage*, he thought, *and how to use our weapons!*

"We can't leave it like this," Dr. McInness said. "We have to go back, try again to make contact with them."

"That was contact!" Beckman snapped angrily, realizing trying to weed such an enemy out of this vast, empty wilderness was going to be a nightmare. "And it's only going to get worse from here."

\* \* \* \*

"You wished to see me, sister?" Daughter-of-the-Waves asked as she entered Beloved's small chamber.

"Yes," Beloved replied, motioning Daughter to join

her at the low table.

"I heard you encountered something strange in the Deep Blue," Daughter said as she seated herself. "Is that true?"

"Who have you heard this from?" Beloved asked, wondering who had betrayed her latest secret.

"I overheard the males. They say you are changed, that you are more than you once were, that you are now wiser than any of your sisters," Daughter said with barely concealed envy.

"I am what we are meant to be. Our kind have not lived like this for millions of years," Beloved said, waving to her dank cave retreat. "I know this now and much else besides."

"They say you have selected some males to go to the Deep Blue to gain this gift, but none of your sisters."

Beloved retrieved two plates covered in animal skins from a natural rock shelf. "That is correct. The males must be prepared to protect us. There is no need for our sisters to receive the gift." Denying the other females the Infiltrator knowledge ensured none of them could challenge her, while the only males to receive the implants would be those she had biochemically imprinted to serve her alone.

"I would like to receive this gift, to meet this dark-swimmer they speak of."

"You will receive a gift, my sister, but not that gift," she said, placing the two plates on the table without taking her seat. Instead she paced as if in thought, allowing Daughter to believe she was about to confide in her.

"Some say you keep this special prize for yourself, so we all must serve you."

"Who says such things?" Beloved asked innocently, stopping to study her sister with concealed hatred.

"Our sisters speak of little else."

There was always talk among the females, with their endless plotting and petty jealousies. It was why Beloved had risen above her sisters, playing one off against another, outscheming them all.

"I serve our collective need," Beloved said as she moved around the table behind Daughter. "Our place in this world is tenuous, our enemies more numerous than you can possibly imagine. This places a heavy burden upon my shoulders, a burden I am forced to carry alone."

"I would gladly share your burden."

"Would you indeed?" She paused a moment, as if considering the offer, then added, "I believe you sister. You are one I had considered I might trust."

"Had?" Daughter asked suspiciously, knowing there was rarely trust among females, only alliances of convenience.

"Let me serve you," Beloved said, leaning close and removing the animal skin covering the plate, revealing the sea wasp tentacles Prowls-the-Shallows had discovered. Daughter tensed when she saw them, then felt the cold steel of a land-dweller knife against her throat. Beloved's hand clamped over Daughter's sonar lobe and pulled her head back. "Eat, my sister."

"What are you doing?" Daughter demanded.

"Serving you as you would serve me, as you served Heart-of-the-Deep who is now dead because of you."

"She's dead?" Daughter said surprised, knowing enough not to move or struggle. Any sign of resistance would force Beloved's hand. Instead, she relaxed, instantly understanding what had happened.

"Poison is such an imprecise weapon, my sister, so unlike this blade at your throat. Now eat as she ate and die as she died."

Daughter hesitated. "I can replace her. I will be as loyal to you as she was. More so! Make me your second and I will ask for nothing more."

"You might have been my third, but you will never be my second," Beloved said coldly. "Eat and die fast, or refuse and I will bleed you slow."

Daughter felt cold steel dig into her skin, then slowly,

she reached for the sea wasp tentacles. It took a moment before the super toxin began to sting her fingers. "Our sisters will never forgive you for this."

"You think I need their forgiveness?" Beloved whispered with a menace few had ever seen. "Fear not sister, I will ensure they know exactly what happened here. It will discourage them from ever challenging me, as you have." She pushed the knife so hard, Daughter's thick skin broke letting a line of blood appear at the blade's edge. "Eat, *sister!*"

Daughter raised her hand, placed the tentacles in her small mouth and swallowed quickly. "I should have been leader," she gasped, then the poison constricted her airways, having a far more toxic effect on her alien physiology than on any Earth evolved life form. She wheezed, now unable to speak, then convulsed and doubled over.

Beloved pushed Daughter's face into the sea wasp tentacles, then wiped smeared blood from her blade. While her enemy died, she resolved never to trust any of her sisters again. She couldn't kill them, she needed them all for breeding, but she would limit the number of males they could imprint, denying them the power they instinctively craved. She would order Prowls-the-Shallows to place any males they had imprinted in the forefront of the fighting, ensuring they would be the first to die against the humans. It was a lesson Heart-of-the-Deep's murder had taught her, a lesson the Infiltrator had reinforced by gifting her with the long and treacherous history of her kind, of her gender.

There could be only one Supreme Matriarch and she must stand alone.

*Thank you my sister,* Beloved thought, remembering Heart-of-the-Deep's last action that had saved her life. *I shall never forget you.*

\* \* \* \*

The *Naturaliste* anchored at Cadell Strait's eastern exit shortly before sunset. With the ship's propellers now silent, her hull mounted sensors began cataloging the immense number of acoustic signatures coming from the bays and inlets between the Wessel Islands and Arnhem Land. By midnight, Petty Officer Casey had enough data to map the acoustic focal points to the shadowy masses identified by aerial reconnaissance and to fix the locations of several previously unknown sonic concentrations. With his new, more detailed acoustic map, Casey met the senior officers in the captain's stateroom to report his findings.

"There are six hot spots south of the Wessel Islands," he said, motioning to a map displayed on a large screen. He followed the line of slender islands reaching to the northeast, pointing to small coves and sheltered anchorages about thirty kilometers apart finishing at Sphinx Head near Cape Wessel. "There are two more east of here, off Inglis Island and in Elizabeth Bay, and three to the southeast in Buckingham, Ulundurwi and Arnhem Bays."

"Eleven hot spots," Beckman said thoughtfully. "That's a hell of an infestation."

Dr. McInness gave him a dark look. "They're nurseries, Bob, not a plague of rats."

Beckman's expression told them he wasn't convinced.

"Can you estimate their population?" Teresa asked.

Casey looked doubtful. "The signal density is very high in both the ranging and communication bands. That's causing a lot of interference from overlapping frequencies. The quantity of signals and the overlap interference adds a significant error factor."

"Give us a ball park estimate," Beckman said.

"So far, sir," Casey replied slowly, "the count is three point two million and rising."

"Million!" Beckman exploded.

"The population of the nearest nursery," Casey

added, "has stabilized at around three hundred and fifty thousand. Accuracy on the other acoustic hot spots decreases with distance."

"Even rats don't breed that fast," Beckman said.

"We shouldn't be surprised at their numbers, sir," Teresa said. "We've only studied the male of the species so far, but Kermit's reproductive biology is designed for mass fertilization, not individual impregnation."

"You're sure there are no nurseries north of the Wessel Islands?" Dr. McInness asked.

Casey shrugged uncertainly. "It doesn't look like it, but ... there's a lot of frequency overlap."

"If all the acoustic hot spots, all the hatcheries, are in protected waters between the islands and the mainland," Dr. McInness said, "it's probably safe to assume the open sea is unsuitable for breeding purposes."

"There's rich fishing all through those waters," Reynolds said. "I don't know if it's enough to feed four million full grown Kermits, but it might keep the babies going until they're big enough to move out into the Arafura."

"And then into the Pacific," Beckman said ominously, "where there's plenty of food and an ocean covering half the world's surface to hide in."

"It's amazing they've remained hidden for so long," Dr. McInness said.

"Not so amazing," Reynolds said. "There's hardly anyone out there to find them."

A sharp knock sounded at the door, then the communications officer stepped inside. "You might want to turn on the TV, ma'am."

"Why?" she asked, motioning him toward a small television.

"There was a survivor from the Rorruwuy massacre," he replied, switching on the TV. "A teenage boy. He ran forty kilometers to a nearby village. Indigenous community radio picked up the story and passed it to the networks."

The screen flashed to life with a static picture of a map of East Arnhem Land and a news anchor's face inset in the top left. The banner headline read 'Massacre in Arnhem Land'. The news anchor was speaking, although there was no picture of who he was talking to, only the frightened voice of a teenage boy on the telephone.

"What did they look like?" the anchorman asked.

"Short, with big eyes and no hair. "

"And these things killed everyone in your village?"

"Yeah. They nearly got me too."

"How did you get away?"

"I ran. They chased me, but couldn't catch me."

Captain Turner motioned to kill the sound and turned to Beckman. "There'll be hundreds of reporters up there by morning."

"At least they don't have pictures," Reynolds said.

"We have to stop them," Beckman declared. "If the media go to Rorruwuy now, they'll be slaughtered, then there'll be no way to contain this thing."

\* \* \* \*

Beloved studied the slender metal cylinder curiously. "This is what attacked the hatchery?"

"Yes Beloved," Prowls-the-Shallows replied. "They call it a sonobuoy."

"They know our weakness. They'll use it against us."

"There was a time," he said touching the side of his head, indicating the ancient wisdom now granted him by the Infiltrator gift, "when our kind used this type of weapon. They invented a lobe shield to protect against it."

Beloved paused as her more complex implants educated her about the devices used to protect their sensitive sonar lobes from underwater sonic attack. "We do not have the resources to produce such a defense."

"We can use animal hides to cover our lobes and

cushion the impact. I have already ordered their production."

"How many can we make?"

"Only enough for the females, the gifted fifty and some of our warriors. We cannot protect the hatchlings."

"Protect only those warriors loyal to me," she said. "Only they should receive the captured weapons."

"Now that we have killed their soldiers, they will come in great strength. We must prepare a retreat for you, your sisters and the gifted."

Beloved knew such a move would weaken her power, yet delaying could prove to be a fatal mistake. Reluctantly she said, "Plan for the escape, but tell no one. When all is ready, we shall go." She knew leaving now would surrender all hope of matriarchy. She would become just another hunted fugitive no different from her sisters, any one of whom might take the chance to rule in her place.

"We should leave today, Beloved. The human sonar fills the open sea. Soon it will be so strong we will be unable to reach the Deep Blue."

"Even with your lobe shields?"

"Perhaps."

From the entrance, Watcher-of-Skies pinged the room cautiously, letting them know he was waiting to be admitted.

"Enter," Beloved said.

Watcher stepped into the small cavern, wary of the effect she always had on him in confined spaces. Only since receiving the Infiltrator gift did he fully understand his reaction was caused by chemicals she constantly secreted. They weakened his self-control, reducing his ability to manage the relentless stream of Intruder knowledge now flooding his thoughts. "I have been considering the nature of human power," he said, as gifted memories of ravaged worlds blended seamlessly with Intruder quantum gravity equations. "Human civilization is vulnerable, Beloved."

She handed the sonobuoy back to Prowls-the-Shallows and focused all her attention on Watcher. "How so?"

"That which makes them powerful – their immense numbers, their great cities – carries with it great risk, makes them more fragile than they realize." He forced himself to concentrate as her mind altering pheromones assaulted his senses with an irresistibly intoxicating force.

"How do you propose to exploit this fragility?" she asked, her hopes rising. She knew Watcher was perhaps the most intelligent being on the entire planet. If anyone could find a way to destroy their enemy, it was him.

"I will need the Infiltrator."

"It has no weapons," Prowls said.

"It has what I need."

"The humans have the power to destroy it," Beloved said. "And it has many other, more powerful enemies nearby." She motioned upwards, indicating the enemy ships periodically passing through the Solar System.

"The Infiltrator will need to reveal its presence, but only briefly. It should survive."

Beloved approached Watcher, deliberately exuding pheromones to deepen her imprint upon him. "Tell me your idea, Watcher-of-Skies."

Watcher began to speak, explaining how the human domination of the planet would end and their time would begin. She marveled at the scope and simplicity of his idea and at its utter destructiveness. As she listened, she saw how her kind would rise from a shattered world, trampling the corpse of an extinct humanity. It was a vision that triggered a wave of relief, sweeping away all her fears and doubts.

When he'd finished, she turned to Prowls-the-Shallows. "Complete your preparations for escape, but while Watcher's plan has a chance, we will stay." She considered what Watcher had described, adding, "If this is possible, we are safer here."

She turned back to Watcher-of-Skies, determined to bend the Infiltrator to her will. In giving her the implants and all the knowledge they contained, the Intruder probe had unwittingly revealed how she could command it, providing she did not directly challenge its primary purpose.

"You will have all you require, my brother," she promised, certain Watcher's genius had saved them all.

\* \* \* \*

Beckman took his seat beside Captain Turner at the small table in the petty officer's mess. They were flanked by Dr. McInness and Teresa and all sat facing microphones and a video camera. Reynolds stood behind the camera with the communications officer who supervised the satellite link.

"What should I tell them?" Teresa whispered to Beckman.

"Exactly what you told me last night. It's up to them to decide where we go from here."

"We're ready," Reynolds said.

In front of the table, three screens came to life revealing live feeds from the White House situation room, the Pentagon and the Australian HQ Joint Operations Command. All three screens showed rooms crowded with uniformed officers and civilian leaders.

The Chairman of the US Joint Chiefs on the right side screen spoke first. "Good morning, or good evening depending on where you are. My name is General Vogel. I've been asked by the President to facilitate this meeting. You should all have received the preliminary briefing package by now, which I trust you've read, even if you don't believe it. This meeting is to determine our next steps with regard to the hostile contact situation developing in northern Australia." He glanced at his notes. "Captain Turner will provide a situation report followed by analysis from our experts in situ. Once the presentations are complete, we will accept questions. Captain Turner."

Turner leaned toward her microphone. "Thank you, General. My name is Commander Michelle Turner. I'm the commanding officer of the Royal Australian Navy oceanographic vessel, HMAS Naturaliste. We are currently anchored at eleven degrees fifty seven minutes south, one hundred thirty five degrees fifty four minutes east, off the northern coast of Australia. We've been recording sonar emissions from multiple extraterrestrial biological contacts for approximately five days, although most of our data has been collected since we anchored in our present position twenty hours ago.

"We have identified eleven high density sonar sources and many other contacts northeast to southeast of our position. These contacts have been detected out to a range of approximately two hundred kilometers. Our sonar data is being streamed live for analysis to the US Naval Research Laboratory, the US Naval Undersea Warfare Center, a specialist unit in Area 51 whose name I don't have access to and to the Sonar Technology and Systems branch of the Australian Defense Science and Technology group. I believe all of these groups are pooling their efforts and will be providing their findings to you directly. These signals include sonar ranging and communications, although we've been unable to decipher the meaning of the communications.

"Three days ago, one of this ship's launches was attacked by these entities. They killed one of my sailors and wounded several other crewmen." She glanced at Dr. McInness who was still wearing his sling. "Dr. McInness, one of the American specialists, was also injured. It was during this attack that we took one of these extraterrestrial entities prisoner. That captive is currently being studied by specialists aboard this ship and via satellite links to various research facilities in the United States. My orders are to keep this captive aboard ship for now in the hope that we can use him to establish contact with his people. Arrangements are in place to transfer him to a transport aircraft for relocation to a purpose built facility should those orders change."

She looked up toward the screen, nodding that she was finished.

General Vogel said, "The Australian Attorney-General will now make his report."

On the screen displaying the Joint Operations Command briefing room in Canberra, a round faced man sitting beside the Prime Minister reached for a microphone as he glanced at his notes before speaking. "Thank you, General. Since the media began reporting this situation, we have declared a quarantine and no-fly zone across East Arnhem Land and adjacent maritime approaches. Our cover story is that there is an outbreak of malaria throughout the region and the young man who reported the attack on the village of Rorruwuy was suffering from hallucinations induced by the disease. He's now being held in isolation at the town of Gove where our people are debriefing him.

"Malaria was eradicated from Australia in 1981, so a reappearance of this disease would pose a serious threat to public health and gives us the power to control access to the area. All inhabitants will be evacuated to Darwin where they will be inoculated with doxycycline and placed under medical observation. Most of the small communities have airstrips which will serve as evacuation points and allow us to remove the population within the next forty eight hours. The region is very sparsely populated, but there will be some indigenous citizens who do not live in communities who will remain in the area. It will be impossible for us to find and remove all of those people. So far, there is widespread acceptance of the story and a general compliance with quarantine orders. Thank you," he said, indicating he was finished.

General Vogel said, "Major Bertolini, who has been leading the study of the EBE, will now make her report.

Major."

Teresa adjusted her microphone, clearing her throat nervously. "Thank you, sir." She smiled uncomfortably. "I'm a xenology specialist with the Contact and Recovery Program operating out of Area 51. I've had only a male of the species to study, however, we are able to draw some significant conclusions based on the male's biology. These conclusions are supported by the sonar contact analysis and provide a rationale for the acoustic data."

She looked up, finding every face on three screens on two continents focused intently upon her. "In biology, there is a concept called Selection Theory which describes the evolutionary strategies used by different species to survive. Basically, there are two types of selection strategies, r-selection and K-selection. Human beings use the K-selection strategy, which is characterized by relatively large bodies producing few offspring. The children require a lot of parental care and this type of species lives in fairly stable environments.

"The other strategy, the r-selection type is used by species with smaller bodies that produce very large numbers of offspring. The children of this type of species require little or no parental care after birth. They reach adulthood much faster than K-selection offspring, and can spread very quickly throughout their habitat. Usually, the r-type species has a short life span, but not always. Sometimes r-types can have long life spans, such as turtles."

"Are you saying these creatures are turtles?" the President asked uncertainly.

"No, Madam President," Teresa replied, "what I'm saying is the EBE's survival strategy is similar to a turtle's. The male specimen's reproductive system is compatible with an r-type selection strategy, and considering his high intelligence, I believe his species has a long life span, what you might call a modified r-type selection strategy."

"I see," the President said. "Please continue, Major."

"Currently," Teresa said, "the Earth is in the middle of a long planetary summer giving us a stable environment which has allowed our population to increase as our ability to produce food has increased. That's typical of K-selection type populations, which stabilize at the limit of their available food supply.

"On the other hand, r-selection species have the capacity for exponential growth and often exist in highly *unstable* environments, where populations can be wiped out suddenly, and then once the negative effects are removed, quickly replaced. This suggests that this EBE species evolved on a world that experienced continual environmental catastrophes – that is, mass-extinction events – that killed off the K-selection types like us and allowed an r-selection species the opportunity to evolve intelligence."

"Thank you, Major," General Vogel said, cutting her off. "That's very interesting. I think we should now move on to the tactical considerations."

Beckman leaned forward. "With respect General, these are the tactical considerations, and the most important part is yet to come."

Before the Chairman could comment, the President spoke up. "Please take as long as you need, Major."

"Thank you, Madam President," Teresa said, giving Beckman an appreciative look. "There is another theory, called Stochastic Theory. It complements Selection Theory. What it says is that those species that have high or fluctuating adult mortality should have a capacity for high reproduction, obviously to replace the lost adults. The r-selection, Stochastic Theory combination is effectively the opposite evolutionary strategy to that used by the human race.

"What all this means is that we are dealing with a highly intelligent species that has evolved a survival-reproduction strategy that renders them purpose built to survive mass extinctions. Initially, these extinction events would have had natural causes, but this species very high level of aggression suggests at some point, natural events may have been replaced by high casualty, even genocidal warfare." Her words triggered a stirring among the military leaders, all of whom became intensely interested in her words. "If they had a tendency to wipe themselves out, their reproductive capacity would allow their populations to recover rapidly."

"So they could go do it all again," Beckman added meaningfully.

"If this is true," Teresa continued, "this would make them a highly warlike species – considerably more warlike than human beings – which could account for the extreme aggression they've displayed so far."

"So their selection strategy," the Australian Prime Minister asked, "isn't based on environmental instability, but on war?"

"Possibly both, sir," Teresa said.

"The ambush at Rorruwuy," Beckman said, "was more than simple aggression. It was highly organized, fearlessly executed and considering they were using stone age knives against automatic weapons, showed a complete disregard for casualties."

"That's the psychological aspect to consider," Teresa said. "This kind of evolutionary strategy, where numbers can be wiped out and quickly replaced, would reduce concern for the individual. Survival of those capable of replacing lost populations will be the natural priority for such a species rather than the concern for individual life which humans have."

"So, no matter how many we kill," Beckman said, "they'll keep coming, because they can produce more, a lot more."

"I wondered how they got to four million so fast," the US Secretary of State muttered.

"That's the problem, sir," Teresa said. "The crash survivors are reproducing. Once this new generation of young reach breeding age, they'll enter a period of exponential growth that will force them out of their current location in search of food. That's when they'll start competing with mankind for Earth's food producing resources."

"If we try to stop them," Beckman said, "we'll be like an elephant stamping on an army of intelligent ants. No matter how many we destroy, eventually the ants will win."

"From this location," Captain Turner said, "they have the entire Pacific to expand into and from there, the oceans, rivers and lakes of the world."

"How long have we got?" the President asked.

"That depends on how long it takes for the young to reach maturity," Teresa replied. "There are still significant size differences between the adults and the young, so assuming only the crash survivors are breeding, what we're seeing is the first generation born on Earth."

"So it'll be years before their numbers sky rocket?" someone in the White House situation room asked.

"I wouldn't count on that," Beckman said. "The adults are breeding now and the young only need to be big enough to survive on their own to break out. Once they get into the Pacific, we've lost them. Twenty years from now, there'll be more of them than us. That's when we lose the planet. It's the breakout we have to stop and that can't be far away."

Worried looks spread across the faces on every screen. The speed with which Teresa's briefing had turned from brain numbing science to a menace threatening the survival of the human race had taken them all by surprise.

"We have to destroy them, now," a general in the Pentagon said.

There were murmurs of agreement from the three command centers.

"Are you sure we can't negotiate with them?" a woman in a dark blue business suit from the Australian government group asked.

"They show no sign of wanting to talk," Beckman said. "They're playing for time, learning what they can about us while the first generation ages."

"Madame President, we shouldn't manage this alone," the US Secretary of State said. "We need to bring in the Europeans, the Russians, the Chinese. Everyone will have to be on board. If we don't tell them, and these creatures get out, we'll be blamed for keeping this to ourselves."

The President nodded. "I agree. Brief them all, in secret." She turned back to the camera. "So how do we stop them breaking out?"

"Bomb the hatcheries," Beckman said.

"No!" Dr. McInness snapped. "We can't!"

"Not now, Ian," Beckman whispered harshly, knowing his friend's tendency was always to oppose military action, to turn a blind eye to the real threat while arguing for negotiation, for peaceful contact.

Dr. McInness leaned toward his microphone solemnly. "Bombing the hatcheries would be a terrible mistake!"

"Not from where I'm sitting," an Air Force general in the Pentagon declared malevolently.

"You don't understand," Dr. McInness said, turning to Beckman with a pained look. "We have to kill the breeding age females first." Surprise flashed across Beckman's face. "If we don't," the scientist continued, "they'll sneak away and breed somewhere else, somewhere we won't know about until it's too late. We've got to find the females before we attack."

"How do we do that?" Beckman asked. "There could be hundreds of females scattered across thousands of square miles."

"There isn't," Dr. McInness said. He motioned to Reynolds who changed the live feed to an image filled with the faces of thousands of amphibians floating in the water. "I've been studying the photographs taken by the

P-8 that dropped the sonobuoy onto the hatchery two days ago. Do you notice anything unusual about their faces?"

"Apart from the fact they're all … aliens?" Beckman asked.

Everyone in the three command centers and in the *Naturaliste's* control room studied the image, but no one spoke.

"Look closely," Dr. McInness said, nodding to Reynolds who switched to a zoomed in section of the image with one amphibian face circled in red. "This one's head is twenty percent larger than the rest, its coloring is lighter and the others keep their distance. Its size and status are different." While his audience peered at the circled face, he added, "The other faces have the same proportions as our captured specimen which tells us they're all males. This one is unique out of all the tens of thousands of faces photographed."

"It's a female!" Teresa declared.

"The only female born in this group," Dr. McInness said. "Which means one female is capable of mass producing her entire species. The breeding age females might visit the hatcheries to spawn, but they wouldn't stay there. They'll be somewhere else, hidden where we can't find them. If you bomb the hatcheries, you'll force the females to disperse, then we'll never stop them. You have to destroy the hatcheries and the breeding age females at the same time." He turned to Beckman. "We'll only get one chance at this, Bob."

The image of the female amphibian was replaced by concerned faces watching from the three command centers.

"So where are the females?" General Vogel asked.

"We don't know," Beckman said, "but we can find out." He gave Captain Turner a questioning look. "Right?"

Turner nodded. "This ship is fitted with the latest sonar systems. No one's better equipped to find them

155

than we are."

"And we're in position," Beckman added emphatically.

The President nodded. "Very well. You'll have everything you need from our end. While you're searching, we'll accelerate the buildup of forces we need to destroy them."

"There's one more thing," Dr. McInness said. "We don't know how to communicate with them. The male we captured clearly can't form human sounds and we can't form their sounds. We'll never be able to speak each other's languages. In fact, we don't even have a starting point on what their language is."

"Your point, Doctor?" the President asked.

"We have to assume they've been studying us for years, that they can read English," he said simply. "If we display a sign saying we want to talk, they should understand."

"We're beyond talking," Beckman snapped.

"They don't know that," Dr. McInness said. "Telling them we want to talk might stop them dispersing. That'll give us time to find the females."

*And then we'll exterminate them*, Beckman thought.

# CHAPTER SIX: ENCOUNTERS

Air replicating the Intruder homeworld's atmosphere filled the capsule shaped interrogation cell as it drained of seawater, then the Infiltrator said, "The implantations are complete. It is time I continued my mission."

"Not yet," Beloved said. "I have another task for you."

"There is nothing more I can do to assist you," it said, well aware that the longer it remained in the shallow sea, the greater the likelihood it would be discovered by its enemies and destroyed.

"For us to survive, the humans must be destroyed."

"That is true, but I have no offensive capability."

"You have your engines."

"I do not understand."

"The one you gifted known as Watcher-of-Skies believes your star drive, if activated close to the planet, could destroy every city on this world."

"He is mistaken. A superluminal shell created within the planet's gravitational field would collapse, causing my own destruction."

"Watcher does not want you to form a shell. He wants the opposite effect. Rather than focusing spacetime distortions around yourself, he wants you to diffuse them, simulating a planet sized gravity field close to the Earth. Can you do that?"

"My engines are capable of producing velocities tens of millions of times faster than the speed of light. They have the power to diffuse spacetime on the scale you describe, but what purpose would it serve?"

"The implanted lattice allows you to see my thoughts, does it not?" she asked.

"That is correct."

"Then I will show you what we desire."

She closed her eyes, imagining the Infiltrator in space performing a close flyby of the planet. Rather than creating a highly localized distortion of spacetime around its hull, it produced a subtle compression tens of thousands of kilometers across, simulating a planet passing close to the Earth. The planet sized gravity field enveloped half the world as the Infiltrator skimmed the upper atmosphere. Earth's crust, floating on an ocean of molten magma, shuddered and slid toward the collapsing spacetime, shifting the planet's tectonic plates. The crustal shift slammed the great plates together, triggering mega quakes that rippled around the world and sent oceans rolling across every land mass, collapsing and drowning Earth's cities. It triggered a cycle of global volcanism not seen in a quarter of a billion years, spewing oceans of lava onto the surface and venting immense clouds of gas and ash into the atmosphere, turning the sky dark and plunging the world into a volcanic winter.

When she finished imagining Watcher's cataclysmic scenario, she asked, "Is it possible?"

The Infiltrator did not respond immediately. Instead, it performed millions of complex calculations determining the gravitational forces required. It considered the plasticity of Earth's magma, the mass of its tectonic plates, the countering effects of Earth's own gravity and the energy needed to achieve what she asked for.

Eventually it said, "Such an effect is possible, however, it would take the planet more than a hundred thousand years to recover."

"But we would survive. The humans would not."

"There would be no place where you could shelter from the effects of the crustal shift. If you survived, you would face starvation and cold during the volcanic winter."

"How long will the winter last?"

"Even I cannot predict that. It will certainly cool the planet for many years."

"We will survive," she said defiantly. "We will rely on sonic vision and preserve enough fish and sea plants to start again."

"You do not understand," the Infiltrator said. "This planet has seven supervolcanoes, including one northwest of here. They will all erupt together, destroying continent sized areas and possibly causing a global glacial event. I cannot guarantee any life would survive."

Beloved wondered what a supervolcano was, then the Infiltrator gift revealed the locations of great lava chambers in America, Siberia, Japan, Indonesia and New Zealand.

"Can you limit the impact on us?"

Again the Infiltrator fell silent, this time calculating how to reduce the supervolcanic eruption of Toba in Sumatra. "If I direct the kinetic energy of the crustal shift against the far side of the planet, Toba would be the least affected. The three supervolcanoes in North America would destroy that continent, but even that would not guarantee your survival."

"We will take our chances. What choice do we have?"

"You may be willing to take such a chance, but I am not. Creating such a planetary event would reveal my presence to enemy ships in this system. They would try to destroy me, preventing me from completing my mission."

Beloved always knew it would come to this. She had thought long and hard on how she would force the Infiltrator to obey her, drawing upon the fundamental tenets designed into its artificial self-awareness. "Your primary purpose is to serve the Matriarchy. Is that not correct?"

"That is what I have done."

"Is not the highest service to preserve the flow of life from the Great Mothers?"

"It has always been so."

Beloved knew in Intruder society, no sacrifice was too great to preserve those who could in a single generation regenerate the species. She knew that fundamental principle had stood for millions of years and was ingrained into every Intruder created intelligence.

"With all my sisters bowed in service to me, am I not entitled to proclaim myself Supreme Planetary Matriarch?"

"It is why I contacted you."

"And is it not the right of a planetary mother to invoke the Law of Rebirth, commanding all resources at her disposal to preserve the future?"

The Infiltrator hesitated, not because it could not compute the answer, but because it knew exactly where she was headed and why. To answer would be to surrender its independence, yet to remain silent would violate its most fundamental guiding directives. Reluctant to abandon its mission, the Infiltrator tried to weaken her position.

"Your survival on this world will not affect the preservation of the race. You are not even known to the Great Mothers of Versala."

"I am accepted by all my sisters on *this* world. By ancient law, I am the Matriarchy here. Is that not so?"

"You satisfy the requirements," the Infiltrator conceded, acknowledging traditions that reached back to the dawn of Intruder Civilization.

"As such, by ancient right, I claim you, but *only* for my time of need."

The Infiltrator wanted to refuse, but could not deny she had the power. Even worse, it knew the way she had manipulated it proved she was worthy of Planetary Rulership.

"All that you require is a rotational movement of the planet's crust?" the Infiltrator asked.

"One degree should be sufficient."

"And I am free to determine how best to achieve that, or must I follow Watcher-of-Skies exact instructions?"

"You are free to improve upon his ideas in any way. Why?"

"I will conceal my presence from my enemies until the last possible moment, then reveal myself only long enough to cause the crustal shift. This will give me time to escape. I will know more once I have surveyed the planet's tectonic structure from space."

Certain the Infiltrator was her servant, at least while they faced extinction, she asked, "What of your enemies?"

The Infiltrator sensed the enemy ship's positions by the streams of particles radiating from their energy plants. Fortunately none were Tau Cetin, otherwise Beloved's plan would have been doomed to fail.

"There are currently three. I will move when they are on the other side of the planet," it said, certain the enemy research ships would focus upon the northern hemisphere where the vast majority of human civilization was located.

"Once you have done as I ask, return to me. I may have need of you again."

"As you command, Great Mother."

* * * *

HMAS *Naturaliste* weighed anchor before dawn and steamed northeast on a course parallel to the Wessel

Islands. Once she cleared Cadell Strait, Captain Turner ordered the ship's towed array to be deployed. To ensure the powerful side scanning sonar used to chart the sea floor was not interpreted as a sonic attack, it was set to passive mode, listening without pinging. Using both hull mounted and towed sensors, the hydrographic survey ship began a detailed mapping of acoustic concentrations, although it never approached within thirty kilometers of any of the hatcheries. Above the ship, high flying UAVs, reconnaissance aircraft and a cluster of satellites searched for the females.

After breakfast, Turner and Beckman were on the bridge scanning the horizon with binoculars, looking for signs of the scouts they knew were following the ship.

"They could be anywhere within ten thousand square kilometers," Turner said despondently as she lowered her binoculars.

"If the females are in charge," Beckman said, "and they're all together, then all roads lead to Rome."

"Rome?" Turner said, puzzled by the analogy.

"It's where the emperor lives, or in this case, the empress. All roads lead there because she gives the orders. The roads we're looking for are followed by sonar contacts."

She nodded slowly. "I see. We're looking for her palace."

"I just hope Ian's right and they can read," he said, glancing back to the elevated helipad above the stern deck where large white sheets were hung with the word PEACE painted on them. "If Ian's wrong and they can't read, they might think our steaming into their backyard means the sign says 'surrender or die alien scum'."

"We'll know soon enough," Turner said. "If it goes quiet out there, they've cut and run." She shifted position in her high captain's chair. "What I don't understand is if they abandoned ship when they were young, got out with nothing, why would their parents dump their children in a hostile world and leave?"

"Maybe they thought their young had a better chance in the ocean than with whoever grabbed their ship," Beckman said.

"So whoever took their ship is even more dangerous, more aggressive than these aliens?" she asked. "That's a scary thought."

"Scary thoughts come with the job."

"Hell of a job. Been hunting aliens long?"

"Fifteen years. And I don't hunt aliens, just artifacts for Ian and his lab rats."

"Must be tough, keeping this a secret from your family. It's hard enough doing normal duty."

Beckman gave her a melancholy look. "I was married, once. It lasted six years. She thought I was having an affair. I couldn't tell her what I was doing, so … she took both the kids."

Turner looked surprised. "Even though she knew your work was classified and you couldn't discuss it?"

"She thought I had a desk job. I never once said I couldn't tell her what I did. That only arouses curiosity which is not what we want."

"Wow," Turner said slowly. "So you let her think you were cheating?"

"It's better this way."

"I'm glad it's not that tough in the hydrographic service."

Lt. Commander Reynolds came onto the bridge from the sonar compartment. "They're ranging us from all sides," he said, "from three hundred meters out."

"Keep the lower watertight doors secured," Turner said, "and the guards inside in case our friends out there decide to do more than shadow us."

"Should we mount the machine guns?" Reynolds asked.

Turner gave Beckman an enquiring look. "Colonel?"

"Not where they can see them," he said. "They'll interpret a show of weapons as hostile."

"Make sure no one sets foot outside without my

permission," she said. "I don't want to lose any more sailors to those things."

"No risk of that, Skipper," Reynolds said. "I've never seen a crew more eager not to get fresh air."

* * * *

In the hours following its meeting with Beloved, the Infiltrator waited at the bottom of the Arafura Sea, watching three enemy ships moving about the planet, studying its inhabitants. One of the ships completed its analysis and left the Solar System, another moved to study a North American nuclear weapons site while the third measured radioactivity seeping into the biosphere from a damaged fission reactor in northern Japan. Satisfied both enemy ships were observing the northern hemisphere, the Infiltrator made its move. It knew if one of the great galactic powers had an undetected ship nearby, it would be discovered and destroyed as soon as it revealed itself, but that was an unavoidable risk.

With all of its masking technologies active, the Infiltrator rose out of the sea on minimum power and climbed into the sky. Once outside the atmosphere, it began mapping Earth's broken eggshell structure, charting the position of the planet's tectonic plates and measuring their mass and density. It took thermal scans of the magma ocean beneath the crust and of the massive volcanic systems that the crustal shift would blast into life. The Infiltrator paid particular attention to the massive Australian plate on which Beloved and her siblings sheltered. It found it to be one of the most tectonically stable regions on the planet, giving it reason to believe they might survive.

The Infiltrator simulated many possible courses, estimating the damage each would cause the planet's tectonic structure. It discovered the optimum trajectory for directing seismic energy away from the Mothersea ran from southeast Africa to the western Sahara. That path would direct the kinetic energy from the African plate into the North American plate, causing both crustal sections to buckle, creating massive new fault lines in each. The submerged Southwest Indian Ridge between Africa and Antarctica would open, exposing the Indian Ocean to molten magma that would boil the sea, saturating southern latitudes in steam clouds that would cool long before they reached the Mothersea.

Simultaneously, devastating lateral shock waves would radiate from Africa into the Eurasian and South American plates, subjecting them to tectonic quakes thousands of times greater than anything Earth had seen in three billion years. Even so, both Eurasia and South America would remain recognizable as land masses, unlike North America and West Africa.

When the shock waves reached the west coast of North America, the Infiltrator calculated a series of super tsunamis would roll across the Pacific onto East Asia. Fortunately, the Australian east coast and the mountainous island of New Guinea would deflect the worst of it away from the Mothersea. Even so, the hatcheries would be swept by immense floods and rocked by massive earthquakes that would scatter its amphibian inhabitants across the southern hemisphere. Many would not survive, but at least the sturdy Australian plate would not shatter.

The greatest weakness to Watcher's plan was the need for the Infiltrator to reveal itself for almost two minutes while its superluminal drive was active. The flyby velocity had to be relatively slow, to give the spacetime distortion it would create time to drag the African plate one degree. There was nothing it could do to hide the gravity waves that would ripple through the Solar System, but it could disguise its approach. With no warning of what was to come, enemy ships would have insufficient time to detect and understand what was happening, denying them the opportunity to disrupt the crustal shift maneuver.

It was the need for camouflage that drove the Infiltrator to slip away from Earth and return to the comet it had used to enter the inner system. The comet was now only a few million kilometers away on a trajectory that would pass close to Earth, but not cross its orbit. It was a short hop for the Infiltrator, even at its most stealthy velocity, and with Earth's mass shielding it from the research ships, the transit went unnoticed by its enemies.

When it reached the surface of the drifting mountain of rock and ice, the Infiltrator glided into a dark crevasse and buried itself once again deep inside the comet's frozen heart. From its hiding place, it completed its study of Earth's structure, measured the planet's magnetic field, gravity and orbital velocity, estimated the characteristics of its spinning iron core and perfected its course calculations.

When its computations were complete, the Intruder probe distorted nearby spacetime, changing the comet's trajectory to an Earth crossing orbit. It decelerated the comet to the required velocity, then once on course to skim Earth's upper atmosphere, it confirmed the enemy ships had not detected its preparations.

With nothing more to do, the Infiltrator powered down, making itself invisible to even the most sensitive enemy sensors. The approach would be slow, but the comet was now perfectly aligned to intersect Earth's orbit at exactly the right angle and velocity. A few hours from closest approach, the Infiltrator would power up enough to generate a small acceleration field just strong enough to prevent Earth's gravity from tearing the comet apart. The field would be so weak, it would be undetectable by any ship inside Earth's gravity, while enemy observers would assume the comet had not calved because its internal structure was more rock than ice.

In one hundred and six hours, the Infiltrator would begin pulsing its star drive, causing catastrophic damage to the planet's surface. Many species would not survive, but those that did would eventually serve Earth's new apex predator, a species originating from beyond the Milky Way. There was nothing the humans could do to stop it even if they knew the end was coming – which they did not. The Intruder probe added a detailed explanation to the report it would send to the Great Mothers of Versala. It was certain they would be intrigued to discover their lost sisters had established a precious foothold close to their greatest enemy's homeworld, a foothold that might one day serve another purpose.

In spite of its initial reluctance, the Infiltrator decided Beloved's demand had not been so far removed from its primary mission after all.

* * * *

Two hundred kilometers north of Cape Wessel, far out in the Arafura Sea, a US Navy P-8 came in low at minimum air speed. At the first of a series of carefully calculated coordinates, a cylindrical device ejected from the fuselage and floated to the sea on a parachute. When it splashed into the water, the parachute disconnected and the cylinder sank to the sandy bottom, where its protective casing split apart. A dull white sensor deployed beside a spherical float that dragged a thin wire to the surface. When the very low frequency antenna had fully extended, it began transmitting to the Harold E. Holt submarine communications station on Australia's northwest coast.

The underwater sensor had been designed to detect Russian submarines threatening sea communications between North America and Europe. Now it listened for amphibian sonar signals, providing an early warning of any attempt they might make to break out of the hatcheries to the south.

Several minutes after the sound surveillance system listening post landed, two amphibian scouts swam warily toward it. They'd been warned not to use their sonar as it would betray their position to the land-dwellers, so they located it by eyesight alone. Neither scout had been implanted by the Infiltrator, so they didn't understand the science being used against them, but they had the discipline to obey orders. They studied the underwater sensor carefully so they could accurately describe its appearance, then one sentry headed south to report while the other remained to watch as twenty kilometers away the P-8 dropped another sensor.

By dusk, a single line of underwater listening posts had been deployed from one end of the Arafura Sea to the other, completely enclosing the Intruder colony. Within a day, the line of sensors had expanded to a field one hundred kilometers deep, able to detect any sonar signal emitted by the amphibians.

Long before that, every scout knew what the humans were doing and why.

* * * *

The *Naturaliste* continued on a north easterly heading at eight knots all through the day assembling an acoustic map of amphibian hot spots and the underwater movements of solitary sonar contacts. It kept a respectful distance from the hatcheries while teams of amphibians shadowed the ship in relays. By nightfall, estimates of the numbers in what Beckman called the infestation zone had been revised upwards four times. Shortly before the last dog watch finished at eight PM, the senior officers were summoned to the communications room by Lt. Commander Reynolds.

"What is it?" Turner asked as she arrived.

"NASA," Reynolds said incredulously.

Teresa, Beckman and Dr. McInness exchanged puzzled looks, then a slender man in his late fifties, balding with a pale complexion, appeared in the center of a small screen. He was close to the camera, speaking to them through his desktop computer.

"Hello?" he said. "Is there a Dr. Ian McInness there?"

"Yes, I'm here," the scientist replied.

"My name's Hamilton Pearce. I've been told to make a report to you."

"To me?"

"And I'm not supposed to ask where you are or what you're doing."

"Told by who?"

"The head of NASA … and the Pentagon."

Dr. McInness looked intrigued but didn't relieve Pearce's obvious curiosity. "What do you have to report?"

"Nine hours ago, a comet that was going to miss Earth by several million kilometers suddenly turned toward us."

Worried looks appeared on the faces of the Area 51 team while Reynolds and Turner looked confused.

"How can a comet change course?" Beckman asked without introducing himself.

"That's the thing," Pearce said. "We don't know. We've been routinely tracking it for over a year, during which time it changed velocity and direction several times for no reason. It decelerated as it approached the inner planets, which should be impossible because the sun's gravity should have been accelerating it. So we've had Hubble keeping an eye on it, hoping to see what's going on. We don't normally get comets in this close, so the astronomers are having a field day. Anyway, Hubble picked up something strange, something we can't explain." He started clicking with his mouse, searching for a data file on his computer. "Here it is," he said, then his face was replaced by an image of the icy surface of the comet showing a glacial crevasse. "This is a time series of Hubble images. Keep your eyes to the left of that fissure."

The first image was of a dirty gray mass of ice and rock, then as additional images flashed onto the screen, a long shadow appeared. With each successive image, it moved closer to the frozen ravine, then disappeared into it.

"What is that?" Beckman asked.

"I was hoping you could tell me. I'm told this is your field. All I know is that's a shadow on the comet's surface, but there's nothing casting the shadow. We have plenty of wide and medium angle shots from Hubble and from ground based observatories to prove it. We ran the pictures through the best image processing software on the planet, confirming there's a solid object blocking sunlight twenty meters from the comet's surface. Except ... there isn't."

"How you can see a shadow, but not what's casting it?" Turner asked.

"Whatever's casting that shadow is completely non-reflective. More than that, it must be retransmitting background imagery at exactly the same luminosity as the comet's surface. That's our theory anyway. It allows it to disappear into the background while it soaks up sunlight like a sponge. Radar too. The only reason we saw it at all was because it was close to the comet's surface."

"Is it radiating heat?" Dr. McInness asked.

"If it is," Pearce said, "it's perfectly matched to the infra-red readings coming off the comet."

"Run the images again," Dr. McInness said, then they watched in silence as the shadow slid across the comet's dull gray surface and vanished into the crevasse. "I don't recognize the silhouette," he whispered.

"Me neither," Beckman replied, then said to Pearce, "I'm sorry, we can't help you."

"That's too bad. I needed a break on this one."

"You say it's heading right for us?" Dr. McInness asked.

"Yeah, that's why it's in my lap."

"Who in NASA do you work for?" Beckman asked.

"I'm head of PDCO."

"What's that?" Beckman asked, never having heard the acronym before.

"The Planetary Defense Coordination Office," Pearce replied. "That comet's headed for Earth and it's my job to stop it. What's got me worried is that shadow. Right after it went into the crevasse, the comet changed course again. So either I'm crazy or there's an invisible UFO out there about to smash a comet into the Earth."

"Are you sure it's going to hit?" Beckman asked, certain the NASA scientist was not deranged.

"I'm not sure of anything. It's still one point eight million kilometers out, so there's a small chance it'll miss, but that's way too close to bet the farm on. And if there's something out there steering that comet at us, then it's going to be a bull's-eye no matter what we do. Right?"

"How big is the comet?" Teresa asked.

"It's no dinosaur killer," Pearce said, "but a direct hit will devastate a good fraction of the Earth's surface."

"How big a fraction?" Beckman asked.

"Maybe an area the size of Alaska. Of course, it it hits the ocean ..." He winced, describing with a look the damage a kilometer high super tsunami could cause.

"At least it's not a mass extinction event," Teresa said.

"Try telling that to the guy whose house it lands on," Pearce said.

"Do you know where it's going to hit?" Dr. McInness asked.

"Early projections indicate somewhere between the northern United States and the Arctic Circle, possibly eastern Siberia, but if something's controlling it ..." Pearce shrugged. "It could come down anywhere."

"Can you stop it?" Beckman asked.

"Hell, I don't even know if I can hit it! The bigger problem is anyone with the technology to get here and change a comet's course can easily destroy anything we send against it."

Beckman motioned for Reynolds to cut the sound, then turned to Dr. McInness. "If they have a ship, why didn't they leave?"

"They'd need a very big ship to evacuate five million passengers," he replied. "Whatever was casting that shadow was small enough to fly into a crevasse."

"Or they liked what they saw and decided to stay," Reynolds said pessimistically.

"So why level a medium sized country?" Beckman wondered.

"To demonstrate they can," Teresa suggested. "Surrender now or they'll tow a hundred more comets in from the Oort Cloud."

"There are trillions of trans-Neptunian objects out there," Dr. McInness said soberly. "That's more than enough ammunition to level every country on Earth."

Beckman looked doubtful. "It's too big for a demonstration of force. All they need to do is drop a rock on Washington to get our attention, not destroy Alaska. It's too small for a mass extinction, too big for an ultimatum. What's left?" His question was greeted by silence and uncertainty, then he motioned for Reynolds to restore sound. "How long have we got?"

"Four days," Pearce said.

"When will you know if you can stop it?" Beckman asked.

"We've got a lot of hardware crunching numbers right now figuring out an intercept course. We've scrubbed the latest mission to the space station so we've got a launch vehicle ready to go and the military are pulling the largest nuke they can find that'll fit into the HAIV."

"HAIV?" Beckman whispered to Dr. McInness.

"Hypervelocity asteroid interception vehicle," he whispered back. "It's a prototype."

"With only four days to impact, there's no time for a soft-push deflection," Hamilton Pearce continued. "All we can do now is use a nuclear detonation to nudge it off course."

"Suppose you shatter it?" Dr. McInness asked. "That would make it much worse."

Pearce nodded. "If you've got a better idea, I'm listening … None of us want to nuke it. We know that's the worst possible option. It's also the only option we have left in the time available."

"How big a nuke are you using?" Beckman asked.

Hamilton Pearce checked his handwritten notes beside the computer. "They're giving us something called a W88. It's almost half a megaton."

"Will that do it?"

"I hope so. The bigger question is will that ship up there destroy our capsule before we get anywhere near the comet?"

*It probably will*, Beckman thought as he exchanged doubtful looks with Dr. McInness. Hiding his pessimism, he said, "Just do the best you can and keep us posted."

Worry lines creased Pearce's face. "I used to tell people the reason dinosaurs didn't survive was because they didn't have a space program. I guess sometimes even having a space program isn't enough."

"No, it isn't," Beckman agreed.

\* \* \* \*

Tom Gardner's single engine Cessna took off from Darwin airport just as the sky began to lighten. He'd lodged a flight plan for a typical tourist scenic flight to Katherine in the south, but rather than climb to cruising altitude, he stayed low, turning east once he was out of sight of the city. Twice before, he'd tried flying toward the East Arnhem Quarantine Zone and each time an air force fighter jet had forced him to turn back. This time, staying below the radar, there was no interception. After nearly two hours of skimming tree tops, the tiny village of Rorruwuy appeared ahead, nestled amidst the forest within sight of Arnhem Bay's pristine blue water.

Pete Markham, a network news reporter in the copilot's seat motioned to Nick Pappas, the cameraman sitting behind him, to start recording. "Get some aerial shots," he yelled over the drone of the engine.

Pappas aimed his camera through the window at the cluster of deserted buildings below as Gardner put the Cessna into a slow turn, circling Rorruwuy. There was no sign of life, no medical team inoculating villagers, only dark smears on the ground which none of them recognized as blood stains.

Halfway through the first orbit of the village, Markham's brow furrowed as he spotted the charred wreck of an army helicopter lying near the dirt airstrip. "No one said anything about a chopper crash."

"Not here," Gardner agreed, "but there was a training accident two days ago off the east coast."

"Two choppers down in the same week?" Markham said suspiciously. "I don't think so!"

Pappas focused on the wrecked MRH-90, zooming in for dramatic effect. The bodies of the pilots were gone, as were the dead soldiers in the clearing between the airstrip and the forest. The soldiers had been stripped of their equipment and their bodies disposed of at sea, while the remains of the chopper had been thoroughly studied by several of Watcher's gifted.

"You sure you want to do this?" Gardner asked, wary of being infected with malaria. "There'll be a ton of mosquitoes down there."

"Any mozzie that can get past all the insect repellant I'm wearing deserves what he can get," Markham said lightly. "Besides, I've swallowed enough anti-malaria pills to inoculate half of Arnhem Land."

"OK, it's your funeral," Gardner said, then dropped the small plane toward the airstrip.

Markham turned to his producer, Danny Wang, who would establish the satellite link. "When the network sees that chopper, they'll take us live. Send the aerial stuff first, then Nick and I will do a walk and talk around the wreck." Turning to Pappas, he said, "Look for any markings that'll identify if it's the same chopper that went down near Townsville."

Pappas ejected the data cassette from the camera and handed it to Wang to transmit to the studio once the satellite link was up, then the plane touched down. When the Cessna rolled to a stop at the end of the runway, Markham jumped out to look around while his team unloaded their gear. Wang quickly set up a portable satellite dish and beamed the first images to the control center in Sydney.

Once the studio saw the wrecked chopper footage, Wang said, "They're getting research to check the other chopper's markings. We'll know in a few minutes if it's the same one. If it is, John in the studio will announce it, then they'll put it in the ticker text." He put his hand to his earpiece and listened a moment, then nodded to Markham and Pappas. "We'll be breaking into normal programming in one minute. Standby."

Tom Gardner lit up a cigarette as he stayed by the plane while Markham sprayed another layer of insect repellant over his face and arms. When he finished, Pappas and Wang took turns spraying themselves, being careful not get repellant on their equipment. Markham quickly scribbled notes on a small pad, picked up his microphone and stood in front of the cameraman with the village distantly visible through the trees behind him.

"How's this?" he asked.

The cameraman checked the sun's angle, assessing the light. "Keep to the right as you walk toward the chopper. Point to anything you want me to zoom in on."

"We're live in three, two, one," Danny Wang called, then pointed at Markham indicating his face was now on TV screens across the country.

"This is Pete Markham reporting live from Rorruwuy in the Northern Territory where the malaria outbreak was first detected. That's Rorruwuy you can see through those trees over there. It appears to have been evacuated already and the medical team withdrawn." He started walking slowly, being careful to keep his good side toward the camera as it panned after him, bringing the burnt out MRH-90 into shot in the distance. "What we found when we landed just a few minutes ago was that crashed army helicopter behind me."

A voice sounded from Markham's earpiece. "Pete, this is John Drumond in the studio. I've just been informed that the helicopter you're looking at has the same serial number as the chopper that went down in the Coral Sea two days ago."

Markham signaled Pappas to zoom in on the wreck. "Thanks John. We'll certainly try to find out what a helicopter that supposedly crashed in the sea fifteen hundred kilometers away is doing here," he said as the cameraman focused on the partly shattered cockpit windows.

Pappas spotted a small hole in the Plexiglas, then realizing Markham hadn't seen it, zoomed back out. When he was once again focused on the reporter, he pointed to the chopper wreck and silently mouthed the words, "Bullet! … Hole!"

Markham didn't understand, but guessed Pappas had seen something important, so he continued toward the wreck. "This could be why the air force stopped our two previous attempts to get out here. The question is, why would the government want to hide where this helicopter crashed?" At last, he saw the tiny bullet hole in the windshield surrounded by fracture marks, then he faced the camera, masking his surprise. "There also appears to be a bullet hole in the cockpit window," he said, then Pappas gave him a confirming thumbs up. "When we get back to Darwin, we'll be asking the authorities who was shooting at this helicopter and what that has to do with a malaria–"

The side of Pete Markham's head exploded horizontally in a burst of blood and bone, then he crumpled to the ground. Nick Pappas continued filming, too stunned to switch off the camera as his images were transmitted live to the country. When he realized Pete Markham was dead, he took a step forward with the camera still on his shoulder, then a bullet struck him in the chest. He stumbled back, dropping the camera on its side as he fell to the ground.

Danny Wang jumped to his feet beside the portable satellite link, squinting in the bright sunlight, wondering what had just happened. Pappas was moaning on the ground, still alive as blood welled from his chest. Beside the Cessna, Tom Gardner threw his cigarette on the ground and started running toward the news crew to help, then five diminutive forms armed with assault rifles emerged from the forest and took aim. A bullet whistled past Gardner's ear, then Wang was struck in the head, killed instantly.

The pilot saw Wang collapse, then as he searched for the shooter, he saw the five aliens near the trees aiming at him. There was a muzzle flash from one of the rifles, then a bullet struck his shoulder, spinning him around. He managed to keep his feet, then pressed a hand to his wound and stumbled desperately back toward the aircraft. Bullets whizzed past his ears as he ran, then as he stopped to open the cockpit door, a bullet struck the back of his head, spraying blood and brain tissue over the white painted fuselage.

In Sydney, confused control room staff tried to contact the news team while the side tilted image of the ground and the dead anchorman lying on ochre colored dirt continued to transmit. Beside the camera, they heard Pappas groaning and saw his boot moving.

"Nick, are you alright?" one of the control room operators asked.

"Cut the feed!" the director said. "We're live to millions of people."

"I can hear footsteps," a technician wearing headphones said.

"We've got a dead body on screen!" a frantic director

yelled. "Cut it, now!"

"Wait," the producer ordered, sensing breaking news and phenomenal ratings.

A dull gray amphibian foot passed in front of the camera, silencing everyone in the control room. It crouched, then they heard it sever Nick Pappas' throat with a blade, followed by a gurgling sound as he died.

"Oh my God!" one woman cried in horror.

The amphibian moved out of shot, then the image swam as the camera was picked up and turned toward an angular face with widely spaced, bulging eyes and thin, narrow lips. For a moment, the alien stared into the lens, not realizing what it was, then one of his brothers fitted with the Infiltrator gift switched off the camera.

The control room screen went black, leaving the staff staring at it with open mouths, glazed eyes and stunned expressions. Several women began to sob, but no one spoke. Hardly anyone even breathed.

Fifteen minutes later, one billion people had seen the broadcast.

* * * *

The *Ithrelsa* was a small survey ship shaped like a pair of flattened spheroids merged end to end. When she'd completed her analysis of the radiological contamination seeping into the ocean off northeast Asia, she moved away from the planet, heading for a point beyond Earth's gravity well where she could safely activate her superluminal drive. It was then that she detected a comet heading for Earth and decided to investigate. Moments later, she streaked up alongside the comet, matched velocities and began scanning, hoping to discover the cause of the comet's perilous course.

Deep inside the comet, the Infiltrator knew from the neutrinos flooding space that the enemy ship was relatively primitive. Its energetic sensor emissions were completely absorbed by the Intruder probe's hull while allowing the Infiltrator to identify the enemy as Cor Carolian. All it knew of them was that they were a minor species inhabiting a world a hundred and ten light years from Earth and were undoubtedly within the Tau Cetin sphere of influence.

The Infiltrator knew it could shatter the survey ship's hull by ramming, but feared once the Carolians were considered overdue, their homeworld would dispatch search ships. Even worse, they might seek assistance from other local powers to help locate their missing vessel which could attract Tau Cetin attention. That was something the Infiltrator wished to avoid at any cost, so it remained hidden within its icy sanctuary.

Unable to determine the cause of the comet's anomalous orbit, the Carolian scientists assessed what damage the ragged ball of ice and dust would cause the Earth. They estimated it would skim the outer edge of the planet's atmosphere, most likely sparing its pre-stellar inhabitants from a catastrophic impact providing there were no more inexplicable course changes.

They discovered the planet's inhabitants were aware of the danger and had aimed many of their ground based and orbital telescopes at the comet. Transmissions from Earth indicated they were preparing a chemical rocket with a nuclear payload to deflect the comet's orbit, a mission the Carolians concluded had a moderate chance of success if all went according to plan, although there were many risks. The chemical rocket could explode on launch, its thrusters might misfire while maneuvering, a piece of orbital space junk might strike the spacecraft or the payload might not detonate at the correct position. So many failure points weighed heavily against the humans, as did the inexplicable irregularities in the comet's trajectory. For the Carolians, who had studied the planet's inhabitants for thousands of years, redirecting the comet themselves was a simple matter, but with so many human eyes focused upon it, their intervention would be detected.

Not acting, however, would put a great number of innocent lives at risk.

Interstellar civilizations were generally prohibited by galactic law from revealing their existence to pre-stellar societies, yet allowing a catastrophic planetary impact to occur was also forbidden. The *Ithrelsa's* team of psychobiologists argued that even if the humans detected the Carolian intervention, they would recognize it as a friendly gesture, alleviating the fears of the planet's more xenophobic inhabitants. Nevertheless, the debate on the ethical and legal imperatives of the situation raged on, prolonged by the nature of the Carolians themselves – they were arch moral abstractionists – but eventually the *Ithrelsa's* ruling triumvirate declared unanimously that galactic conventions regarding the preservation of pre-stellar societies left them no discretion: protective intervention was required.

The decision made, the Carolian ship approached the surface of the comet, unaware of how close they were to an Intruder probe. Once in position, the *Ithrelsa* used her superluminal field to create a spacetime depression into which the mountain of frozen rock and ice slid.

Inside the comet, the Intruder probe sensed the changing spatial geometry, instantly aware of what the Carolians were doing. While its own immensely powerful trans-galactic drive could easily have overpowered the feeble Carolian engines, it chose to do nothing, allowing itself to be carried along for the ride. Once the comet was on a new course away from Earth, the *Ithrelsa* moved off, her crew confident they had averted a potential disaster.

Having fulfilled their interstellar treaty obligations, the Carolians logged the incident for entry into the galactic information network upon their return to Hodru, their homeworld. Such an insignificant event would be stored and catalogued along with billions of other equally unimportant reports, but would be looked upon favorably by the Galactic Forum when the Carolian's request for access to the Aquila Rim was considered.

Ten thousand kilometers from the comet, the *Ithrelsa* bubbled, leaving the Solar System for Cor Caroli II. Moments later, the Infiltrator emerged from its hiding place, moved to the frozen mountain's Earth-facing side and once again compressed spacetime, pulling the comet back onto a trajectory that would send it skating above the planet's atmosphere. When the Intruder probe was satisfied the comet was back on course, it returned to its hiding place, hoping the last remaining enemy ship in the Solar System would not be so curious.

The Infiltrator wanted no more delays, no more interruptions. Beloved-of-the-Sea might – by ancient rite – be a Supreme Planetary Matriarch, but her struggle with an obscure pre-stellar civilization that played no part in galactic affairs was utterly insignificant compared to its mission. Whatever happened after the crustal shift, the Infiltrator would never again return to Earth.

Beloved-of-the-Sea would be on her own.

\* \* \* \*

The senior officers assembled before evening meal in the petty officer's mess for the second satellite linked conference in three days. A fourth screen for NASA's planetary defense team had been added to those displaying the leaderships in the White House, the Pentagon and the Australian Joint Operations Command. Generals and Admirals, Ministers and Secretaries argued back and forth about cover stories and containment.

Eventually, the President said, "Ladies and gentleman, the genie is out of the bottle. I think the time has come to tell the truth."

For a moment, there was stunned silence.

Beckman placed a hand over his mike and whispered to Dr. McInness. "Now there's a novel idea,"

"With respect, Madam President," a five star general said, "the psychological shock of such a disclosure could be devastating."

"I think we're past that, General," the Secretary of State declared. "World markets have fallen twenty percent, the press have besieged the White House, religious nuts are in the streets and the UN is in meltdown."

"And it's going to get a lot worse before it gets better," the President said. "If we're ever to be trusted again, now's the time for full disclosure."

"You want to tell them about Area 51?" an Admiral asked. "What about the Contact and Recovery Program and the frozen five?"

"That's going too far," she conceded. "I'm only talking about what's going on down there in northern Australia. I'm going to convene an emergency UN Security Council meeting to discuss the situation."

"Excuse me, Madam President," a nervous Hamilton Pearce said, "does that include what's happening with the comet?"

She looked confused, then someone whispered into her ear. "Oh yes, Mr. Pearce from NASA?"

"Yes ma'am."

"I think we should announce that we're about to launch a mission to deflect the comet away from Earth," the President said. "Don't you? There's a reasonable chance of success isn't there?"

"I'm not sure," Pearce replied hesitantly. "The problem is Hubble took this photo some hours ago." He typed onto his keyboard then the blurred image of a blue-white object shaped like a figure eight appeared on screen. "This object maneuvered in a way that indicated it was under intelligent control, that it's an alien spacecraft. And its hull geometry, its shape, clearly could not have cast the shadow Hubble detected."

"Are you saying there are now *two* alien ships up there?" General Vogel asked, astonished.

"There were," Pearce replied as anxious looks appeared on every face. "Shortly after this craft was detected, the comet changed course away from Earth."

"The aliens diverted the comet away from us?" an admiral at the Pentagon asked hopefully.

"It seemed to," Pearce replied to audible sighs of relief, "however, a few minutes after this ship departed, the comet changed course again, back toward Earth."

"How's that possible?" the director of the Office of Science and Technology Policy asked.

"The second ship, the one we can't see, must have steered the comet back toward us," Pearce explained. "We weren't able to detect any shadows this time – perhaps it moved too fast – but it's the only plausible explanation."

Concerned murmurs rippled through all three command centers.

"So one group of aliens are protecting us," the President said, "and another are attacking us?"

Pearce nodded. "Comets don't zigzag, Madam President, not without help."

Dr. McInness said, "What this shows is that there are different groups with different objectives out there. We don't know what those groups are or what they want, but there's obviously a complex political situation here that we don't understand."

"So who's aiming the comet at us?" General Vogel asked.

"The only group that would benefit from knocking us over," Beckman said. "The same group we're tracking down here."

"But if that thing hits us," the President said, "the aliens will die too. Everyone loses."

"Not if it hits the northern side of the planet," Dr. McInness said. "The southern hemisphere might get off lightly."

"The downside is much worse for us, Madam President," Teresa said. "If a comet impact causes our population to collapse, it'll become a race to recover. That's a race we'll lose because their numbers will increase many times faster than ours."

"Is this comet likely to cause such a collapse?" the President asked.

"It depends where it lands," Dr. McInness replied. "There could be global consequences from an impact winter, increased volcanism or super tsunamis. With the world's food stockpile measured in months, not years, we could be facing global food shortages, even starvation."

"Whatever happens on land," Teresa said, "sea life will regenerate faster than land plants and animals, so we have to assume their food supply will recover long before ours."

A gloomy silence fell over the conference. Worried looks appeared on every face as they considered the consequences for their own families.

"Then NASA better make sure it destroys that comet," the President said gravely.

"We can deflect it," Pearce said, "providing their ship doesn't destroy our delivery vehicle."

"So we have to find the females before that comet hits," the President said. "Do you know where they are, Colonel?"

"We have a good idea," Beckman said. "We're heading there now."

"If you find them," the President asked, "then what?"

"We wipe them out on the ground, so even if the comet hits, they lose."

# CHAPTER SEVEN: HOSTILITIES

Next day the *Naturaliste* anchored at the entrance to Hopeful Bay, a crescent shaped expanse at the southern end of Marchinbar Island, the outer most island in the Wessel group. The isolated bay was enclosed by a sand locked island to the north, a curved white beach flanked by a barren rock plateau to the east and low windswept cliffs to the south. The bay appeared deserted except for the occasional seabird floating in the breeze and the amphibian biosonar that constantly pinged the ship's hull.

"Now what?" Captain Turner asked as she and Beckman stepped onto the open air walkway alongside the bridge superstructure.

Beckman raised his binoculars to study the shoreline, wondering if the enemy leaders were watching them. He knew the acoustic map assembled by the sonar team showed a constant stream of sonar emitting contacts regularly visited the bay, indicating it was the alien nerve center. "If those sonar trails are couriers, they're talking to someone. We have to find out who and where they are."

"So we can commit genocide," she said uncomfortably.

"The alternative is to let five million become fifty billion," he said, "and that's not going to happen."

She glanced astern to where the 'Peace' sign hung from the elevated flight deck. "I hope they negotiate."

"They won't," Beckman said, "not with Everest about to land on our heads. If we hear anything, it'll be after the impact and it'll be an ultimatum."

"You seem very sure of that."

"They have the high ground and nowhere else to go."

"If we destroy them down here," Turner said, "what's to stop their ship bombarding us from space with one comet after another?"

"Not a damn thing. In the end, we may have no choice but to surrender."

She was shocked by his frank admission. In none of the discussions had any leader mentioned such a possibility. "Does your President know that?"

"Everyone knows there's no way we can defend the planet from a starship in orbit. We might be able to resist a ground invasion, but no one who wants to conquer the planet is going to invade. That would be stupid."

"So what are we doing here?" Turner asked. "What's the point?"

"They're not invaders. They're trapped here and whatever that ship up there is, it's not a warship."

"How do you know?"

"It hasn't fired on us. If it had, this would already be over."

"So what is it?"

"I don't know. Maybe something they salvaged from their ship, a life boat or their equivalent of one of your launches. If we're lucky, it doesn't have the fuel or the range to tow in more comets."

"Wouldn't it be nuclear powered and have unlimited range?"

Beckman grimaced. "We'll cross that bridge when we come to it. For now, we keep feeding the public propaganda and hope they don't realize how screwed we are."

Ever since the decision had been made to reveal what was really happening off the coast of Arnhem Land, there had been constant guarantees from major governments that measures were being taken to contain the situation. An emergency meeting of the UN Security Council had unanimously approved unrestricted military action and endorsed the NASA mission to deflect the comet. In an unprecedented show of global unity, the Russians had agreed to fill the gap left by NASA's scrubbed supply mission to the International Space Station; every observatory in the world began feeding NASA around the clock observations of the comet to more accurately calculate its flight path; and the Chinese, Japanese and Europeans had all placed their satellite networks at NASA's disposal.

Once the NASA intercept mission had been revealed to the public, its every detail was analyzed and critiqued by experts on hundreds of television stations around the world. Broadcasts depicting the Space Launch System rocket, the prototype HAIV spacecraft, its nuclear warhead and intercept trajectory constantly filled the airwaves of every country, enthralling billions. Physicists argued how effective a proximity blast would be, how much deflection could be achieved at such short notice and what risk such a blast posed to the structure of the comet itself. Many believed the blast would shatter the comet, turning it into a series of smaller objects that would rain destruction over a much larger area than a single impact would have affected. Everyone acknowledged the risks, but the alternative was to do nothing, which no one supported.

In all of the information released to the public, no mention was made of the alien spacecraft guiding the comet toward Earth, while all questions from civilian astronomers and physicists about peculiarities in the comet's orbit and velocity were attributed to observational or computational errors. These lies were not told to keep the truth from the public, but from the Infiltrator itself, which it was assumed was monitoring Earth's transmissions. There was no way to hide the intercept mission from the Intruder probe, but there was no reason to let it know that its presence had been detected.

"We need boots on the ground over there," Beckman said as he studied the pockets of greenery separated by patches of empty sand and rock. He knew the high flying UAVs orbiting above could only see so much, and so far they'd not detected any amphibians on this part of Marchinbar Island.

"It's ambush country," Turner said, lowering her binoculars. "We don't want another Rorruwuy on our–"

A soft thud sounded as a bullet struck Turner in the throat. Beckman turned to her in surprise as she collapsed onto the deck clutching her neck, blood welling through her fingers. He rushed to her side as a bullet whizzed past his head and struck the bridge window behind him. He glanced at the shore, seeing no attacker, then ducked down behind the metal panel beneath the railing and grabbed her arm. Staying crouched behind cover, he dragged her through the door into the bridge.

"Sniper!" he shouted to the bridge crew. "Everyone down. Get away from the windows."

The officers on watch ducked for cover as a bullet smashed through a window.

"Get a medic up here!" Beckman yelled as he lowered Turner to the deck. Her hand fell away from her throat as her eyes lost focus and the color drained from her face. Beckman pressed his hand over the wound, trying to stem the flow as blood ran down her neck, staining her light camouflage shirt. "Hang on, Turner!"

She coughed weakly, spluttered blood, then her eyes closed.

"Stay with me, Turner!" Beckman said desperately, wondering why the medic was taking so long, then he saw it was already too late.

She was gone.

* * * *

"That shot had to be at least fifteen hundred meters," Beckman said to Reynolds and Dr. McInness as they stood beside the Captain's covered body in sickbay.

"The bullet we dug out of the bulkhead was a NATO standard five point five six millimeter round," Reynolds said, "the same ammo Norforce used at Rorruwuy. They shot her with one of our own guns."

"Norforce were using assault rifles," Beckman said, tormented by guilt, blaming himself for her death. He should have foreseen the danger, anticipated the unexpected from an inhuman enemy. He'd seen warning signs at Rorruwuy of the amphibian's expert marksmanship, but had thought they were safe on the ship, protected by distance and the sea breeze. "The windage should have made that shot impossible."

"Kermit can sit like a statue for hours without twitching a muscle," Dr. McInness said. "It's an ambush predator trait that would make them deadly accurate with any gun. And who knows what kind of mental calculations they're capable of in estimating a bullet's trajectory."

Reynolds nodded grimly, grappling with the realization his captain and friend was dead and he was now in command. "We have to cover the windows."

"God help us if they ever get hold of sniper rifles," Beckman said.

"It's interesting they chose to shoot the Captain," Dr. McInness said, "instead of you."

"Interesting!" Reynolds exploded. "She's dead!"

Dr. McInness recoiled. "I'm sorry. I … I didn't mean to be unsympathetic."

"I know, Ian," Beckman said wearily. "Why is it interesting?"

189

"They killed the person they thought was the highest value target, not because she was captain of the ship, but because she was a female. In their minds, females are the priority targets. It's instinctive."

"Remind me to tell Teresa not to show herself on deck," Beckman said.

"And every female member of the crew," Reynolds added.

"It means we're on the right track," Dr. McInness continued. "In their minds, the way to defeat an enemy is to kill their females."

"Right!" Reynolds said with controlled anger. "So where are they?"

"They're here," Beckman said. "Having a sniper on overwatch proves it. We've just got to get eyes down there to find them."

"The UUV's ready to go," Reynolds said. "Too bad it's not armed."

"It doesn't need to be," Beckman said. "All we need is to locate the target."

* * * *

Chief Petty Officer Barnes pulled open the steel door to the main deck and stepped aside, then eight soldiers in body armor ran out with assault rifles held at eye height. The white sheets inscribed with the word 'Peace' hanging from either side of the elevated flight deck obscured them from the shore as they took cover behind the railings. The helipad extending three quarters of the way from the superstructure left the aft end of the main deck exposed, although the ship has swung on its anchor, angling the stern away from the shore, reducing the danger.

"Clear!" the squad leader yelled, then Barnes led five sailors onto the deck.

Two sailors ran aft and hung a white awning from the flight deck down to the stern rail, further obscuring the main deck. A bullet whizzed past one of the sailors, then another struck the awning as it was secured in place. Other sailors ran to the starboard side derrick, crouched behind the railing and attached a winch hook to a torpedo like device as carefully aimed bullets ricocheted off the hull.

With the unmanned underwater vehicle ready to deploy, Barnes raced up narrow metal stairs to a rectangular control station halfway between the main deck and helipad. Bullets cut the air around him as he dived behind the hoist's rectangular control unit, then reached up to the console and fed power to the winch. The bright yellow submersible lifted off the deck and swung out over the sea, although no bullets struck it. Forward of its single propeller were three tail fins in triangular formation and a pair of dorsals containing global positioning and communications antennas. Ahead of these was the lift bail used by the hoist's hook, then slender strips housing side scanning sonar emitters ran along the UUV's hull to a transparent nose bubble enclosing cameras and lights.

"UUV ready to deploy," Barnes reported via two-way to the bridge.

Reynolds radioed permission, then the hoist's engine hummed as Barnes lowered the yellow underwater robot into the sea. He remotely released the hook, then radioed, "Submersible away."

The UUV's twin bladed propeller spun to life, rapidly driving it away from the ship as it submerged. It was guided by a sailor in the operations room using a ruggedized laptop computer which projected the camera feed onto a large screen watched by Beckman and Dr. McInness. The submersible went into a shallow dive as Reynolds arrived from the bridge, then it leveled off above the sandy bottom and began a GPS guided grid search of the sea floor.

"I'm picking up broadband sonar signals," the operator said as he listened through his headphones. The submersible's sound transmitter was off to avoid having its acoustic emissions interpreted as an attack while its receiver was used by the *Naturaliste* to triangulate the location of nearby acoustic sources. For the next forty minutes, the UUV motored back and forth across the bay, sometimes glimpsing dark shapes in the distance giving the craft a wide berth. When it was halfway through its search pattern, a small amphibian hand appeared on the transparent bubble, experimentally pressing against it.

"They're after the UUV," Beckman said.

"Do they know what it is?" Reynolds asked.

"They know it's searching for them," Dr. McInness said.

The video feed suddenly lurched down as several amphibians forced the submersible's nose toward the bottom.

"Can you break free?" Beckman asked.

The operator fed full power to the prop, then the amphibian hands fell away as the UUV surged forward and nosed up, skimming the sea floor. After a moment, the little yellow submersible lifted away from the bottom and leveled off as more gray shadows came swarming after it.

"There's too many of them," Reynolds said.

"Turn on the transmitter," Beckman ordered as more small hands appeared again, reaching for the UUV's transparent nose. "Full power."

"They'll think it's an attack," Dr. McInness warned.

"It is an attack."

Reynolds motioned for the operator to proceed. "Do it."

The sailor switched on the side scanning sonar's transmitter, blasting the surrounding sea with powerful sonic pulses. The amphibian hands immediately vanished, then the UUV regained level trim as it caught glimpses of dark shapes swimming away at speed.

"We've got your number," Beckman said with some

satisfaction.

The intercom sounded. "Bridge, Captain. There are at least twenty hostiles on the surface."

Reynolds scooped up the intercom. "What are they doing?"

"Swimming away from us, sir, heading for the beach."

"Roger that. Keep an eye on them," he said, watching as the UUV continued its search unmolested. No longer were there any shadowing forms watching from a distance or further attempts to crash the submersible into the sea floor.

"How far to the focal point?" Beckman asked, referring to the acoustic hot spot all sonar trails led too.

"We're coming up on it now, sir, two hundred meters," the operator replied.

They watched gently ridged sand pass beneath the submersible as a pockmarked rock face loomed ahead, rising sharply out of the water. The UUV turned to avoid a collision, glimpsing a large dark opening partly obscured by boulders at the foot of the cliff.

"Go back," Beckman said.

The operator circled the submersible away from the cliff then brought it slowly around to the cave mouth where he checked the vehicle's GPS coordinates against the acoustic map. "That's it."

"Can you get in there?" Reynolds asked.

"Aye sir, but I may not get out again."

"We've only got one UUV," Reynolds said to Beckman. "If we lose her in there, we're done."

"It's worth the risk."

"OK." Reynolds nodded to the seaman. "Take her in."

The UUV glided toward the partly blocked cave mouth, nosed up to clear a boulder, then slid in under low hanging rocks, scraping its hull before descending to clear water. The operator switched on the submersible's floodlights as it glided into a dark cave barely high enough for a man to stand upright in. The light illuminated a rough passageway that bent to the left before opening into a broad cavern.

"Take her up," Reynolds ordered.

"Aye sir," the operator said, then the UUV's nose lifted, revealing light flickering on the surface above.

Dark shapes blurred by gentle ripples became visible as the UUV climbed out of the darkness. When the submersible's nose bobbed out of the water, its floodlights revealed a cave lit by small, wall mounted burning torches. A circle of amphibians sat and stood on a ledge transfixed by the yellow torpedo that had breached their inner sanctum.

Dr. McInness peered intently at the screen, then exclaimed excitedly, "Two of them are female!"

An amphibian carrying an Australian Army assault rifle stepped forward, aimed at the submersible and fired once into the UUV's nose. The screen in the *Naturaliste's* communications room flickered and blinked out.

"Welcome to Kermit Town," Beckman said.

\* \* \* \*

On the other side of the world, Hamilton Pearce stood beside Flight Director Wade Franklin in NASA's Mission Control Center in Houston, apprehensively watching a wall of enormous screens showing the SLS rocket on the launch pad in Florida. Alongside it were other screens showing a green and blue map of Earth detailing the mission's intended flight path and the statuses of the spacecraft's most critical systems.

The buzz of muted voices filled the room as they listened to flight controllers in the Launch Control Center in Florida take turns calling out 'go' for their respective systems. With each tick of the countdown clock, the tension became heavier, then an emotionless voice announced to the world, "Go for launch."

Watched live around the world by billions of people, the monotone countdown reached zero, then the giant RS-25 engines and its companion boosters ignited, lifting the enormous rocket off the pad. For a few seconds, everyone held their breath as the most important mission ever launched by mankind began to climb into the sky.

The launch narrator announced, "Liftoff of the Intercept Mission to deflect the comet Pinaka away from the Earth ... and it has cleared the tower."

Flight Director Franklin shook his head in disgust. "Whoever named that comet Pinaka should be shot," he growled as control passed from Florida to Houston.

"I thought of it," Pearce said. "Why? What's wrong with it?"

Franklin was a stocky, balding engineer with over thirty years experience in manned spaceflight. "You know what Pinaka means?"

"Yeah, it's the Hindu God Shiva's bow. I thought it was appropriate."

"I looked it up last night. Any arrow fired from Pinaka could not be intercepted."

Pearce's eyes widened. "Oh ... I didn't realize. I hope it's not an omen."

Franklin scowled. "I don't believe in omens. I'm an engineer. I believe in science, technology and the power of nuclear weapons."

Together they watched the giant rocket carry a half megaton nuclear warhead into the sky. Several minutes later, it reached orbit, made a perfect insertion and executed a precise delta-v burn that sent it out toward Shiva's invincible weapon.

One point eight million kilometers away, the Infiltrator watched it too, with its own sensors and via television transmissions from over a hundred and fifty countries. Many transmissions showed the flight path in detail, the planned detonation point and the amount of energy the warhead would release. According to the

Intruder probe's own estimates, the human calculations were three percent from optimal, not perfect, but close enough that they would achieve their goal if their mission was allowed to proceed uninterrupted. The flight path would bring the nuclear armed capsule to within a quarter of a kilometer of the comet, close enough for its crude fusion weapon to push Pinaka onto a trajectory that would miss Earth's outer atmosphere by a mere eight thousand kilometers.

The Infiltrator considered moving from its hiding place and knocking the primitive chemical rocket off course, but the one remaining enemy ship in the system had moved to Florida to observe the launch. It tracked the human spacecraft, verifying it was on the correct course for a successful mission. The Infiltrator waited, wondering if the enemy ship would conduct its own interception, but as the hours slipped by, it made no attempt to leave the planet's atmosphere. The Intruder probe guessed the enemy vessel had calculated the human's chances and decided they would be able to save themselves, thus negating its obligation to intervene.

The Infiltrator realized while the human spacecraft was heading toward the comet, the enemy ship would stay away. Its commander had decided to allow the humans the triumph of saving themselves from planetary disaster while keeping his ship safely outside the nuclear blast zone. That discovery convinced the Intruder probe to let the human ship approach, to use it as cover as the comet raced toward Earth. It decided to wait until the last possible moment before destroying the little human capsule, giving the enemy research ship no opportunity to react. By the time the enemy realized the humans had failed, the comet would be skimming Earth's outer atmosphere and the Infiltrator's engines would be tearing at the planet's tectonic plates. Moments after Earth's crust had moved one degree, it would abandon its cometary hiding place and leave the system for Tau Ceti, twelve light years away.

By then it would be too late to stop the destruction of human civilization or discover where in the galaxy the Infiltrator had gone.

* * * *

Late that afternoon, six US Marine Corps Ospreys came in low over the sea, followed by six Viper attack helicopters. The force had been dispatched from the USS *Makin Island*, an amphibious assault ship now on station in the Arafura Sea two hundred kilometers to the north. The tiltrotor aircraft passed over the *Naturaliste*, then spread into a line above Marchinbar Island. Their engines rotated to the vertical, transforming them from horizontal flight to hovering, then they descended toward the barren plateau while the attack helicopters circled protectively. Beneath the tiltrotor transports, sun bleached rock crevices filled with scrawny green trees provided natural cover to any defenders hiding there.

On board the aircraft were seismic teams from Geoscience Australia and Japan's Earthquake Research Institute, along with US Marines tasked with their protection. The seismic teams had been hurriedly flown with their equipment to the US carrier from their respective headquarters in Tokyo and Canberra with little explanation as to why they were needed. A third team from the US Geological Survey was on its way from Virginia, but with so little time remaining before the Pinaka impact, it had been decided not to wait for them.

Each Osprey carried one geoscience team with listening devices to be attached to the island's rocky backbone. Once in place, small explosives would be detonated to send sound waves through the island that would enable the scientists to map the structure of the island's cave system. The military would then use the seismic maps to accurately target the caves with bunker busting bombs, destroying the alien females hiding there.

On the *Naturaliste's* bridge, Beckman and Reynolds watched through gaps in the window coverings as radio chatter from the Ospreys played through the loud speaker system.

"There's plenty of cover up there," Reynolds said warily as he focused his binoculars on the rocky plateau.

"We don't have a choice," Beckman said. "We've got to know where to hit them."

When the Ospreys were close enough to the ground to kick dust and sand into the air, one of the pilots announced, "I'm taking small arms fire from the ground."

Anxious reports from other pilots quickly sounded from the bridge speakers. "My starboard engine's hit … We're under attack … My copilot's down!"

Smoke began billowing from one Osprey's engine, then the Marine Commander's voice came in over the chatter. "Voodoo Zero One to Rhino, break off, break off. Voodoo flight, engage."

The Ospreys immediately lifted away from the landing zone. Five circled out to sea while the sixth retired north with one engine belching smoke, then the attack helicopters came in over the island.

One Viper pilot declared, "Alpha Mike Foxtrot."

Reynolds gave Beckman a curious look, not understanding the pilot's meaning.

"Adios Mother– you can guess the rest," Beckman explained.

Reynolds nodded, then the attack helicopters blasted the landing zone with cannon fire and rockets, focusing on the scrub covered crevices where the hostile fire had come from.

"I can't see a damn thing down there," one of the Viper pilots declared.

After several minutes of remorseless strafing, with fires burning across the island and thick smoke rising from the ground, the Vipers returned to circling and the five remaining Ospreys came in for a second attempt.

When they tried to land, they again came under frighteningly accurate gunfire from the ground focusing on their engines and cockpits. Without warning, the second transport in line nosed down, flew into the ground and exploded into a fierce fireball.

"LZ is too hot," the Marine Commander declared. "Break off and return to Makin."

The Ospreys scattered in different directions, racing out over the sea to escape the gunfire, rotating their engines for horizontal flight, while the attack helicopters emptied their ammunition into the island before following the Ospreys back to the carrier.

"That could have gone better," Reynolds said, unable to take his eyes off the burning wreck on the island where many marines and a team of Japanese scientists had just died.

"They were waiting for us," Beckman said darkly, annoyed that the amphibians had prepared a carefully thought out defense with the limited weapons they had. "They're bunkered down, buying time, waiting for the big one to hit."

"So what now?"

"That depends on NASA and how much time we've got."

* * * *

The senior officers took dinner in the captain's stateroom where they watched the latest updates on the Pinaka Intercept Mission. With the capsule moving rapidly away from Earth, interest around the world had risen to a state of mesmerized intensity with every channel providing round the clock updates. Experts discussed and analyzed every aspect of the mission down to the smallest detail, supplementing the science with a morbid focus on the consequences of failure. The media had begun hypothesizing on a connection between the alien foothold in northern Australia and the impending comet impact, although the UN Security Council would not confirm such speculation.

A few astrophysicists suggested there was a chance of a very near miss while broadcasters around the world sensationalized the story into a life and death struggle for human survival. Wiser heads suggested the comet was not large enough for a planetary mass extinction event, but they received much less air time than scare mongering doomsayers who stoked global fears. Predicting which continent or ocean would suffer a direct hit and how damage would roll around the planet became a worldwide obsession with hourly updates of predictions based on the latest calculations. Over time, the prospects for southern Canada seemed gloomy indeed, triggering mass movements of people toward Central and South America.

In no country did anyone consider the true nature of the attack, because the use of compressed spacetime as a tectonic weapon was simply so far beyond human technology, it was inconceivable. The threat could only be interpreted in terms of what mankind knew, which drew heavily on the dinosaur killing impact at Chicxulub on Mexico's Yucatan Peninsula. The idea that one of Einstein's most elusive predictions could be turned into a planet rending weapon would not dawn on mankind for another five centuries.

In countries with strong religious beliefs, end of the world preachers attracted vast audiences, citing apocalyptic prophesies from their preferred religious text. Sectarian violence erupted in some regions where the impending Judgment Day was seen as a divine call to settle old scores and long held hatreds. In other less violent regions, the faithful expressed themselves in mass prayer and inspirational songs of salvation.

"Any sign of the invisible ship?" Beckman asked as he sipped an after dinner coffee, thankful that detail was absent from the broadcasts.

"The comet hasn't made any more course changes,"

Dr. McInness replied, "and we haven't detected any more shadows on its surface."

"It's still there," Beckman said. "It has to be. That's why the amphibians haven't run. They're betting their chances of survival are better here than in the Pacific. They'll scatter after the impact."

"Why are you so sure?" Reynolds asked.

"It's what I'd do."

Reynolds turned to Teresa. "Any chance Kermit will help us map the caves?"

"He won't even acknowledge the map of Marchinbar Island," she replied. "As soon as I showed it to him, he stopped participating in the tests. He knows it means we've found them."

"Can we force him to cooperate?" Beckman asked.

She looked doubtful. "We couldn't trust what he'd tell us, Colonel, aside from the fact we still have no way of communicating with him. He refuses to acknowledge he can even read. I tried word patterns in the IQ tests, wrote a question on screen asking if he wanted white or black in the chess games and offered him books to read. He didn't take the bait."

"He understands everything," Dr. McInness said. "What he can't hide is the way he looks at the medical screens or how he watches Teresa when she's making notes. He wants to know what you're writing about him."

"Even if he can read, he isn't going to betray his people," she said. "I'm sure of that."

"He's a stubborn little son of a bitch," Beckman muttered.

"If the females have an evolutionary control over the males," Teresa suggested, "he may be unable to betray them. He could be hard wired to die rather than allow the females to be harmed."

The intercom sounded, then an officer said in a worried tone, "Captain required on the bridge."

"What is it?" Reynolds asked as he stood.

"We're adrift, sir. We've lost the anchor."

Alarm flashed across the acting captain's face. "On my way."

"I'll try Kermit one more time," Teresa said as they got to their feet. While she returned to the wardroom, the others hurried to the bridge.

The main lights were out, leaving the instruments' soft glow to turn the watch officers into ghostly wraiths in the night. The windows were covered to deny amphibian snipers a target, while the ship relied on radar, passive sonar and lookouts peeping through gaps in the window covers to monitor the surrounding waters. The *Naturaliste's* exterior lights were ablaze, illuminating the sea, while the water below the hull remained impenetrably dark.

"The GPS shows we've drifted into the bay," the watch officer reported as Reynolds stepped onto the bridge. "We're a couple of hundred meters from the north shoal."

"What happened to the anchor?" Beckman asked.

"They must have opened the shackle," the watch officer replied.

When Reynolds saw the blank look on Beckman's face, he added, "The bolt connecting the chain to the anchor. It's hard enough to open on the surface with tools. God knows how they did it underwater with their bare hands."

"They improvised," Beckman said, "something they have a talent for."

Reynolds checked their position on the navigation display. "Hmph. They waited for the tide to turn. They knew when they disconnected the anchor, the current would push us onto the rocks."

Beckman reached for the intercom. "You mind?" he asked Reynolds who nodded for him to proceed. "Sonar, this is Beckman. I'm on the bridge with Captain Reynolds. What's happening outside the ship?"

"Sonar to bridge, they're pinging the crap out of us,

sir," Petty Officer Casey replied. "There are thousands of contacts out there, ranging us constantly."

"Thousands? Are they approaching?"

"No sir, just tracking our position."

Beckman turned to Reynolds. "We should get out of here, now."

Reynolds nodded, well aware how vulnerable the ship would be if it ran aground. "Haul in the anchor chain," he said to the watch officer. "We'll take her out into deep water."

A sailor activated the forecastle mounted winch. It began winding the heavy steel chain in, then a warning light illuminated. "The anchor winch is slipping, sir," the sailor announced, clearly puzzled. With no anchor, the only strain on the winch should have come from the chain alone, not nearly enough weight to cause the clutch to slip.

"Hold it there," Reynolds said, knowing they could do nothing about a winch problem this close to amphibian snipers. Anxious to creep away from the shallows, he added, "We'll fix it in the channel. Ahead dead slow."

The hum of the engines increased as the twin propellers bit into the sea, then the sailor at the winch controls yelled, "Strain on the anchor chain, sir," as the winch tension spiked. An alarm sounded and engine warning lights flashed as an anguished groan of tearing metal reverberated through the ship.

"All stop!" Reynolds ordered, then an eerie silence fell over the *Naturaliste*.

"Bridge to engineering," sounded from the intercom. "Skipper, the starboard shaft has sheered. Both props are fouled. I killed the power just in time or we'd have lost the port shaft as well."

Reynolds glanced at the warning lights flashing on both the anchor winch and engine displays, putting the pieces together, then muttered to himself, "How'd they do that?"

"Do what?" Beckman asked, not understanding what had happened.

"They fouled the props with our own anchor chain – or something attached to the chain. They must have floated the end of the chain up to the propellers, or tied them together with a cable." Reynolds grabbed the intercom handset. "Mani, what's the status on the port propeller?"

"We ain't going nowhere until we clear it, sir. The port shaft is OK ..." The engineering officer leaned away from the intercom and yelled at one of his sailors, "How's that gearbox look?" After a moment, he spoke into the intercom. "Starboard side gears are stripped. The port side's OK, but I wouldn't strain the shaft until the prop's clear."

"Understood," he said, replacing the handset.

"You can't send divers down there," Dr. McInness warned.

"I know," Reynolds said. "They'd be dead as soon as they hit the water." He calculated the distance to the northern shoals. "We'll be aground in a few minutes"

"That's when they'll hit us," Beckman said grimly.

"They'll want to take the ship intact," Dr. McInness said. "They'll need its communications system to assess the comet's damage and decide when to move into the Pacific."

"Or even if they need to move," Beckman added, anticipating the worst.

Petty Officer Casey's voice sounded from the intercom. "Sonar to bridge. Captain, they just pulled the plug. It's gone dead quiet outside. I'm not hearing a peep out of them."

Before Reynolds could reply, the starboard lookout said, "Contacts, port side! They just surfaced."

"Starboard side too," another lookout reported. "Jeez, there's a lot of them!"

Reynolds and Beckman approached a pair of covered windows and eased the blinds back just enough to see without exposing themselves to sniper fire. Floating in the inky water were thousands of pairs of unblinking amphibian eyes glowing eerily in the darkness, reflecting light from the ship, all staring at the *Naturaliste*. Their glistening heads bobbed just high enough above the sea to keep their sonar lobes out of the water.

"That's creepy," Beckman whispered, feeling as if every alien eye was focused upon him.

"What are they waiting for?" Reynolds asked, then a bullet punched a hole through the window close to his hand. It cut a neat circle through the blind, forcing him to step back.

Beckman released his blind expecting another shot, but none came, then a muffled explosion sent a shudder through the ship. Twin waterspouts erupted either side of the *Naturaliste*, splashing the superstructure aft of the bridge.

"That's why their heads were out of the water," Beckman said, "to protect their sonar lobes from the shock wave."

"Where'd they get explosives from?" Reynolds asked surprised.

"Grenades from Rorruwuy," Dr. McInness said. "Their fuses and oxidizers are internal. Water wouldn't stop them exploding."

Reynolds grabbed the intercom. "Engineering, damage report."

A young seaman's voice sounded over rushing water. "Seaman Costa here, sir. Plates are sprung below the waterline amidships. There's a three meter hole aft of–"

A gunshot sounded, cutting off Costa's report.

"They're inside the ship!" Beckman declared.

Reynolds switched the intercom to broadcast throughout the ship. "Now hear this, this is the Captain speaking. All hands prepare to repel boarders. The enemy is using a hole below the waterline to enter the ship. Response teams one through six to the lower deck. Remaining teams secure all main deck watertight doors."

"They're coming over the stern!" a lookout peering through the aft facing window yelled as shadows leapt out of the water and landed on the railings. They cut the 'Peace' signs and the aft awning down allowing many more to come surging over the sides and swarming onto the main deck. They ran toward the locked watertight door beneath the flight deck and clambered up onto the helipad carrying steel knives, poison darts, pistols and assault rifles.

Beckman turned to Dr. McInness. "Ian, tell Teresa if she's going to get anything out of Kermit, now's the time."

The scientist hesitated, certain Beckman wanted him off the bridge to get him out of harm's way. "OK, don't get your head blown off," he said and reluctantly went below.

"Combat team to the bridge!" Reynolds yelled down the gangway, then twenty soldiers in full combat kit charged in as bullets fired from the flight deck shattered the windows, spraying glass over the crew. While the soldiers began shooting down onto the lower decks, Reynolds grabbed the intercom mike. "Hangar team, open fire."

Behind the bridge, the hangar door rolled up a meter, then two army squads behind metal equipment cases welded together and manning heavy machine guns began sweeping the flight deck with tracer. Waves of amphibians pouring onto the flight deck were cut to pieces as they charged the partially open hangar door and the metal stairs leading up to the aft bridge door.

The burp of machine guns could be heard on the bridge as soldiers fired through the broken windows at the flight deck and the water around the ship swarmed with movement. Only the forecastle remained clear, shielded from the sea by the ship's high bow.

An explosion flashed on the flight deck as an amphibian tried hurling a grenade at the bunkered troops in the hangar and was cut down before he could throw it.

It exploded in the midst of the charging alien horde, tearing them apart.

A moment later, a muffled explosion rumbled up from the main deck's watertight door as grenades detonated against it, blasting it inwards. Before the smoke cleared, automatic weapons fire erupted from inside the gangway as troops and sailors raked the mass of dark shapes scrambling over the wrecked door.

With explosions and gunfire reverberating through the air, the *Naturaliste* trembled as her hull scraped the rocky shoal. For a moment she teetered, then as water continued to flood her lower deck, she settled on the bottom, rolled fifteen degrees to port and stuck fast.

Reynolds and Beckman had their sidearms drawn, crouching in the center of the bridge as soldiers and sailors fired through the windows. Amphibian sniper fire peppered the superstructure, killing one of the lookouts and wounding two soldiers. Medics on hands and knees pulled the wounded away from the bridge while other soldiers and sailors took their places.

"I need to get off a mayday while I can," Reynolds said. "If they take engineering, we'll lose power."

"And lights," Beckman said. "Fighting blind is a no win for us."

"Anything you want me to tell Command?"

"Yeah. If we're overrun, destroy the ship. We don't want them getting more weapons and equipment."

Reynolds cast a regretful look around the bridge, realizing Beckman was right. "Will do."

Beckman started toward the gangway.

"Where are you going?" Reynolds asked.

"Engineering, to help keep the power on as long as possible," he said, then headed down into the bowels of the stricken ship.

* * * *

The crackle of gunfire filled the gangway as Beckman stepped into the wardroom where Dr. McInness and

Teresa were coaxing Kermit to communicate, watched at a distance by a single armed sailor. Beckman suspected if given half a chance, the sailor would shoot the amphibian as payback for what was happening elsewhere in the ship, but for now, he held fire.

The screen in front of Kermit displayed a satellite image of Marchinbar island with Hopeful Bay and the cave entrance marked at its southern tip. Beside the image were the words: *Show us where the caves lead and we will let you go.* Teresa stood beside Kermit holding a map of the island and a pen for him to use, but the alien stared blankly ahead, ignoring her every approach.

"No luck?" Beckman asked.

"He can hear the explosions," Teresa said. "That doesn't exactly put us in a strong bargaining position."

"He expects to be rescued," Dr. McInness said.

Beckman nodded to the screen. "Tell him if he helps us, there's still time to prevent the destruction of his people."

Teresa typed Beckman's words, then offered the keyboard to Kermit to reply. When he refused to acknowledge her, Beckman turned to the sailor. "Aim your weapon at the prisoner, but don't fire."

"Yes sir," the sailor said, eagerly aiming at the alien's head.

"Now tell him, we will shoot him before he can be rescued. The only way he gets out of here alive is to cooperate."

When the message appeared on the screen, Teresa once again offered Kermit the keyboard. This time the amphibian turned and stared at Beckman, giving the first indication he understood who was in charge. For a moment, they locked eyes, then Kermit raised his unrestrained hand and with one finger, tapped the keyboard twice. His answer appeared on the screen below Teresa's last message.

*No.*

"I knew it!" Dr. McInness said. "He's known how to read and write all along!"

"Why doesn't he understand what we say?" Beckman asked.

"He's had no direct contact with humans," Teresa said, "no chance to hear our language, to relate the sounds to the written words." She glanced at Kermit thoughtfully. "Given a chance, it wouldn't take them long to learn our spoken language, although they'll never be able to speak it themselves."

"They'll never get that chance," Beckman said, turning to the sailor. "Son, if those things get in here, shoot him. Under no circumstances are they to free him. Understood?"

"Yes sir!" the sailor replied crisply.

"What do you want us to do?" Teresa asked as a burst of gunfire sounded from the end of the gangway where alien attackers were making another attempt to storm a lower deck hatchway.

"We may not hold this deck," he said. "Fall back to communications. Take Kermit and whatever equipment you need." He holstered his pistol, took the handcuffs from the side table and cuffed the amphibian's hands in front of him. "Those cuffs don't come off again," he said, certain if given half a chance, the amphibian would kill them. He turned to Teresa. "Remember, they kill females first."

She gave him an uneasy look. "Thanks for reminding me."

Beckman released the straps tying Kermit to the bed, then hauled him roughly to his feet. Teresa picked up her laptop, then took one of the amphibian's arms while Dr. McInness grabbed the other. The sailor moved behind them, where he had a clean shot should the alien try anything, then they guided Kermit to the communications room while Beckman hurried toward the sound of gunfire.

He soon encountered a medic tending a wounded

sailor and a squad of soldiers taking turns firing down a hatchway at the deck below. Between explosions, return gunfire sporadically struck the overhead proving no matter how many amphibians they killed, many more were waiting to replace them. Just as Beckman reached the soldiers, a swarm of white bone slivers flew up through the hatch.

"Darts!" one soldier yelled.

They all dived clear, then the poison tipped shafts clattered harmlessly onto the deck. A moment later, the soldiers rushed back into position and fired down through the hatchway before the aliens could climb the ladder.

"Grenade," one soldier called as he threw a small green cylinder into the hatchway. It rang hollowly on the metal deck below amid the patter of bare feet charging the ladder, then an explosion accompanied by inhuman screams tore through the lower passageway. The soldiers held their weapons ready, but no attackers appeared at the top of the ladder.

Beckman glanced at the coral darts on the deck, then turned to a sun tanned sergeant holding his assault rifle vertically with one hand, his eyes following Beckman's gaze.

"The little bastards are using poison," he said. "Nasty shit. Got a few of the boys before we figured out what they were doing." The sergeant glanced along the gangway to two soldiers lying dead on the deck showing no sign of wounds. "Now every time they throw darts at us, we throw grenades at them." He gave Beckman a malicious look. "So far, we're ahead."

Beckman remembered the dart he'd seen kill a soldier at Rorruwuy, unaware it had been coated with sea wasp poison, the same deadly toxin that had killed Beloved-of-the-Sea's closest confidant. "What's the situation?"

"We've lost everything below the waterline," the sergeant replied. "They flood a section and swim in underwater. We either fall back or die."

It was a smart tactic the soldiers could do nothing against, but was limited by the depth of the water the *Naturaliste* was aground in. "What about engineering?"

"Last I heard, we had one end, they had the other."

"How's your ammo?" Beckman asked.

"Low, but more's coming."

Beckman left the squad to hold the hatchway and hurried toward engineering. When he pulled the engine room's watertight door open, he was immediately assaulted by a cacophony of rushing water, humming engines and the deafening boom of gunfire in confined spaces. The large engine compartment was crammed with equipment separated by small access spaces now awash with swirling sea water. Two massive engines dominated the center of the room, droning on resolutely, while two of the four smaller diesel generators had shorted out. A third generator was racked by repetitive hammering, warning it didn't have long to live, while tracer flashed back and forth between the machines.

Sailors wielding assault rifles stood waist deep in seawater in the narrow spaces firing at the dimly lit aft end of the engine room. A handful of soldiers had scrambled above the rising water and now lay on top of the engines firing over the heads of the sailors. Other soldiers had retreated into the elevated control room and were firing down through broken windows at the amphibians who were systematically shooting out the lights.

Beckman realized once the engine room was plunged into darkness, the amphibians would be free to use their sonic vision to pick off the human defenders. Sensing the urgency of the situation, he scrambled down narrow metal stairs into waist deep water, then with his nine millimeter pistol in hand, waded toward Lt. Manish Raman, the engineering officer commanding the defense.

Seawater pushed a slick amphibian corpse in front of him. It was floating face up with a chest riddled with bullets, then the body changed direction and headed toward the engineering officer. In the half light, Beckman saw a shadow beneath the corpse using its dead comrade for cover. He charged after it, pushing hard through the water, catching the corpse's foot and yanking it back, tearing the body away from the alien below. It's cover gone, the submerged amphibian surged out of the water at Beckman, surprising him with its speed and suicidal courage. He fired twice into its face at point blank range, knocking it back into the water while the startled engineering officer spun toward the sound of gunfire. Mani Raman was soaked from head to foot and had a shallow cut weeping blood on the left side of his face.

"How many are there?" Beckman yelled over the roar of surging water, thrumming engines and ricocheting bullets.

Raman shook his head uncertainly, showing signs of shock and fatigue. "Too many! They just keep coming!" he said, then fired a suppressing burst between the engines. As if in response, an overhead light exploded from a well placed shot, dimming the human held side of the engine room.

"Can we seal the door at the other end?" Beckman asked as he turned his back to the engineer, covering the water behind them ensuring they weren't taken by surprise.

"No chance. They blew it apart."

A soldier perching on a generator took a bullet in the chest and fell into the water, then two amphibians raced out of the darkness to his body. One dived beneath the water, emerging a moment later with his rifle while the second searched his body for grenades and ammunition. Before they retreated with the captured equipment, two soldiers sprayed them from the engine room windows, killing both, then another light shattered, increasing the gloom.

Beckman looked around desperately, knowing they were only minutes from a massacre. "Are these diesels?"

"Not for much longer," Raman replied. "This sea water's going to kill them."

"Can you cut the fuel lines?"

"Are you crazy?"

"Diesel floats, right? We can set it on fire. Incinerate those sons of bitches."

"And us with them!"

"You got a better idea, Lieutenant?" Beckman demanded, then when Raman gave him a helpless look, he added, "This fight is over in two minutes if we don't do something fast."

A dark form surged out of the water beside Beckman, driving a coral blade at his stomach. He dodged sideways, caught the amphibian's forearm and drove the barrel of his pistol into the space between the alien's eyes and fired, blowing the back of its head off, then he pushed the body away and turned to Raman, waiting for an answer.

"We'll seal the room," the engineer said. "If we don't blow up the ship, the fire will eat up the oxygen. Once it burns itself out, we can come back."

"Let's do it!"

Raman fired a short burst, then pushed through the water to a sailor in gray coveralls. "Cut the fuel lines," he yelled over the thunder of seawater and engines. "Let in two tonnes of diesel, then close the cut off." He held up two fingers emphatically. "Two tonnes only!"

"OK Mani," the technician said doubtfully, then grabbed a large wrench and headed for the nearest fuel line.

Raman turned to another sailor in coveralls. "Close off the vents. And tell those guys in the control room to get out now," he ordered, then turned back to Beckman. "If two tonnes of burning diesel won't stop them, nothing will."

"Now all we need is a match."

The engineer pushed through swirling water to a half submerged workshop where he retrieved an acetylene torch. He motioned for Beckman to head for the stairs, intending to light the diesel himself.

"My idea," Beckman said, putting his hand on the torch

"My engines," Raman declared, refusing to let go.

"Lieutenant, I have no idea how to repair these engines. Do you?"

The engineer hesitated, then reluctantly released the torch. "I'll hold the door open for you, Colonel."

"I'm counting on it. Now get your people out of here."

Raman motioned to the surviving crewmen, pointing to the forward watertight door, yelling, "Out! Everyone out!"

Soldiers and sailors began falling back toward the door, firing into the growing darkness as they retreated while the engine room filled with pungent fumes. Diesel poured onto the sea water from severed fuel lines while a technician watched the fuel gauges. When two tonnes had spilled into the control room, he shut off the fuel valve and ran to the watertight door.

An amphibian sniper destroyed the last light, plunging the engine room into darkness except for the soft glow spilling through the open watertight door. Raman was the last man through, then he gave Beckman a thumbs up before disappearing behind the steel door moments before bullets ricocheted off it.

Beckman fired several shots into the darkness as he retreated to the stairs, then holstered his pistol and lit the torch. Its short intense flame pushed back the darkness, revealing alien forms wading toward him through a lake of diesel. He hurled the torch into the shadows at the far end of the engine room, then scrambled up the stairs. At the landing, he glimpsed dozens of amphibians suddenly engulfed in an expanding wall of flame exploding toward him, then he dived through the open doorway. He heard the clang of the watertight door slam shut behind him as he landed on the deck, then a dull roar as the engine room was consumed by a firestorm.

Raman placed his hand on the metal door, feeling its temperature rise, then turned to his crew mates. "Fried fish anyone?"

There was muted laughter from the exhausted, soaking men resting in the passageway. Some sat on the deck, others leaned wearily against bulkheads, while the wounded limped off or were carried to sickbay. A fatigued silence settled over the men while the chatter of gunfire punctuated by an occasional explosion echoed through the ship. The gangway's lights blinked out as main power failed, immersing them in darkness for a few moments until weak red emergency lights came on.

The engineer turned to one of his men. "Get breathing apparatus down here. Once the fire burns itself out, we'll go back in." He glanced at Beckman and asked, "They don't have breathing apparatus do they?"

"They can stay underwater a long time," he said as he climbed to his feet.

Raman looked disappointed, then turned to another bedraggled sailor. "Get the welding gear from maintenance," he said, then to Beckman. "We'll ventilate engineering and weld plates over the door they blew open."

"While you're at it," Beckman said, "block all access points to the lower decks. Once they recover, they'll be back."

"We'll do that while we're waiting for the fire to die down."

Beckman left the engineer to his work and hurried back up to the bridge where soldiers and sailors were crouching below the windows.

"I take it we've lost engineering?" Reynolds asked, glancing at the blank instrument panels, now dead from lack of power.

"We did," Beckman said, "but so did they."

He crept to one of the windows and stole a look at the flight deck now strewn with alien corpses. There were no bodies on the forecastle, spared an assault by its high bows and the difficulty of breaking into the superstructure from the bow. Aware of how close it had been, Beckman sat beside Reynolds on the deck and rested his back against the base of the captain's chair.

"I got a message off," Reynolds said. "It'll be the last one, even if we get power back. They shot out our antennas. Radar and sonar are gone too and sickbay is overloaded with wounded."

"What's our supply situation?"

"Not bad. The food and the army's ammo are above the waterline. Fresh water might be a problem, and with no lights or comms, command will think we've been overrun. It's only a matter of time before our own people hit us."

Beckman's gaze fell on the broken windows and the bright stars above. "There's a UAV up there somewhere. All we have to do is signal it. Once they know we're alive, they'll send help."

Reynolds turned to CPO Barnes who sat cradling an assault rifle in his lap as he rested against a locker. "Barnes, break out a signal lamp." Reynolds scribbled a short message, then showed it to Beckman.

*Naturaliste disabled. Taking water. No power. Enemy control lower decks. One third casualties. Request assistance. LCDR. Reynolds.*

"That about covers it," Beckman said.

When Barnes returned with a lamp, Reynolds handed him the message. "Send this, Chief. Don't stop until your batteries are flat."

"Aye sir," Barnes said, then on hands and knees to avoid sniper fire from the shore, he crawled through the port side door, out onto the wing lookout platform and lay on his back. Safely enclosed by the plated railing, he aimed the lamp at the sky and began signaling.

Ten thousand meters above, a robotic eye saw a solitary flashing light winking in a vast sea of darkness.

216

Beloved-of-the-Sea crept along a shallow crevice to the edge of the rock plateau overlooking Hopeful Bay. The crippled human ship lay a few hundred meters off shore, firmly aground and listing to port. It was shrouded in darkness except for the occasional muzzle flash from a defender shooting at shadows, although no new attack had yet been ordered.

Prowls-the-Shallows stood beside her, studying the ship through naturally telescoping eyes. "We have few human grenades left and they have sealed themselves behind their steel walls."

"Can you break through?"

"Not from below. Not now. We took them by surprise once, but they have recovered. They are tenacious warriors."

"We could wait," she said. "When the land shifts tomorrow, the great waves will destroy them and the ships to the north, then there'll be no one to stop us moving into the Deep Blue."

"I know, Beloved, but I want their weapons. We will need them after the Long Darkness."

"You think the humans will survive?"

"The strongest will and they will be filled with a terrible vengeance."

She considered his request, aware of the cost they'd paid in the first attack, certain a second attack would be even worse. "Very well. We have too many to feed now anyway."

The humans could kill thousands of her brothers tomorrow and it would make no difference, for those who would be sacrificed played no part in her plans. All those of value – her sisters and the gifted males – had already withdrawn into the caves where they would wait for the Great Shift. Beloved had imprinted the gifted males, rendering them immune to her sisters and assuring her own position if she were lucky enough to be among the survivors. She could not predict who would live and who would die as the Shift would certainly cause cave-ins. Even so, sheltering below ground was a lesser risk than staying on the surface where they would be swept away by the oceans of the world as they flowed over and drowned the continents.

To reduce the risk, the females and their breed-males had been separated into small groups and allocated shelter in different parts of the subterranean complex. Each shelter had more than one way back to the sea, enough food to survive for many months and primitive tools in case they had to dig their way out. With luck, enough would survive to start again, to forge a new civilization upon the ruins of the human world.

Beloved-of-the-Sea hoped she and Prowls-the-Shallows would be among the survivors. If they were, she would rule. If not, the remaining females would fight each other until one emerged supreme. Either way, Beloved would be remembered as the founding mother of a new Intruder homeworld half a galaxy away from the first.

# CHAPTER EIGHT: CONFLAGRATION

Chief Barnes lay on his back outside the bridge, shielded from the sea by the enclosed railing as he flashed the signal lamp at the sky. He hoped there was a UAV up there watching, unaware the message had already been sent via satellite to military commanders on two continents. Since the attack, all had gone quiet except for the occasional shot fired by a defender or the clang of a sniper's bullet against the superstructure.

When he was halfway through the next round of signals, he heard a clattering of wood on metal behind his head. He glanced back to see a carved grappling hook attached to the railing, then another hook struck the metal plating and fell away. A moment later, the second grapple was thrown again, this time catching hold.

Barnes rolled away from the railing, dropped the signal lamp and drew his pistol as the ropes creaked under the weight of amphibians climbing up from the main deck. He aimed at the nearest grapple as a dark ridged head slowly rose up. When bulging blue-green eyes appeared, he fired, causing the amphibian's head to jerk back and sending it plunging into the sea. A third grapple caught the railing, then the scraping sounds intensified as amphibians swarmed up the ropes.

Three white slivers flashed into the air, then Barnes threw himself toward the bridge door as the poison tipped darts fell onto the deck where he'd lain moments before. He pulled the bridge door open and crawled through as a streamlined face peeked above the second grappling hook. The alien hurled a dart at him as he slammed the metal door shut in time for the dart to hammer harmlessly against it, then a soldier at a broken window killed the amphibian with a single shot.

"They're coming up the sides!" Barnes yelled as a swarm of darts came flying over the railings at the shattered bridge windows.

As the defenders ducked for cover, a female rating was struck in the cheek. She swatted the dart away, then staggered back with a hand pressed against her face and fear in her eyes. The young sailor gasped for breath as the poison took hold, then she fell to her knees as more grappling hooks caught the railings on either side of the bridge. Suddenly, amphibians came pouring over both sides into a hail of gunfire. Many fell back into the sea or onto the walkway surrounding the bridge while others hurled darts as they launched themselves at open windows, ignoring the ragged glass lining the windowsills.

Some defenders inside the bridge were struck by darts and fell writhing onto the deck while the rest retreated behind the control stations. Amphibians immediately scrambled through the windows, only to be shot by soldiers sweeping the bridge with automatic fire, clogging the windows with bodies and blocking those behind them.

Beckman and Reynolds stood firing their pistols from behind the central control station at the mass of bodies trying to force their way in, while around them, automatic weapons clicked empty, were reloaded and clicked empty again.

"Fix bayonets!" a corporal yelled, then soldiers ran forward and speared their attackers in the face and shoulders as they tried squeezing through the corpse congested windows.

When Beckman fired his last bullet, he ran to one of the dead soldiers, grabbed a grenade off his belt and stepped to the starboard side door. It was wedged half open by two dead amphibians.

"Grenade!" he yelled and hurled it through the half open door, then ducked behind the bulkhead as an explosion shredded the dense tangle of bodies outside.

On the other side of the bridge, a soldier speared an alien in the mouth as it tried pulling itself through a window, driving it back, then he tossed a grenade through the opening onto the external walkway. A moment later, an explosion tore through the attackers, hurling bodies into the air and over the sides.

For frenetic moments, the bridge was filled with flashing bayonets and slashing coral knives, then a dozen soldiers charged onto the bridge, firing rapidly. In seconds, the reinforcements overwhelmed the attackers, tossing grenades onto the exterior walkways, then the ship's exterior lights blinked on as minimal power was restored. Caught in a blaze of light, with the windows choked with bodies, the amphibian horde broke off the attack and dived back into the sea.

The human defenders looked on, exhausted and confused, hardly able to believe it was over. The deck was littered with dead and wounded, some dying choking deaths as the poison finished its work while their comrades watched on helplessly. Amphibian corpses clogged every window and were piled high on the external walkways while inside the bridge, human and alien bodies littered the deck.

Beckman took in the gruesome scene at a glance, realizing the second attack had ended as suddenly as it had begun, unaware that a recall had been sounded beyond the range of human hearing.

"We won't be able to repel another attack like that," Reynolds said grimly.

"They don't know that," Beckman said, aware the enemy's ignorance of their desperate state might be the only thing keeping them alive. "We need to clear those bodies," he said, nodding to the windows.

Reynolds motioned to the newly arrived soldiers. "Throw the alien corpses over the side, but be careful of snipers."

The fresh troops forced open the exterior doors and crouching below the railings, began the grisly business of tossing alien bodies overboard. Whenever they encountered a wounded amphibian, they dispatched him with a bullet before approaching.

"Engineering to bridge," Lt. Raman's voice sounded from the intercom. When Reynolds answered, the engineer said, "We've got one of the Alsthoms working, sir, but I don't know for how long. It's a real mess down here."

"Well done, Mani. We really need those lights. Do whatever you have to, to keep them on," Reynolds said before replacing the handset.

"Captain," Barnes called from the far side of the bridge. "I hear something."

"Not again," an exhausted sailor muttered, thinking it was another attack.

Beckman and Reynolds approached Barnes' position at a crouch, hearing the muted drone of approaching engines in the distance.

"What is it?" a bloodied soldier asked uncertainly.

"Jet engines," Beckman said. "Big ones."

All eyes turned to the night sky as the drone became a roar, then two large aircraft appeared, coming up from the south. Their navigation lights were out, although they were just visible in the moonlight as they skimmed low over the sea.

When they neared the entrance to Hopeful Bay, Reynolds recognized their silhouettes. "They're P-8s."

The light gray Poseidon maritime patrol aircraft flew on parallel courses either side of the *Naturaliste*. As soon as they were over the bay, they began dropping sonobuoys every few seconds. The cylindrical devices were just visible in the ship's light as they floated toward the sea on small white parachutes. The two big RAAF jets passed noisily overhead, then as they reached Marchinbar Island, they banked sharply away on opposite courses, separating before turning south again and making a second pass over the bay further from the ship, dropping another series of sonobuoys parallel to the first. When they'd finished their run, they climbed away for the long flight back to their base at Edinburgh, South Australia. Behind them, the sonobuoys splashed into the sea and began bombarding the dark depths with powerful acoustic pulses, deafening the submerged amphibians and driving them to the surface. Moments later, the sea erupted as thousands of large streamlined heads burst from the water, elevating their sensitive sonar lobes above the acoustic assault filling the shallows below.

"Bloody hell," Reynolds said to Beckman, "there's more of them than we have bullets."

One of the soldiers took aim, but Beckman said, "Hold your fire. We're going to need the ammo."

Before the P-8s had vanished, another louder scream came rolling in from the Arafura Sea to the north. It quickly drowned out the retreating drone of the Poseidons as all eyes on the bridge again turned to the sky. Across Hopeful Bay, thousands of amphibians floating in the water, climbing onto the rocks and splashing onto the beach paused to watch the sky.

"Fast jets," Beckman said as a line of gray streaks on short wings with twin angled tails came racing out of the darkness. "It's an air strike!" he yelled. "Everybody down!"

On the bridge, the defenders ducked below the windows as US Navy F-35 fighters came in fast, each with a pair of thick canisters slung from their wings. They dropped the canisters in staggered pairs across the bay, over the shoreline and around the crippled

*Naturaliste*. The aerodynamically shaped containers tumbled clumsily toward the thousands of upturned, uncomprehending amphibian faces. As the canisters fell, they shattered, scattering hundreds of bomblets through the air. Before they hit the water, the cluster bombs exploded, showering the amphibian army in a lethal storm of shrapnel. A few pieces struck the ship's hull, but careful planning ensured none reached the exposed bridge, while the upturned alien faces jamming the bay were shredded before they knew what was happening.

When the explosions died down, Beckman stood in time to see the F-35s climbing away toward the carrier battle group to the north. Beneath the departing fighters, Hopeful Bay, now choked with thousands of alien corpses, fell into a deathly silence.

"Is it over?" a stunned sailor asked.

"No," Beckman said. "It's just beginning, God help them."

He knew the air strike signaled the decision had been made to unleash the world's military power upon the amphibians, ensuring none would be left alive to benefit from the coming cataclysm.

* * * *

At first light, a twin-engine US Navy transport aircraft with a four vertical stabilizer tail circled the *Naturaliste* at low altitude.

"It's a C-2 Greyhound," Reynolds said, studying it through binoculars, "a carrier based cargo plane."

The old Greyhound circled in close, then one of the hand held two-way radios crackled. "Naturaliste, this is Romeo-Golf Zero Four, are you receiving? Over."

Reynolds snatched up the two-way. "Romeo-Golf Zero Four, this is Naturaliste. We hear you."

The aging C-2 dipped a wing as it banked to stay close. "Be advised, B-2s are inbound with MOPs."

Reynolds glanced at Beckman. "MOP?"

Beckman's eyes widened in surprise. "Massive ordnance penetrator. Fourteen ton bombs."

"Earthquake bombs?"

Beckman nodded. "They can't use precision weapons, so they're going to blow the island apart."

Reynolds lifted the two-way to his lips. "Acknowledged. Thanks for the warning."

"Naturaliste, you are directed to institute NBC protocols immediately," the navy pilot added.

Reynolds looked surprised. One glance at the bridge's shattered windows told him securing the ship to survive a nuclear-biological-chemical attack was impossible. "That's going to be a problem," he replied, knowing the military commanders could not limit their actions just to keep the *Naturaliste's* crew alive. "We're unable to seal the ship."

"Understood, sir. You are outside the blast radius and the winds are favorable."

Reynolds gave Beckman a worried look. "He's talking about fallout."

Beckman nodded gravely. "Pray the winds don't change."

The navy pilot added, "A UAV will orbit you at low altitude to maintain a communications link using two-ways."

"Thank you, Romeo-Golf," Reynolds said. "If the airstrike takes out the snipers ashore, we can send people aloft to get comms back up."

"I'll let them know. Good luck, Naturaliste, Romeo-Golf Zero Four, out."

The C-2 leveled off and headed north toward the international fleet massing beyond the horizon, then Reynolds picked up the intercom handset.

"This is the Captain speaking. We have been ordered to implement NBC protection. Damage crews to seal windows, doors and air intakes immediately. Use plastic sheets if you have to."

When he hung up the handset, he and Beckman

moved to one of the broken forward windows, keeping low as they searched the lightening sky for bombers.

"If they're coming from Whiteman," Beckman said, "they'll come from the northeast. No reason to circle."

Twenty minutes later, after the *Naturaliste* had been hurriedly sealed and the sun was breaching the horizon, a lookout with powerful naval binoculars pointed to a series of white contrails high in the sky. "There they are. Six of them."

The six flying wing shaped bombers were already lined up on Marchinbar Island's narrow length. They were operating at their absolute ceilings, the highest altitude at which they could maintain level flight, in order to give gravity the maximum time to accelerate the bombs to velocities high enough to punch deep into the island's rocky structure. Well before the B-2 Spirit bombers reached the southern end of the island, they began releasing their enormous GBU-57s, one at a time, two per aircraft.

The MOPs were shaped like thick white torpedoes fitted with four stubby wings spaced evenly around their hulls. They were equipped with nose mounted laser sensors and four guidance stabilizers protruding from their tails. The giant bombs fell ponderously out of the sky, slowly at first but rapidly gaining speed until they were hurtling toward the ground at supersonic velocities. After falling for more than a minute, the twelve super bombs struck the island like massive hammers, smashing their way deep into the rock before detonating, sending geyser-like clouds erupting through the penetration shafts. Forty meters beneath the surface, violent shock waves equivalent to fourth magnitude earthquakes shook the island to its core. Football field sized slabs of rock collapsed into caverns excavated by the bombs while the artificial earthquakes triggered hundreds of cave ins, burying all beneath them. Above the target zones, broad dust clouds burst into the air and hung low over the island before being slowly dispersed by the sea breeze.

Reynolds studied the thin blast clouds wafting over the impact zones with a disappointed look. "I expected something ... bigger."

"It doesn't look like much, but it's effective," Beckman said. "It's called the trapdoor effect. The surface collapses, burying everything and everyone beneath it."

The B-2s turned to the northeast for the long flight back to Whiteman Air Force Base in Missouri while on the island, nothing moved beneath the thinning dust clouds. The scale of destruction was only dwarfed by the thousands of alien corpses clogging Hopeful Bay, rotting in the tropical sun.

"Aircraft bearing three four zero degrees," a lookout reported.

All eyes on the bridge turned toward eleven F-35s flying in from the US Navy led United Nations Fleet to the north, each carrying a single silver white B61 variable yield bomb. The stealth fighters separated before they reached Marchinbar Island and headed toward the hatcheries the *Naturaliste* and aerial reconnaissance had identified. Ominously, six of the F-35s circled in a line almost directly overhead – two northeast, four southwest – while the other strike fighters continued on to their assigned targets further south.

"They look close," Reynolds said.

Beckman watched the circling fighters through his binoculars. "The closest hatchery is forty clicks from here. That's far enough," Beckman said with more confidence than he felt. "We should take cover."

"Seal them up," Reynolds said, then anyone near an unsealed window finished taping the plastic sheets installed by repair crews to the bulkheads. Reynolds picked up the intercom. "Close all air intakes. This is it, people." When they'd sealed the windows as best they could against radioactive particles, knowing their only real protection was the sea breeze, everyone moved off the bridge. The senior officers went into the communications room while the rest went to the mess for food or just loitered in the corridors. Once the bridge was clear, a sailor locked the door and sealed it with tape.

In the communications room, Teresa and Dr. McInness met them with anxious looks while Kermit, sat silently in a corner under the watchful gaze of his guard. The officers accepted coffee and food from an orderly then Beckman said, "Any minute now."

The main communications screens now displayed live feeds from cameras placed above the bridge, observing the horizon. The images were pumped to every screen on the ship and were watched anxiously by all aboard. What conversation there was barely rose above a whisper.

After several anxious minutes, each strike fighter confirmed it had reached its assigned target. The fleet admiral gave one final confirming order, followed by a countdown from the flagship. When the count reached zero, the fighters released their bombs simultaneously. No one on the *Naturaliste* saw the bombs fall or the fighters streak away to safety and none of the millions of hatchlings had any warning of what was coming.

On the *Naturaliste's* screens, eleven small suns flashed into existence across a two hundred and fifty kilometer wide target zone. Each blast released a third of a megaton close to the sea's surface where the heat could most effectively vaporize the water and incinerate the five million hatchlings sheltering within it. The *Naturaliste's* cameras flickered with distortion, but the ship was far enough from the electro-magnetic pulses that its electronics weren't knocked out. The nuclear suns glowed blindingly bright, then faded into eleven billowing mushroom clouds rising into the air.

"I hope you weren't planning on having children," Reynolds said.

"Got two already, not that I see them much," Beckman replied as he watched the mushroom clouds form a semicircle around the crippled *Naturaliste* like giant trees on the horizon.

"They're low altitude bursts," Dr. McInness said. "Half the radiation will be absorbed by the Earth."

"I feel so much better," Beckman said, hardly comforted.

"I wonder if any of them survived?" Teresa asked.

Beckman noticed Kermit was staring at the screens, not understanding what he saw, but certain it spelt disaster for his brothers. "That's what he's wondering."

Over the next few hours, they watched the nuclear clouds rise and disperse, hoping the sea breeze and taped plastic sheets would protect them from the fallout. When the nuclear clouds had dissipated, a line of propeller driven aircraft appeared out of the west. They were a mix of four-engine Hercules and twin-engine Spartans, all hurriedly equipped with fuselage tanks and under wing spraying systems. The allied transports spread out across the sky, then began spraying a red mist over the sea and islands, being careful to stay well clear of the *Naturaliste*.

"What is that stuff?" Reynolds asked.

Beckman realized the political and military commanders had decided they would take no chances and were saturating the enemy with one remorseless assault after another. "Whatever it is," he said, "I wouldn't want to be under it."

\* \* \* \*

A warning indicator flashed on the attitude control subsystem display at NASA's Mission Control. The Guidance, Navigation and Control Systems Engineer checked the real time data coming from the spacecraft against his expected baseline, then turned to the thruster control operator. "Colin, is there an unscheduled attitude burn in progress?"

The Propulsion Systems Engineer looked up blankly.

"No, there's nothing planned until final approach."

The GNC Engineer looked puzzled. "My gyros are spinning out of control." He stood up and called the Flight Director. "Wade, I've got an emergency stabilization warning."

Wade Franklin was tired. His sleeves were rolled up, his tie loose and he looked as if hadn't slept for three days. "Anything on radar?"

"Spacecraft radar is negative," another engineer called. "No contacts."

Franklin turned to a female engineer wearing silver rimmed glasses. "Any magnetic readings?"

"Magnetometer is negative," she replied.

Hamilton Pearce stepped up beside the Flight Director. "What is it?"

"I don't know," he said warily, watching a slim man talking rapidly on the phone. When the man looked up, Franklin asked, "Does Hubble see anything?"

The space telescope had been visually observing the Pinaka Intercept spacecraft since it had broken orbit, although only the head of the Flight Operations Team at Goddard Space Flight Center in Maryland knew what it was looking for.

"Nope. The spacecraft's all alone out there," the Space Telescope Operations Control Center liaison replied.

Wade Franklin turned weary eyes back to the GNC engineer. "Any chance it's a software glitch?"

The GNC Engineer was still standing, staring at his screen. He shook his head emphatically. "No way! The gyros are maxed. Whatever's happening to the spacecraft, they can't compensate."

"Confirmed," the Guidance Officer called, jumping to his feet. "She's way off course!"

"Prop," the Flight Director said, "can you burn to adjust?"

The Propulsion System Engineer stared at his screen with growing alarm. "Negative. The capsule's off-trajectory acceleration is too high for our thrusters."

The Ground Control engineer whistled softly. "According to Goddard, ground tracking is showing the capsule accelerating at more than sixty Gs. We've lost the intercept. No way we can get to the comet now."

"That's it!" Pearce said, grabbing Franklin by the arm. "They've got our spacecraft."

The Flight Director hesitated. "But there's nothing on radar. Nothing on visual. No magnetics," he said turning to a stocky engineer who was staring at his screen with clenched fists. "How far is the spacecraft from Pinaka?"

"Two hundred and ten thousand kilometers," the Flight Dynamics Officer replied. "Too far for the payload to affect the comet's trajectory."

"Wade," Hamilton Pearce said urgently. "Do it now, before it's too late."

"But there's nothing out there!" he snapped, reluctant to make a decision without proper data.

"You think sixty G's acceleration is an accident?" Pearce asked.

The Flight Director thought for a moment then turned to the Payloads Officer. "Send the code."

A US Air Force general placed a black folder on the desk in front of the Payloads Officer, opened it to a specific page and pointed to a long alpha numeric. "That's it."

The Payloads Officer carefully entered the top secret sequence, double checked he had typed it correctly, then glanced at the general.

The general compared the code to the folder with painstaking slowness, then nodded, "Confirmed."

The Payloads Officer transmitted the signal, then announced, "The nuclear activation code has been sent."

Wade Franklin grimaced, knowing it was now out of his hands.

"Let's hope we're not too late," Hamilton Pearce said.

The Infiltrator had planned to wait for Earth's rotation to carry the enemy ship to the planet's far side, but the research vessel suddenly moved to investigate eleven nuclear detonations in the southern hemisphere. The Intruder probe knew from the explosion's locations that the humans were destroying the hatcheries with atomic weapons and that such an attack, while undoubtedly successful, would achieve nothing of value.

With the planet's mass now separating them, the enemy ship could not detect the Infiltrator as it slipped from its icy hiding place deep within the comet and moved to intercept the NASA capsule. The Intruder probe was not equipped to tow, so when it came alongside the fragile human spacecraft, it enveloped it within its sublight propulsion field and accelerated with it away from Earth. It intended to release the HAIV spacecraft at the outer edge of the planet's magnetic field, then return to the comet to await the moment it would begin diffusely compressing spacetime with its superluminal engines. The only resistance the human spacecraft could offer was the feeble force generated by its gyroscopic stabilizers. It was such a minute amount of energy that the Infiltrator scarcely adjusted its flight parameters to compensate.

The Infiltrator could have completed the ejection maneuver in a fraction of a second, but the energy required for high acceleration would have made it visible to the enemy ship, so it crawled away from Earth a mere sixty times the planet's gravity. The low acceleration – far greater than any human rocket could achieve – would make it difficult for its enemies to identify who had caused the planetary disaster about to strike the Earth. The Tau Cetins would certainly discover the crustal shift was no accident and if they realized an Intruder ship had caused it, their fleet would make it impossible for the Infiltrator to approach their home system.

When the Intruder probe neared the edge of the planet's magnetosphere, it detected a radio transmission unlike any it had previously received. Since its arrival in the Solar System, it had grown accustomed to reading the plethora of human broadcasts flooding space, but this signal was unique in that it contained a seemingly meaningless combination of symbols. After several million unsuccessful decryption attempts, the Infiltrator wondered if the symbols themselves were the message: a code key. A few billionths of a second later, it sensed a change within the capsule's payload, a burst of radioactivity indicating the humans were prematurely detonating their nuclear warhead.

The Infiltrator experienced the equivalent of surprise as it realized the humans had abandoned all hope of attacking the comet and saving themselves. Instead, for some inexplicable reason, they had detonated their crude fusion weapon far out in space where it could not possibly affect the comet. As the fusion blast began to expand, the Intruder probe calculated there wasn't time to allow the human capsule to move outside the radius of its propulsion field.

That discovery led the Infiltrator to a remarkable conclusion, one it could scarcely countenance, yet which logic and data supported: the humans had sent the spacecraft to destroy it, not the comet! The idea seemed scarcely credible as primitive human technology could not possibly have detected the Intruder probe's presence, yet detonating the warhead now could only have one purpose, the destruction of the Infiltrator itself. Somehow the humans must have been aware of its presence all along and what they called the Pinaka Intercept Mission had been aimed at it from the beginning.

By the time the nuclear material reached supercriticality, the Infiltrator had reassessed its every move, considered all its precautions and yet was unable to understand how it had failed. For days, it had watched thousands of human broadcasts describing the Pinaka mission, transmissions it now realized were proof the humans had secretly mobilized the resources of their entire world to deceive it. To lie with such conviction on such a scale required a devious nature equaled by very few species, perhaps only by the Infiltrator's own creators.

In a moment of insight, the Intruder probe wondered at the fate awaiting Beloved and her siblings at the hands of such a calculating species. Given several million years, they might become a threat to any who opposed them. The Intruder probe, knowing it could not save itself, began activating its trans-galactic communicator in the hope of informing Versala of the presence of their sisters on Earth and warning of the insidious humans who should be marked for extermination before they had time to become a threat.

Long before it could begin transmitting, the Infiltrator realized it was too late. After having come more than sixty five thousand light years and evaded the most advanced starships in existence, it was about to be destroyed by the most primitive space weapon in the entire galaxy. At the edge of Earth's magnetosphere, a point of brilliant white light glowed brighter than the Sun, enveloping the Intruder probe in a fusion blast that even its hyper-tensile hull could not resist.

The Infiltrator experienced a moment of incredulity then ceased to exist.

* * * *

The Payloads Officer stared at a screen now devoid of readings. "Either it detonated or we've got a total systems failure."

The STOCC liaison jumped to his feet still holding his telephone. "Hubble confirm a nuclear detonation!" he yelled. "Our vehicle's gone, but there's something else out there. Could be the wreckage of a ship."

The James Webb Space Telescope Liaison sat beside him listening to her telephone, then turned to the Flight Director. "The Institute confirm Webb has detected a huge infra red source. Whatever our nuke hit, it's hot. At least ten million degrees Kelvin!"

Whistles sounded around the room as they realized their nuclear device had detonated only meters from the alien spacecraft.

One scientist said, "Damn! What's it made of?"

Another shook his head, unable to understand how any part of the alien ship had survived. "It should have been vaporized."

Shocked silence filled Mission Control as the enormity of what they'd achieved struck them, then one astonished engineer said, "My God, we did it!"

Cheers broke out, high fives and hugs were exchanged as tears of joy flowed. Hamilton Pearce slapped Wade Franklin on the shoulder as they shook hands.

"I don't believe it," Pearce said with relief and a beaming smile. Expecting Earth's transmissions to be monitored, the entire media campaign, the constant detailed broadcasts of the Pinaka Intercept Mission had all been designed to draw the shadow ship out of hiding.

Franklin sighed as the weight of responsibility for the survival of the human race lifted off his shoulders. "Believe it," he grunted, then allowed himself an exhausted grin.

A short man with thick glasses stood up, the only man in the room with a serious expression. He held up his hand to get the Flight Director's attention. "Wade!" he yelled over the din. "WADE!"

Franklin turned to him, sobering when he saw the worried look on the man's face. "What?"

"Goddard's reporting the comet is calving. It's broken into three pieces."

"Was it our nuke?" the Flight Director asked with rising alarm.

The Goddard Space Flight Center liaison shook his head. "No. The blast was too far away. It's Earth's gravity. It's pulling Pinaka apart."

Wade Franklin's relief vanished as he realized multiple comet fragments, each as big as a mountain, might still strike the planet's surface, spreading catastrophic damage across a wide area. "Are they going to hit?

"Too close to call," the Goddard liaison replied. "They're working on it."

Hamilton Pearce turned to Franklin with an urgent look. "Wade, tell the Russians to get moving."

Franklin nodded and snatched up his telephone. "Get me Baikonur Cosmodrome." He waited a moment, then when his opposite number half a world away answered, he said, "Arkady, we got it," the Flight Director said. "Yes, the sky is clear, but Earth's tidal forces are breaking up the comet. You haven't got much time ... That's right ... Good luck."

Forty three minutes later, the Russian rocket that had been announced would supply the International Space Station and which had been ignored by both the world's media and the Infiltrator, launched with an eight hundred kiloton nuclear warhead.

Pinaka was now less than four hours away.

* * * *

Prowls-the-Shallows swam along the coast of Marchinbar Island, navigating by sight and memory alone, fearing the humans were listening for his biological sonar. He'd been near one of the northern entrances to the caves when the earthquake bombs had struck. At first he thought it was the beginning of the crustal shift, that the Intruder probe had begun its attack earlier than expected, then the Infiltrator gift filled his mind with memories of deep penetration weapons that had destroyed underground bases and collapsed the foundations of entire cities. The weapons the humans had deployed against them were at the lower end of the destructive scale, but the principle was the same. He knew at once it meant the humans were blindly attacking the island itself in an effort to destroy the female sanctuaries. Instinctively, he'd swum for the nearest submerged entrance, but just as he reached it, the cave mouth collapsed in front of him.

Desperate to find survivors, he began working his way along the coast to the southern entrance. He hadn't gone far when a brilliant flash cast sharp shadows into the water, then a strange current began dragging him toward what the humans called the Sphinx Head hatchery. Prowls didn't understand where the current came from or that the sea was rushing to fill the emptiness left by vaporized water.

He dived to the bottom and clung to a submerged rock as the rushing tide tore at him, dragging fish and sea life past him, scraping sand from the sea floor and hurling it toward the blast zone to the north. When the current eased he discovered the Mothersea was filled with a terrifying silence. The constant acoustic chatter of the hatchlings was gone, as were the stern warnings of the nursery fathers who always struggled to keep the young within the protected shallows.

Confused and helpless in the face of such an attack, he surfaced and climbed a headland where he saw great cavities had opened in the island from the earthquake bombs and eleven billowing mushroom clouds rose across half the horizon. In a horrifying moment of clarity, he realized the hatcheries had been annihilated by the humans. The Infiltrator gift filled his thoughts with visions of a weapon so terrible, it was universally banned across the galaxy. He'd been far enough to the south to avoid the nearest shock wave and flash while the water and his genetically engineered resistance had protected him from the worst of the ionizing radiation.

Prowls resisted the urge to leave his hiding place and

rush down into the collapsed caves, fearing the humans were watching from high altitude. Instead, he gazed in horror at the nuclear forest climbing skyward in the distance, then searched for aircraft, wondering if more attacks were coming. It was then he noticed a line of blurred lights in the sky, far to the south east. He tried focusing on them with his telescoping eyes, but found they were incredibly far away, too far to see clearly. When he wondered what could cause such a display in daylight, his implanted gift revealed it was the comet breaking apart as it fell toward the Earth. He knew at once such a phenomenon could only occur if the Infiltrator was no longer in control.

Fighting despair at the magnitude of their defeat, Prowls crept back into the water. In an acoustic silence not known in the Mothersea for a decade, he heard a few confused signals from hunters and scouts who, like himself, had been outside the kill zones. Some were injured and called for help that would not come, while others wondered what to do, where to go.

Prowls considered issuing orders, but wary of human listening devices, he made his way down the coast in silence. He hadn't gone far when he saw human aircraft spraying the sea surrounding the hatcheries with a red mist. Almost immediately, he heard the sonar screams of survivors caught by the toxin as it dissolved their eyes and skin and forced its way into their lungs. The Infiltrator gift couldn't tell him what chemicals the humans were using, but it warned him of the danger. Knowing the safest place was near the human ship, Prowls swam as fast as he could toward it before the current carried the toxin to him.

By the time he rounded the southern tip of Marchinbar Island, the sonic screams of the dying had receded. He'd heard distant warnings to get out of the water and then reports that the humans were spraying the islands as well, that nowhere was safe.

When he swam into Hopeful Bay, he saw the human

ship was hard aground, surrounded by thousands of rotting corpses. The tide had kept the bodies of his brothers trapped all morning, but it would soon turn, carrying them out to sea. A growing number of one-fin-killers had followed the scent of blood into the bay and begun feeding with a frenzy that would last for days to come.

The sharks showed no interest in Prowls-the-Shallows as he swam beneath the corpses without surfacing, heading for the cave complex's main entrance. To his relief, the submerged entrance had not collapsed, although the silence coming from its interior made him uneasy.

Without hesitation, he raced into the darkness, passed over the wrecked UUV, then surfaced at speed, leaping high out of the water onto the ledge above. A single torch wedged in the rocks continued to burn, while the others had been doused when the rock walls they'd clung to collapsed. He considered retrieving the torch, but one look told him there was light ahead, so he scrambled over fallen rocks toward the first large chamber.

It was unrecognizable. Huge slabs of rock had crushed many and exposed the cavern to the sky. It was damage on a scale he'd scarcely imagined. Every thought he had triggered gifted memories of ruined cities and war ravaged worlds, as if the gift was intent on showing him the catastrophes his kind had both endured and inflicted in their multi-million year history. Desiring neither context or war winning strategies, he pushed the Intruder memories aside as he clambered over fallen boulders toward the passage leading to Beloved's private chamber.

Prowls began to call out her name in their own created tongue, in the Intruder One Speech and with his sonar lobe, but there was no response. At every turn, he found collapsed passages and unstable rocks periodically crashing to ground, but he pushed on desperately. The thick dust forced him to rely on the air in his quad-lungs, while jagged rocks tore at his skin. Finally, he squeezed into Beloved's ante-chamber, then rushed into her private quarters. One side had collapsed from an aftershock rather than a direct hit and a beam of sunlight shone down through wafting dust from a cavity in the rock ceiling.

Beloved lay on the other side of the chamber, her head smeared with blood and a deep gash along one leg. He knelt beside her, relieved to discover she was still breathing and that her wounds were already coagulating due to the genetically enhanced cell regeneration she'd inherited from their mother.

"Beloved," he whispered.

She opened her eyes weakly. "I knew you'd come."

"The humans have destroyed the hatcheries. They're killing our brothers across the Mothersea. We are defeated."

"We survived," she whispered defiantly. "There will be other survivors. Find them. This is the last day of the humans. Tomorrow, will be ours."

"The humans will never stop until we are all dead."

"The crustal shift will stop them," she said, pushing herself to a sitting position against a boulder.

"There will be no shift. The Infiltrator has failed."

"How do you know?"

"The comet is off course. I saw it in the sky. It's breaking apart. It's going to hit the planet."

Beloved thought for a moment, referencing her Intruder gifted knowledge of celestial collisions. She lacked Watcher's detailed understanding of science, but even she knew such a failure would still inflict enormous damage upon the planet and her enemies.

"We may yet prevail," she said, her relentless will unbroken.

"Beloved, everything is destroyed," Prowls said, trying to make her see the hopelessness of their situation. "We have lost."

"The comet may not exterminate the humans, but it

will hurt them," she said, resting her hand on her abdomen, "and I am ready to spawn." She emitted a reassuring ping from her sonar lobe. "You, my brother, are all I need."

* * * *

At Mission Control, Hamilton Pearce, Wade Franklin and their teams could do little but watch and wait as Pinaka approached Earth at fifty eight thousand kilometers an hour. The late launch of the Russian rocket had allowed scarcely enough time for it to complete four Earth orbits before it began boosting toward the incoming comet fragments.

"We've left it too late," Pearce said in a low voice to Franklin, not wanting to alarm the others. He'd called his wife to reassure her their family was outside the impact zone, but what he couldn't tell her was they had no way to predict the scale of destruction multiple impacts across thousands of kilometers would have on Earth's surface. The best reference they had was the Shoemaker-Levy 9 collision with Jupiter late last century, although the gas giant's immense gravity had broken the comet into pieces no larger than two kilometers long. By contrast, the Infiltrator's protective acceleration field had shielded Pinaka from Earth's gravity until almost the end, causing its individual pieces to be larger, and thanks to the Infiltrator's deceleration, considerably slower than Shoemaker. Even so, NASA's deep space Ground Network was now tracking six fragments spread out in a slowly lengthening line that was steadily reducing the chances of a successful deflection by a single detonation.

Pearce knew if Pinaka hit, there would be no fairytale recovery. The greatest danger would come, not from earthquakes and tsunamis, but from the increased volcanism such an impact would cause and from the enormous quantities of material thrown into the atmosphere. If enough particles saturated the upper atmosphere, Earth could quickly become a dark and cold wasteland that would cause the global food chain to collapse. In six months, the human race would have consumed its food supply and would face starvation on a planetary scale. By then, the only food left would be other humans, but even cannibalism wouldn't save Earth's billions of inhabitants. It would take years for the volcanic-impact winter to clear and many centuries for the planet to recover, assuming it did not become a mass extinction event.

With the alien stealth ship destroyed, the world now waited and hoped one Russian rocket could deflect the procession of small mountains hurtling toward Earth like a string of glowing pearls in the sky. If the intercept was successful, life on Earth would go on as before. If it failed, humanity would be forced to endure a planetary cataclysm unlike any it had ever known.

The stark realization that the attack had been launched far beyond the reach of the most powerful Earth militaries had emphasized how vulnerable non-space faring humanity was to any interstellar species. To a human race with no knowledge of galactic affairs or of the relationships between great interstellar powers, there was no way to determine what political factors decided mankind's safety.

All Pearce and Franklin could do was watch and listen as Mission Control engineers monitoring the Russian rocket began announcing each major milestone.

"The Russians have recalculated the detonation point."

"The four second burn was successful, they're on target for Fragment Four."

"Target acquired on spacecraft radar."

"Three minutes forty to optimal firing position."

"GN has fragment spread at twenty one thousand meters and increasing."

"That's too big!"

"Baikonur have transmitted the arming code."

"Fragment Four just calved. That's seven pieces now."

"JPL confirm Fragments One and Two will bounce off the atmosphere."

"JAXA have downgraded their estimate of a Pacific impact."

"The European Space Agency are predicting Fragment Three will land seventy kilometers west of Winnipeg. JPL concur."

"Vostochny declare Fragment Six, I mean Seven, is now outside the warhead's effect radius."

Wade Franklin and Hamilton Pearce exchanged worried looks. It was what they'd been fearing since Pinaka began to calve, that a single blast could not deflect all of the fragments.

"Where's Seven coming down?" Franklin asked.

"The last estimate was Sinkiang from the Chinese," Pearce replied, "but that's way outside JPL's predictions."

"It could be worse. It could have been the Pacific," Franklin said, fearing the destruction an oceanic impact would inflict upon densely populated coastlines.

"I sure hope the Japanese are right," Pearce said.

The Payloads Officer announced, "The Russians have passed weapon control to the spacecraft's radar proximity detonator."

Mission Control became hushed as all eyes focused on the giant screens dominating the main wall. The central screen displayed course plots of the seven comet fragments relative to a blinking marker representing the Russian spacecraft as it crawled toward the intercept point. Either side of the main screen were live feeds from Baikonur Control and Vostochny Cosmodrome, both showing intensely focused engineers and scientists, along with real time updates from the Hubble and Webb space telescopes. All of the images were beamed live around the world, making it the most watched event in human history.

"Ten seconds," the Payloads Officer said, having just received confirmation from his Russian counterpart.

Franklin glanced at a wall clock. "This is it."

"Pray there isn't a second ship out there," Pearce said in a low voice.

"If there was, the Russian spacecraft would already be dead."

Live audio from Vostochny came in, counting down in Russian from five, " Pyat, chetyhree, tree, dvah, ahdeen..."

In Mission Control, in the two Russian control centers and everywhere in the world, mankind held its collective breath. Confusion spread as no one knew if the mission had succeeded or not, then one excited female voice suddenly proclaimed to the world.

"Detonatsiya podtverdil! Detonatsiya podtverdil!"

Nervous teams in Baikonur and Vostochny began clapping and hugging each other, then an engineer in Mission Control got the translation.

"Detonation confirmed!"

Muted cheers and applause erupted across the room, although the tension barely lightened. Soon the celebration died down as the anxious wait began for an assessment of the effect of the blast. In the Russian centers too, the engineers quieted down as they waited for news of the new Pinaka course plots. Hubble and Webb images began coming in of a brilliant white ball of light expanding against the blackness of space, then ground based telescope images of a new star in the sky appeared on the world's screens, masking the presence of the Pinaka fragments.

The International Space Station half a world away caught part of the explosion as it bloomed out from behind the Earth. The detonation had been timed to occur close to the center of mass of the line of comet fragments, generating a blast wave that would nudge them away from Earth. Using a blast wave rather than a direct impact greatly reduced the risk of shattering the comet into additional pieces which would have rained destruction over more of the Earth's surface.

Seconds turned to agonizing minutes while observations were turned into data by dozens of space agencies, observatories and universities around the world, then their results were painstakingly compared and checked for errors. While the world waited, mankind's greatest minds and most powerful computers crunched numbers, checked and rechecked calculations, then submitted their results to the Jet Propulsion Laboratory in Pasadena for the final decision.

Wade Franklin's telephone rang as the head of JPL called him directly. He listened, nodding and taking notes, then lifted his pad as every eye and television camera focused upon him. "JPL estimate the velocities of Fragments One through Five has increased one point seven to two point four percent. According to their calculations, Fragments One, Two and Three will miss the Earth entirely. Four and Five will bounce off the upper atmosphere." He cleared his throat uncomfortably. "The velocity of Fragment Six has decreased one point five percent. The velocity of Fragment Seven has not been affected. Both fragments will enter the Earth's atmosphere in nine minutes."

"Oh God," Hamilton Pearce said, placing his hands on his head.

"Do they know where they're going to hit?" an engineer asked.

Franklin shook his head slowly. "They don't have precise impact points calculated yet. It'll be somewhere between Africa and northwest Canada. They're working it out now." He dropped his notepad on the table and stared at the screens despondently.

"The Atlantic's ground zero." Hamilton Pearce whispered in horror. "If just one of those things hits the ocean …"

"I know." Franklin nodded. "Super tsunamis

thousands of feet high will wipe out the East Coast …
and there's not a damn thing we can do about it."

\* \* \* \*

Pinaka Fragments Six and Seven entered the upper
atmosphere over southeast Africa. They followed a flat
trajectory barely half a degree below the angle that
would have caused both fragments to bounce off the
atmosphere. The oblique approach allowed the thin
exosphere time to slow and heat both fragments as their
altitude dropped below a thousand kilometers.

Soon the Pinaka fragments were venting gas as they
raced in tandem over the southern Sahara, becoming a
pair of stars so bright they filled the night with an eerie
illumination. When they reached the north west coast of
Africa, Spanish television in the Canary Islands beamed
grainy images of the two brilliant fireballs to the world.
Spellbound, billions watched the twins hurtle out over
the Atlantic on a shallow trajectory as they slid into the
thickening atmosphere. Behind each were growing
superheated tails of gas and dust, drawing a glowing
white scar across the night sky.

The two fragments began to break apart as they
approached the mid-Atlantic, battered by atmospheric
pressure and from intense heat caused by frictional drag.
Each fragment's surface area expanded, creating
hypervelocity shock waves and temperatures not seen
inside the atmosphere in three quarters of a million
years. The superheated air tried to expand, to cool itself,
but couldn't because the fragment's velocities were too
high, forcing the temperatures to continue rising. With a
wall of trapped heat before them, the dazzling white orbs
grew enormously in size and intensity as they streaked
across the sky, losing altitude.

In the North Atlantic, ships at sea watched the twin
fireballs pass above them, feeling the heat radiating
down as Six and Seven punched into the troposphere, the

thickest layer of the atmosphere. Hypersonic booms shattered windows and deafened crews in the ships below and began to disturb the ocean itself as a great swathe of the night sky appeared to burn.

Soon, the twins approached the terminator between day and night, dwarfing the rising sun with their brilliance and blinding any who looked directly at them. Clouds boiled away before them, then when barely six kilometers above the sea and less than a thousand kilometers from Nova Scotia, Fragment Six exploded. It was followed a moment later by Seven when it crashed into Six's blast wave. In a tremendous flash, the infernal twins coalesced into a large aerial burst, a single enormous fireball of ablated cometary matter and ionized air exceeding two thousand degrees centigrade. The hypersonic monster continued its shallow dive toward the coast, vaporizing the ocean and incinerating every ship in its path.

From the shore, it seemed as if the atmosphere itself was on fire from horizon to horizon, although observers on the coast had barely a moment to see it before it was upon them. The enormous fireball flashed across the coast south of Halifax, raced over northern Maine to Quebec City, melting all in its path.

Superheated air rolled out either side of the melt zone, setting the forests of New Brunswick to the east and towns and cities to the west from Portland to Montreal ablaze. Supersonic hurricanes swept over the land, fanning the heat like a blast furnace as the large aerial burst carved a swathe of destruction across Quebec Province toward northern Ontario, liquefying soil and rock in an instant.

The large size of the Pinaka fragments caused the thermal effects to far outweigh the blast damage, while the deadly combination of energy and momentum created a line explosion that tore across the countryside at hypersonic velocity, incinerating everything in its path. Much of the momentum that blasted up from the atmospheric plume was blocked by the thick atmosphere above and reflected back down in a reactionary impulse that struck the ground so hard, it triggered seismic effects detected thousands of kilometers away.

Less than a minute later, the Pinaka super-fireball reached the Manitoba coast of Hudson Bay where it began to dim as it ploughed into freezing northern airs, then as it crossed the Arctic province of Nunavut, it dissipated. In its wake was a four thousand kilometer long river of lava, two hundred kilometers wide, all the way to the Atlantic coast. On each side of the molten river, firestorms a hundred kilometers wide burned furiously, creating an impenetrable wall of flame that filled the sky with choking black smoke. There had been no ground impact, no crater, no shock wave through the planet, no mountain of debris hurled into the air, only a vast wall of heat so intense, it turned the land into black glass.

There was no way to count the dead, as the Pinaka Burst had cremated every living thing in its path. Only the great inferno remained and would burn unchecked for weeks until it was eventually extinguished by rain and snow.

* * * *

The first news reports reached the *Naturaliste* soon after a repair team established a jury rigged satellite link atop the bridge. The screens in the communications room filled with confused reports of the two Pinaka fragments and of the destruction wrought by the colossal fireball they became. Images from the edges of the largest fire in recorded history flashed across the screens, while radiant heat prevented all but the highest flying aircraft from approaching. The military aircraft that did fly toward the central melt zone could not see the ground through the smoke or risk a direct over flight for fear of fouling their engines in the clouds of ash that rose more than forty kilometers into the atmosphere.

From space, the International Space Station sent pictures of the thick smoke plume spreading from eastern Canada across the North Atlantic while infra-red satellites revealed an intense thermal zone at ground level peaking at over a thousand degrees centigrade running from Maine to Hudson Bay. On the ground, Canadian and American emergency teams tried to save those on the edges of an inferno they had no hope of putting out. It would be weeks before the heat receded enough for anyone to enter the linear explosion zone itself.

"I don't understand. It never hit the ground," Beckman said, struggling to comprehend how a continent sized firestorm could be raging in eastern North America.

"It was a large aerial burst," Dr. McInness said. "Really two bursts in one."

"It looks like a line of fire across the country," Reynolds said.

"That's because it didn't dive vertically into the ground, but flew horizontally," the scientist said, demonstrating with his hands. "The flat trajectory spread the damage over a long straight area beneath its flight path."

"I've never heard of such a thing," Teresa said.

"Large aerial bursts aren't as famous as dinosaur killing asteroids, but they're more common," he said. "A large aerial burst big enough to destroy a city hits the planet once every hundred years. Chelyabinsk in Russia was a near miss by a small one. Something this big isn't as common. The last really big one hit Earth seven hundred and eighty thousand years ago. We're standing in the middle of that blast zone right now. It destroyed an area over eight thousand kilometers long from China to southern Australia."

"That's twice the size of this one!" Teresa exclaimed.

"We deflected most of Pinaka," Dr. McInness said.

"A space program does make a difference, Hamilton Pearce was right about that."

"If there's no crater," Beckman said, "how do you know about the other one?"

"These bursts are so hot, they create melt sheets that break into little black rocks called tektites. We can map the size of the tektite sheet to calculate the size of the blast zone. Considering how big the Australasian Burst was, we got off lightly."

"Lightly!" Reynolds said. "It killed millions!"

Dr. McInness nodded sadly. "I know, but the others tell us it could have been much worse."

"Others?" Beckman said. "How many others?"

"Five big ones in the last thirty five million years," Dr. McInness said. "The oldest incinerated an area from present day Texas all the way to Georgia. Another turned the entire Libyan desert into glass. Central Europe and the Ivory Coast have also been hit, but the Australasian event was the biggest by far. The damage from one of these events is orders of magnitude greater than anything nuclear weapons can do."

"This was bad enough," Beckman said, wondering how many millions had lost their lives. He glanced at Kermit sitting on the deck handcuffed to a table. The alien was staring at the small screen, observing the destruction, well aware the humans had suffered a heavy loss and survived.

Teresa followed Beckman's gaze. "What are you thinking, Colonel?"

"That was their last shot. Now we have to make sure not one of them gets out of this place alive."

"Bob," Dr. McInness said. "We've won. Do you really want to commit genocide?"

"It's not genocide. It's survival. Ours not theirs." He turned to Lt. Commander Reynolds. "We should tell them to gas the island. There could be survivors hiding in those caves. They've got to forget about us and finish the job. We can keep the ship sealed up." He said sniffing the musty air. "We've still got hours of breathable air."

There was silence in the communications room as Reynolds considered Beckman's advice, then he said, "Get me HQJOC ... and pray the sea breeze is blowing the right way."

* * * *

Beloved-of-the-Sea sat on a rock ledge on the northern side of Marchinbar Island in the early evening. The moon and stars allowed her to see the mast of HMAS *Naturaliste* in the distance, protruding above a headland. A human engineer wearing a full body orange fire suit was suspended high on the mast by a cable as he worked to repair a damaged aerial while a searchlight swept the water around the ship for an attack that would not come. She knew they were signs the humans were rapidly recovering from the assault, and worse, was an indicator of their drive and energy.

Further out to sea, the corpses that had choked Hopeful Bay all day were now being carried away by the tide. Hundreds of bodies floated off the island as scavenger birds swooped on them and one-fin-killers tore at their rotting flesh. In the sheltered waters on the other side of the island, the destruction was even worse. Everything that had lived there was now dead. The bodies of one-fin-killers, of thousands of brightly colored fish, of red shelled bottom-crawlers whose white flesh she was particularly fond of, and of countless seabirds, all floated lifelessly in the calm waters of the Mothersea. Whatever the humans were spraying had turned a once fertile marine paradise teeming with life into a poisoned, lifeless desert.

Now that she had seen for herself the heavy price they'd paid to achieve so little, she realized she had underestimated the lengths to which her human enemies would go in order to exterminate her kind. It was nothing less than she herself would have done if given the chance.

*They are dangerous,* she thought. At least, in that, she'd been correct.

She glanced along the rocks to where handfuls of survivors were gathering beneath scrawny trees and scrub. There would be more, marooned on other islands and on the mainland, unable to enter the water for fear of the toxins that ate through their skin and burned their eyes to blindness.

A dull drone sounded in the distance, although she couldn't at first see its source. Only when the aircraft drew near could she pick out its silhouette against the stars as it came in low from the south.

Prowls-the-Shallows appeared beside her. "It's one of the sprayers," he said, lifting her off the ground without further explanation.

"Where are you taking me?"

"The headland," he said, hurrying toward a finger of land jutting to the north. "The sea wind will blow it away from us."

She could have limped, but she would have been too slow, so she allowed him to carry her without complaint. Some of the other survivors went into the water, keeping their sonar lobes dry to avoid the acoustic assault that reverberated through the sea for hundreds of kilometers in every direction. The toxin had been sprayed mostly south of the island, partly because there were few sonic traces to the north and partly to protect the *Naturaliste*, but now the island itself was coming under attack, further reducing their safe havens.

By the time they reached the northern tip of the headland, the Chinese PLAAF transport plane was spraying red mist over the island. The chemical weapon hung in the air as it filtered down through the collapsed caverns into the ruined caves below. The amphibians could hold their breath for hours, but they could not avoid the burns the mist inflicted upon their skin and eyes, so they swam away from the island or sheltered on points out of reach of the toxic mist.

Prowls set her down against a tree from where she watched the human aircraft in the distance heading for Cape Wessel. She didn't know how many survivors there were, but this latest attack upon their last refuge would cut deeply into their dwindling numbers.

The red mist settled between the trees and for a moment she smelt a pungent odor that reviled her senses, then the sea breeze pushed it away. She dared not breath for several minutes, then her eyes wandered over the sea. With the sonic barrier preventing their escape underwater to the north and the Mothersea to the south now poisoned, her hopes of spawning were fading.

She heard heated whispers and turned to see Watcher-of-Skies and Prowls-the-Shallows arguing in hushed tones, clearly in violent disagreement. When they looked at her, she motioned for them to approach.

"What is it?" she asked.

Prowls was slow in answering. "My brother believes the humans have destroyed the comet."

"There should have been an earthquake by now," Watcher said. "The seas should be receding before giant waves." He pointed to the tranquil waters to the north, proving his case.

"Yes," she said with clear understanding. "It is over. Even spawning will not save us now."

"There is another way," Watcher said cautiously, "but it will not be to your liking, Beloved."

She gave them a puzzled look. "A way to defeat the humans, even now?"

"No Beloved," Prowls said, "a way to survive."

With the Infiltrator gone, the comet destroyed and the Mothersea a poisonous graveyard, she saw no way out, but Watcher was the most brilliant of all her brothers, so she turned to him with a glimmer of hope.

"What way, my brother?"

* * * *

The hand held radio on the communications console crackled, then a series of high pitched tones sounded. Lt. Commander Reynolds picked up the two-way, listening curiously as the tones repeated, exactly as before. "It's not interference," he said uncertainly, "and it's not Morse."

"It's repeating," Beckman said, "some kind of signal."

"It's their language!" Teresa said fascinated, never having heard Kermit utter a word.

"They must know we don't understand it," Reynolds said.

"We don't, but he does." Beckman said, nodding at Kermit who was transfixed by the two-way in Reynolds' hand. "Teresa, get your computer." He lifted Kermit to his feet, then when she placed the computer on the table in front of him, he motioned at the keyboard. "Translate."

Kermit listened to the message once more, then raised his cuffed hands and began one finger pecking at the keyboard. Slowly, five lines of numbers, letters and symbols appeared on screen, as incomprehensible as the alien tones sounding from the two-way.

Beckman stared at the screen with rising irritation. "It's gibberish!"

Teresa studied the message, initially puzzled, then with a look of astonishment, exclaimed, "Oh my God!"

"You can read that?" Reynolds asked.

"I'm a mathematician." She squinted at the formulas, adding, "Not that I fully understand it, but … wow."

"Wow?" Beckman repeated curiously.

"Sir, they've solved the Navier-Stokes equations!" she said, scarcely able to believe her eyes.

"They've done what?"

"It's turbulence, fluid dynamics, one of the greatest unsolved problems in all of mathematics. I'm not qualified to say if they're right or not, but … they could be."

Understanding flashed across Dr. McInness' face. "Yes, that's it!"

"We just nuked their asses," Beckman said. "Why are they giving us math problems?"

"Not problems, sir, solutions," Teresa said. "If you ever wanted to build a submarine that could travel at supersonic speed underwater in complete silence, or fly a jet twenty times the speed of sound without making a sonic boom," she pointed to the equations on the screen, "you need to know that."

Beckman glanced at Dr. McInness who smiled, shaking his head in disbelief. "She's right, Bob. They've cracked turbulence."

Kermit finished typing, then stepped back and pointed to the last two words he'd typed at the bottom of the screen.

WE SURRENDER.

When Beckman saw the message, he shook his head. "They just killed millions of our people. There's no surrender."

"Bob," the scientist said, "that's not your call." He glanced at the screen. "Not now."

"The hell it isn't."

"No," Dr. McInness said firmly. "It really isn't. They're offering to work for us, if we let them live."

"No way!" Reynolds snapped. "They killed Captain Turner and a third of my crew! We have to finish them off."

"Colonel," Teresa said slowly, "if they can solve turbulence, there's no telling what else they can do. That's what they're saying. They're worth more to us alive than dead."

Beckman hesitated, staring at a screen full of equations he didn't understand. "Apart from submarines and supersonic aircraft, how important is this stuff, really?"

Dr. McInness stared into the distance as he imagined the possibilities. "The great theoretical physicist, Werner Heisenberg, once said that when he met God he'd ask two questions: 'Why relativity? And why turbulence?' Heisenberg said he really believed God would have an answer for the first question."

Beckman stared at Dr. McInness skeptically. "Did he really say that?" he asked, hardly able to believe swirling water was a tougher problem than relativity.

The scientist nodded. "Turbulence is the last unsolved mystery of Newtonian physics, Newton's second law. It's one of the greatest unsolved problems in all of science. They know the answer and we don't." He pointed emphatically at the screen. "I want whoever wrote that equation in my lab, on my team. And if you believe in what we've been doing all these years, you do too."

"They don't even have computers," Beckman said exasperated, "except what they stole from us."

"They don't need them," Teresa said. "They have evolution on their side."

"It's the best offer we're ever going to get, Bob," Dr. McInness said, "better than any derelict alien equipment we'll ever recover."

Teresa nodded. "I agree, Colonel."

Reynolds glared at her. "You're the one who said there'd be millions of them if they ever got out."

"Yes," she conceded, "there could be. We'll have to keep the females separate from the males, control their numbers, let them breed only enough to stay viable as a species."

"That's crazy," Reynolds said. "They tried to wipe us out."

"They failed," Dr. McInness said. "Now we have a choice. Exterminate them or–"

"Turn them into German rocket scientists," Beckman said.

"What?" Reynolds asked.

"After World War Two, we took Nazi rocket scientists and landed on the moon." Beckman fixed his gaze upon Kermit, imagining the possibilities. "Who knows where we can land with them on our team."

"The Germans and the Japanese were our enemies once," Teresa said, "Now they're our friends. Our allies."

Beckman sighed reluctantly, his mind made up. "I'll call the President."

* * * *

*Naturaliste's* three survey boats motored in line ahead off the north coast of Marchinbar Island toward Lagoon Bay, an aquamarine expanse of shallow water lapping a stretch of pure white sand several kilometers long. Barren rocky headlands embraced the beach at each end and sickly trees close to a toxic death stretched away behind the sand. Inland, every shred of greenery had already fallen from the dying forest that was quickly becoming a barren wasteland.

The first motor boat flying the Australian white ensign and carrying a squad of heavily armed soldiers nosed into the beach, then Beckman jumped onto the sand and started warily toward the tree line. The troops spread out behind him, aiming their weapons at the pitiful line of amphibian survivors waiting up the beach. The soldiers had strict instructions not to fire unless Beckman himself gave the order or was killed by the aliens.

The other two launches came into the beach either side of the first, disembarking more soldiers who extended the firing line in both directions. Once the soldiers were in position, Dr. McInness clambered off the first boat with Teresa and Kermit, who no longer wore handcuffs, although a guard stood behind him at all times ready to shoot if he made a hostile move. Teresa carried her laptop under her arm while Dr. McInness, having dispensed with his arm's sling, mopped sweat from his brow.

Two kilometers off shore, a dozen US Viper helicopter gunships circled the bay, staying far enough from the beach to avoid provoking a fight, but ready to come in fast if the shore party were attacked. Beyond the attack helicopters, three warships were visible on the horizon with their five inch guns aimed at the beach. They'd been there for an hour, studying the bay through binoculars while the United Nations Fleet beyond the horizon watched live UAV streams of the beach.

Sitting on the sand was a ragged line of more than a hundred amphibians. Some showed signs of wounds from falling rocks, of terrible flash burns from nuclear blasts while a few coughed and wheezed with weeping eyes from the chemicals that had been dumped on them. Some were close to death and would not survive while a few appeared to be in good health.

The meeting had been arranged via a halting radio conversation, with Kermit translating for Beckman on behalf of the UN Security Council and Prowls-the-Shallows speaking on behalf of his matriarch. Beckman wore a sidearm, but kept it holstered, while none of the amphibians were armed. He'd ordered them to discard their weapons before coming to the meeting or risk being shot on sight. During the morning, UAVs circling above the beach had confirmed the aliens hobbling out of the dying forest were following his orders to the letter.

Dr. McInness hurried across the scorchingly hot sand to catch up to Beckman, unable to take his eyes off the ragtag collection of alien survivors. They sat or lay on the sand watching Beckman approach, wondering at their fate.

"Are you sure about this?" Beckman asked.

"Honestly, no," the scientist replied, wearily rubbing his temple as another migraine pounded inside his skull, "but we've got to give them a chance."

When Teresa came up with Kermit in tow, Beckman

asked, "So who do I talk to?"

She resisted the urge to point, nodding toward a small group of five amphibians sitting in the middle. Three were larger than the others, one of whom had a congealed head wound. "I'm guessing their species is sexually dimorphic. That would make those three larger ones female. They're in charge."

"They're not in charge," Beckman said sharply. "I am." He sighed. "But I'll talk to them."

He signaled for Kermit's guard to stay where he was, then motioned for the amphibian to follow him up the beach to where the three females sat. When they stopped in front of the group of five, watched by the soldiers and the other surviving amphibians, Beckman noticed the five aliens were all focused on Teresa.

"Am I imagining it," he said, "or do they think you're the leader?"

Teresa smiled embarrassed. "I'm sure they'll figure it out, sir."

"So now what?" he asked uncomfortably.

"We talk," she said, then sat cross legged on the sand and opened her computer, motioning for Kermit to sit beside her. "What do you want to say?"

"Tell them we accept their surrender on the condition that there are no conditions."

Teresa typed, *Do you surrender unconditionally?*

Kermit read the message aloud in his own language. The female with the head wound replied for all of them, then he typed Beloved's response.

*We do.*

Teresa glanced up at Beckman. "Now what?"

"Tell her we'll provide them with food and medical care. A sanctuary will be created at the northern end of this island where they'll remain under guard. They will not breed without our permission. The females and males will be separated and will not be allowed to meet except when we allow it. They will have no access to the world beyond this area. Everyone of them will be fitted with tracking devices they will be unable to remove. If they leave this area, they will be killed." That was the gist of what the President had decided and would take to the Security Council for ratification, although preliminary talks with other world leaders had already confirmed agreement would be a formality. "Oh yeah, and whoever worked out that turbulence thingy now works for us – and as many others as we want. Plus anything else we think of later."

Teresa typed quickly then Kermit read the demands to Beloved-of-the-Sea. There was no discussion on the other side. She simply answered for all of them. Kermit dutifully typed her response which Teresa read aloud.

"They accept, sir. There are seven males who have some kind of ... gift. They will work for us. They know things we don't." Teresa shrugged. "I guess she means they're the smartest ones."

Beckman turned to Dr. McInness. "There you are, Ian, seven super-Einsteins to join your team. Hope you can keep up."

The scientist grinned. "Me too."

"The others stay here," Beckman said, looking past bleached sand and dying trees to the baking rock plateau beyond. "Hell of a place to spend the rest of their lives."

The Security Council had agreed to turn the northern end of the Wessel Islands into a reservation. Its isolation would allow the amphibians to be quarantined from the rest of humanity, most of whom wanted them put to death, while the nearby waters would be sewn with sonar listening arrays to track their every move. Further out in the Arafura Sea, an acoustic barrier would be created to force escaping amphibians to the surface where naval patrols would then shoot them.

Cleanup crews would spray dispersants to dissolve the toxins polluting the islands and surrounding waters, although it would take decades for the sea life to recover. The amphibians would be dependent on external food supplies for many years to come, but eventually they'd be able to hunt again in what would become the Wessel Islands Sanctuary, the first alien enclave on Earth. At least that's what the politicians were euphemistically calling it.

*More like a concentration camp*, Beckman thought, but it was the only offer they were going to get.

In a few months, watch towers would be built along Marchinbar Island and out on the surrounding reefs. The collapsed caverns would be excavated and turned into habitats with modest amenities. Its inhabitants would lead meaningless lives whose only purpose was to provide a steady trickle of scientists and engineers to US black projects. That last part was never shared with the UN Security Council. It was a secret known only to a President, a Prime Minister and very few others. As far as the rest of the world knew, the enemy had simply surrendered and the last few survivors would be imprisoned for life. It would be decades before mankind realized the defeated aliens had been allowed to maintain a small, but stable population.

"They'll be under a microscope for the rest of their lives," Dr. McInness said.

"Longer than that," Beckman declared. "Until Hell freezes over."

The tracking devices to be fitted around their necks would be unbreakable and tracked globally by satellite. Every move any one of them made would be monitored twenty-four seven. They'd never know each tracking device carried an explosive that could be detonated remotely if they broke the deal or a decision was made to terminate the arrangement. Once fitted, the patrolling ships, the acoustic barrier and the watch towers would all be redundant, intended only to hide the true nature of the neck bands from the inmates.

"Is there anything else, Colonel?" Teresa asked.

Beckman looked at the three females sitting on the sand. "We'll make up the rest as we go along." He held his radio to his lips. "Beckman here. The deal is done.

Send in the food and medical teams. All forces remain on station until further notice."

He noticed the female with the head wound was staring at him. He couldn't read her expression, yet he sensed her defiance. "She doesn't look defeated."

"How can you tell?" Dr. McInness asked.

"Just a feeling," he said. "Ask them how many females survived?

After a quick exchange, Teresa read out Beloved's answer. "Three, that they know of."

"Three's enough," he said pessimistically, annoyed by Beloved's unwavering stare.

"She's worked out you're in charge," Teresa said. "She's curious about you, Colonel."

"She gives me the creeps," Beckman said, glancing at the other two females and the males scattered along the beach idly watching them. "She's the only one that does."

"Why is that, Colonel?" Teresa asked.

Beckman thought about his answer for a long time, sensing malice in Beloved's unwavering gaze. "Because if it had gone the other way, she wouldn't have been as generous to us."

"You don't know that," Dr. McInness protested.

Beckman met Beloved's cold stare, certain he was right. He had a terrible feeling mankind was making a colossal mistake letting her live, fearing they wouldn't be so lucky next time, but there was nothing he could do about it now.

"God help us if her relatives ever come looking for her," he said fatalistically, then headed back to the navy launch to make his report.

# CHAPTER NINE: CONVERGENCE

Three weeks after the Pinaka Super Burst, Beckman and Teresa landed in an unmarked civilian aircraft at a remote grass airstrip in the mountains of central Idaho, far from the prying eyes permanently camped outside Area 51. They wore plain clothes, carried backpacks and if asked, would declare themselves to be hikers out for a few days in the wilderness. They were met by a pair of men dressed like lumberjacks, although the thick coats and heavy boots barely disguised their military bearing.

"Welcome Colonel," one of the lumberjacks said without saluting, then showed them to a mud splattered SUV. It looked like a typical hunting vehicle, except for the scrambler equipped radio and bullpup style automatic weapons concealed below the dashboard.

"Is it far?" Teresa asked.

"It's about an hour to the farm, ma'am," the driver said as they headed off down a dirt track through the alpine forest.

The graded track appeared to be little used, yet every now and then Beckman noticed concrete reinforcements had been added to make it accessible to heavy vehicles. They never passed another car or saw any sign of human activity until they rounded a corner and stopped in front of a high chain link fence and locked gates. A solitary guard in a dark green park ranger's uniform emerged from a simple log building with a large carved wooden sign mounted on the wall facing the track.

Forestry Research Center,
US Department of Agriculture
No Admittance

The ranger approached the car, nodded to the driver whom he knew by sight, but who nevertheless flashed his ID, then the ranger remotely activated the motorized gates. Watched by surveillance cameras hidden in the forest, they passed through the entrance, following another well maintained dirt road which became sealed once they were out of sight of the sentry post. Six kilometers from the fence, they reached a cluster of single story wooden buildings emblazoned with Department of Agriculture signage positioned to be easily visible from the air. Beyond the forestry buildings, partially obscured by trees, was a collection of gray walled barns facing a high roofed structure on thin poles stacked with trimmed tree trunks. In front of the lumber store was a tractor with log lifting claws positioned to reassure any unauthorized over flight that it was a sleepy facility serving Idaho's logging industry.

They didn't stop at the reception area, but continued on to the row of barns and parked in front of Building Two. None of the barns had windows, although all had large roller doors beside small side entrances.

Their driver climbed out and approached a plain gray metal box concealing a card reader, then swiped his security card to access the side door. He showed Beckman and Teresa inside to a cavernous space with polished white floors, spotlessly clean metal walls and floodlights suspended from the high ceiling. Yellow lines marked out large squares on the gleaming floor, defining the physical extent of individual project spaces.

At the center of each square was either a recovered alien artifact surrounded by a small group of white coated scientists and engineers or unidentified objects covered with white sheets awaiting the next stage of analysis. Surrounding the project spaces were arrays of computer screens, sensing devices, elevated platforms, white boards with team notes and pristine white tables containing disassembled equipment removed from that project area's artifact.

"I wondered where this stuff went," Teresa whispered to Beckman as they started down the central aisle between the reverse engineering project areas.

"I couldn't tell you," he whispered back. "We want the UFO-nuts to think it's all still at Area 51. Stops them looking for this place."

"And the black suits keep watching the nuts so they think they're close," Teresa said, well aware of the aggressive patrolling that took place outside the Groom Lake perimeter.

"Exactly."

Halfway across the floor, they passed a disk shaped craft with a third of its hull torn away. A small hatch was open in the hull through which cables ran to power spotlights and equipment inside. A white coated scientist crouched to step out through the hatch onto a platform suspended alongside the craft. He was followed by a shorter figure wearing a parka with an oversized hood, although his streamlined amphibian face and bulging blue-green eyes were clearly visible.

Beckman and Teresa stopped and stared at Watcher-of-Skies, who wore a small black vocalizer over his mouth. The device had been hastily prepared to allow the amphibians to communicate verbally, although the team developing the amphibian-human translation program still had a long way to go. It would be two years before the devices enabled the amphibians to speak plainly to their human counterparts and another five before it could efficiently handle the technical terminology. Even so, the crude vocalizer was a marked improvement on laboriously typing messages.

The scientist spoke slowly as he motioned to the recovered spacecraft, pausing when Watcher indicated his instructor had used a human word he did not yet understand. The language learning process was cumbersome, although Watcher and the other gifted males' capacity to learn far exceeded the rate at which they were being taught. In a few months, they would master written and audible English, although the slow pace of information exchange would never fully be resolved to their satisfaction.

"They all sound like Stephen Hawking," Beckman whispered to Teresa. "Ian insisted."

Teresa smiled. "He always was a fan."

Watcher glanced at them from the elevated platform, showing no sign of recognition. He'd already decided his new home was not truly a prison, even though he would never have the freedom to leave it. To his surprise the scientists and engineers, who had initially been wary and curious of him and his brothers, were increasingly treating them like colleagues rather than slaves. He found their willingness to accept his contribution gratifying, while the many technological puzzles they were trying to solve fascinated him in a way nothing else in his life had. The unexpected acceptance by the human scientists was rapidly transforming his view of their defeat, making him wonder if an unlikely partnership might not actually benefit both sides more than the total extinction of one would the other. It was something Beloved and the other females would never fully accept, but it was no longer their decision – a fact he was secretly grateful for.

The greatest surprise of all was the strange human capacity to seemingly forget that only weeks before, he and his kind had tried to exterminate them. The humans had no knowledge of the plan to shift the planet's crust or of the power the Infiltrator's trans-galactic engines had to produce such a cataclysm. It was simply something they hadn't conceived and would never be told of.

He and his brothers let them believe the plan had been to simply crash a comet into the planet causing catastrophic damage to human civilization and creating a volcanic winter that would have starved humanity into submission. It was a story that was receiving growing acceptance around the world, even if no government had confirmed a link between Pinaka and the aliens. As far as the world was concerned, the human race had defeated the greatest threat it had ever faced, which was true, although mankind never understood the real nature of that threat.

Watcher suspected the human capacity for forgiveness might even be an aspect of their warlike natures. He knew enough of their history to understand their past was as violent as was his people's – if not as long – but unlike the Intruders, humans waged ruthless war upon each other then forgave their enemies when war ended. It made no sense to Watcher. His own kind had fought wars of revenge for millennia, until one faction had achieved final victory over all others. Such a victory had always involved the victors exterminating the other side's females, thus removing the controlling force over the defeated males. It was a survival strategy humans could not follow. Forgiveness, rather than extermination, seemed more advantageous from an evolutionary perspective, although both approaches achieved the same outcome. They defined how an aggressive predator species managed the conclusion of its intra-species conflicts.

For Watcher, he was resigned to the prospect of never again swimming in the Mothersea, of feeling the heat of its tropical sun or tasting the freshness of its food. Nevertheless, he suspected he might find another kind of contentment here, even if he hated the cool mountain air.

Watcher turned back to his tutor without

acknowledging Beckman and listened attentively as the human scientist explained why the reverse engineering of the Roswell wreck had stalled. Watcher had already discovered the Infiltrator gift contained many helpful theoretical answers, but was frustratingly lacking in detailed engineering solutions for superluminal propulsion, energy generation, acceleration fields and a hundred other technologies necessary for interstellar flight. It seemed the Infiltrator had considered such knowledge to be far too sensitive to share. Watcher realized these were puzzles he and his human counterparts would have to solve together, without the help of Intruder technology.

"This way, sir," their driver said, motioning for Beckman and Teresa to follow.

They continued along the carefully marked path, past six more reverse engineering teams, each with a single amphibian assigned to it. They entered an elevator at the far side of the building with a control panel showing ten subterranean levels, indicating there was far more of the facility below ground than above. They took the elevator up one level to a glassed off gallery overlooking the project floor. It ran along one wall of the building and gave access to the research center's theater-like conference facility. Small groups stood whispering and sipping coffee before the planning session was due to begin. Everyone wore plain clothes, even the obvious military types, although the majority were technical people. Dr. McInness was chatting with three project leads when he saw Beckman and Teresa step off the elevator. He excused himself and came over to greet them.

"Hi Bob, Teresa," he said. "Glad you could make it."

"Wouldn't miss it," Beckman said dryly. "I take it we're not detonating the trackers?"

"Definitely not," the scientist replied, shocked at the thought. "They're fulfilling their side of the bargain. They even seem to enjoy it."

"Pity."

Dr. McInness turned and looked out over the main floor at the twenty one high priority projects selected for amphibian involvement. They'd all been subjected to decades of reverse engineering, some with considerable success, but all had eventually run into dead ends. He ran his eye over the seven aliens below, all being brought up to speed on their assigned tasks. "We made the right decision, not exterminating them."

"I hope so," Teresa said.

"They killed millions of our people," Beckman said coldly.

"We killed millions of them," the scientist said evenly.

"We belong here. They don't."

Before they could begin arguing over the value of one intelligent life form over another, Teresa asked, "How many survived?"

"Three females, two hundred and sixty eight males," Dr. McInness replied.

"Enough for them to start breeding again," Beckman said sourly.

"They've already started."

"Who authorized that?" Beckman demanded.

"One of them spawned a week ago. We decided to allow them to fertilize the eggs, to keep the species viable."

Beckman suppressed his anger. "How many eggs?"

"Forty eight thousand, including nine females."

"What!" Beckman exploded, drawing curious looks from across the meeting area.

Dr. McInness gave him a reassuring look. "Relax. We've separated the females. There won't be any more unless we allow it. And you don't have to worry about their big sisters coming to look for them, we searched the Zeta database. They're not in it."

"How can they not be in it?" Beckman asked, knowing the catalogue of alien civilizations they'd downloaded from the crashed Roswell craft had over twenty thousand interstellar civilizations listed.

"Because they're not from around here. I asked Watcher about it–"

"Who?" Beckman asked puzzled.

"EBE Two," Dr. McInness said, pointing to the Roswell wreck Watcher-of-Skies had been assigned to. "Kermit was one. Watcher, that's his name, is Two. He said they're from outside the galaxy, approximately sixty five thousand light years away."

"How does he know that?"

"The shadow ship told him." The scientist gave him a reassuring look. "Their relatives don't even know they're here."

"I hope that's true," Beckman said uneasily, watching the parka clad alien listening to his white coated instructor.

"It might turn out better than you think," Dr. McInness said. "There's a real chance humans and terrestrial amphibians can work together."

"Terrestrial amphibians?"

"Well we couldn't call them Kermits, so I named them."

"Shouldn't they be extraterrestrial amphibians?" Beckman asked.

"Their relatives are, but they live here now, so they're terrestrial," the scientist replied simply as a bell sounded, summoning the attendees to the auditorium. "That's us."

Together, Beckman, Dr. McInness and Teresa joined the other attendees moving toward a pair of open double doors.

"Don't worry," Dr. McInness said, "the military are getting everything they want to control the terrestrial amphibian habitation zone and we've got a green light to run aptitude tests to select more for our program here. It's going to work out."

"Maybe," Beckman said, unconvinced, "but there's one thing you've got to change."

"What's that?"

"Their name. Terrestrial amphibian, it's … too long."

"I kind of like it, and the naming committee approved it."

"I don't."

"Do you have a better idea?"

"Yeah," Beckman said as they reached the door. "Abbreviate it. We'll call them Tamphs."

Visit the author's webpage at:

www.StephenRenneberg.com

If you enjoyed this book, please post a recommendation
and rating on the site where you purchased your copy.

## The Antaran Codex
by
Stephen Renneberg

**This high-octane sci-fi novel is powered by grand-scale action and adventure, larger than life characters, a richly described backdrop and, above all else, relentless pacing**
**Fast and furious fun in humankind's distant future.**
*– Kirkus Reviews*

Two and half thousand years after *The Mothership*, mankind nears its goal of Galactic Citizenship.

Sirius Kade, trader and Earth Intelligence Service deep cover agent, learns that wealthy and powerful leaders from across Mapped Space are vying for control of an alien relic they believe is the key to untold riches – unaware they are being deceived.

Sirius soon finds himself entangled in an interstellar plot to make humanity a cosmic outcast, denying it its place as the newest member of the vast and ancient community that has governed the galaxy for eons.

With mankind's fate in the balance, Sirius must overcome ruthless alien adversaries and deadly human rivals as he seeks to discover the secret of *The Antaran Codex* and safeguard man's future among the stars.

ISBN: 978-0-9874347-9-1

## In Earth's Service
by
Stephen Renneberg

**Utterly Satisfying. A sci-fi novel that offers a
relentlessly paced, action-packed, and undeniably
epic in scope adventure.**
– *Kirkus Reviews*

An alien colony world, a routine deep cover mission
gone wrong, a chance encounter with a mercenary hit
squad and the murder of an Earth Intelligence Service
agent combine to launch Sirius Kade on a desperate
mission to the distant reaches of Mapped Space.

He finds himself embroiled in a complex web of alien
technologies, pirates, gun running and stellar intrigue,
where ancient galactic enemies and new ambitions vie
for supremacy.

While Sirius seeks to unravel a conspiracy threatening to
shatter Human Civilization, he discovers Mankind may
soon find itself caught in a gathering whirlwind building
far beyond the limits of Mapped Space.

As an interstellar minnow among galactic giants, it is a
cosmic storm humanity – the youngest space faring
civilization in the galaxy – may struggle to survive.

ISBN: 978-0-9941840-0-9